RIVER'S HOLLOW

A RIVER COLLINS FBI MYSTERY THRILLER
BOOK 4

KATE GABLE

BYRD BOOKS

BE THE FIRST TO KNOW ABOUT MY UPCOMING SALES, NEW RELEASES AND EXCLUSIVE GIVEAWAYS!

Want a Free book? Sign up for my Newsletter!

Sign up for my newsletter:
https://www.subscribepage.com/kategableviplist

Join my Facebook Group:
https://www.facebook.com/groups/833851020557518

Bonus Points: Follow me on BookBub and Goodreads!

https://www.goodreads.com/author/show/21534224.Kate_Gable

ABOUT KATE GABLE

Kate Gable is a 3 time Silke Falchion award winner including Book of the Year. She loves a good mystery that is full of suspense. She grew up devouring psychological thrillers and crime novels as well as movies, tv shows and true crime.

Her favorite stories are the ones that are centered on families with lots of secrets and lies as well as many twists and turns. Her novels have elements of psychological suspense, thriller, mystery and romance.

Kate Gable lives near Palm Springs, CA with her husband, son, a dog and a cat. She has spent more than twenty years in Southern California and finds inspiration from its cities, canyons, deserts, and small mountain towns.

She graduated from University of Southern California with a Bachelor's degree in Mathematics. After pursuing graduate studies in mathematics, she switched gears and got her MA in Creative Writing and English from Western New Mexico University and her PhD in Education from Old Dominion University.

Writing has always been her passion and obsession. Kate is also a USA Today Bestselling author of romantic suspense under another pen name.

Write her here:
Kate@kategable.com
Check out her books here:

www.kategable.com

Sign up for my newsletter:
https://www.subscribepage.com/kategableviplist

Join my Facebook Group:
https://www.facebook.com/groups/833851020557518

Bonus Points: Follow me on BookBub and Goodreads!

https://www.bookbub.com/authors/kate-gable

https://www.goodreads.com/author/show/21534224.Kate_Gable

- amazon.com/Kate-Gable/e/B095XFCLL7
- facebook.com/KateGableAuthor
- bookbub.com/authors/kate-gable
- instagram.com/kategablebooks
- tiktok.com/@kategablebooks

ALSO BY KATE GABLE

Standalone Psychological Thrillers
The Other Mother
The Neighborhood Watch

FBI Agent River Collins Mystery Thriller
River's Edge (Book 1)
River's Shadow (Book 2)
River's Hollow (Book 3)
River's Reckoning (Book 4)

Detective Kaitlyn Carr Psychological Mystery series
Girl Missing (Book 1)
Girl Lost (Book 2)
Girl Found (Book 3)
Girl Taken (Book 4)
Girl Forgotten (Book 5)
Gone Too Soon (Book 6)
Gone Forever (Book 7)
Whispers in the Sand (Book 8)

Girl Hidden (FREE Novella)

FBI Agent Alexis Forest Mystery Thriller
Forest of Silence
Forest of Shadows
Forest of Secrets
Forest of Lies
Forest of Obsession
Forest of Regrets
Forest of Deception

Detective Charlotte Pierce Psychological Mystery series
Last Breath
Nameless Girl
Missing Lives
Girl in the Lake

ABOUT RIVER'S HOLLOW

She escaped once. Now they want to finish what they started.

Twin boys found dead in Virginia's mountains. Bodies arranged in ritual patterns. Symbols carved into ancient oaks.

FBI Agent River Collins has seen horrors before. But this case is different.

The victims attended programs run by a respected foundation.

The methodology matches a 1994 cold case.

And the killer knows details about River's childhood abduction that were never made public.

Twenty years ago, River was held captive for two years before escaping. She thought she'd left that nightmare behind.

She was wrong.

The deeper River investigates, the more she realizes: her abduction wasn't random. She was chosen. Prepared. And the same people who took her then are targeting children now—including her six-year-old nephew.

With the winter solstice approaching and more children at risk, River must stop a cult that's been planning this for decades.

But their leader believes River is the unfinished work. The bridge that must be crossed.

And he's been waiting twenty years to complete her transformation.

Perfect for fans of Melinda Leigh, Kendra Elliot, and Robert Dugoni. Book 3 in the River Collins FBI series—each book is a complete investigation with series-long character development.

CHAPTER ONE

Three months later, winter has settled over Virginia like a heavy blanket. The FBI field office hums with the familiar energy of Monday morning caffeine and case files, but today feels different. Today, I'm officially back.

The ceremony was small, just Special Agent in Charge Eric Siwak and a few colleagues in Conference Room A. No fanfare, no speeches longer than a minute, no uncomfortable applause that goes on too long. That's exactly how I wanted it. Daniel's replacement, Agent Garrett Landry, stood respectfully in the back with a container of homemade beignets he'd brought for the occasion—his way of welcoming me back, I suppose. Emma squeezed my hand when Siwak read the commendation aloud—something about "exemplary service" and "dedication above and beyond"—words that felt both too big and too small for what actually happened with Sarah Earhart.

The commendation sits in a frame on my desk now, next to Sarah Earhart's drawing and a photo of Aiden and me at

Leslie's housewarming party last weekend. In the photo, I'm actually smiling—not the tight, practiced smile I use for professional situations, but a real one. Aiden's arm is around my waist, and Leslie's new apartment spreads out behind us, boxes still half-unpacked but full of possibility. Small tokens of a life that's finally taking shape.

I straighten the frame, studying the drawing for a moment. It's a crayon picture of a girl with dark hair holding hands with a taller woman wearing a badge. The girl drew a sun in the corner with rays that look like fingers reaching across the page. Underneath, in careful block letters: THANK YOU AGENT RIVER. She gave it to me at the hospital after we found her, before the therapists and the lawyers and the long road of recovery began. I keep it here to remind myself why I do this work. Why I keep opening folders full of nightmares.

"Collins."

I look up. Siwak appears at my cubicle, holding a manila folder that's already worn around the edges from handling. His expression is grim in a way that makes my stomach tighten—not the usual Monday morning grimness of bureaucracy and budget meetings, but something heavier. Something that's kept him up at night.

"We've got something unusual in the Blue Ridge Mountains," he says, his voice low enough that it doesn't carry to the other cubicles. "Local sheriff requested federal assistance."

I take the folder, noting the weight of it. Thick files usually mean complicated cases, and complicated cases tend to stick with you long after they're closed. The tab reads: CAINE, TITUS & MATTHEW - HOMICIDE.

"What kind of unusual?" I ask, though part of me already

knows I won't like the answer. Sheriffs in the Blue Ridge don't call in the FBI unless they're dealing with something they can't explain, something that keeps them looking over their shoulders in the woods.

"Twin boys, age eight. Found dead yesterday morning by hikers." Siwak pauses, choosing his words carefully. "No obvious cause of death, but the positioning..." He shakes his head. "You need to see it."

I open the folder. The crime scene photos are waiting inside like small windows into a nightmare.

Two identical boys with sandy brown hair and freckles across their noses, lie in a perfect circle in a clearing surrounded by ancient oak trees. Their arms are positioned at precise angles—left arms at forty-five degrees, right arms at ninety, like hands on a clock that stopped at different times. Their faces are peaceful, eyes closed, as if they're simply sleeping under the winter sky. They're wearing matching winter coats, one red and one blue, and their boots are unlaced but still on their feet.

But sleeping children don't arrange themselves in geometric patterns. And they don't usually die without explanation in the wild.

I flip through the photos slowly, forcing myself to look at each one with professional detachment. The clearing is roughly thirty feet in diameter. The oak trees—I count seven of them—form an almost perfect circle around the perimeter. Snow covers the ground except where the boys lie and a narrow path leading into the clearing. There are no signs of struggle. No visible wounds. No footprints except those of the hikers who found them and the first responders.

It's the kind of scene that raises more questions than it answers.

"Coroner's preliminary?" I ask.

"No external trauma. No defensive wounds. Waiting on toxicology, but the ME found nothing obvious." Siwak leans against the edge of my desk. "Local sheriff says he's worked that area for twenty years and has never seen anything like it. The parents are devastated. No known enemies, normal family, boys were just playing in their backyard."

I close the folder and look up at Siwak. Six months ago, these images would have sent me into a spiral of panic and self-doubt, triggering memories I couldn't control and fears I couldn't name. The faces of dead children used to look like accusations. They were reminders of every person I couldn't save, every case that came too late.

Today, I feel something different. The familiar weight of responsibility settles on my shoulders, but it's a weight I've learned to carry. The images hurt—they should hurt, that's what makes me human—but they don't paralyze me. They don't send me reaching for the pills I used to keep in my desk drawer, the ones I haven't needed in months.

"When do I leave for the scene?" I ask.

"First thing tomorrow morning. Emma will meet you there. She's already coordinating with the local sheriff's department." He pauses, studying my face with the careful attention he's always paid to his agents' mental states. There's something else in his expression too—something that looks like pride. "You've come a long way, Collins."

He's right. The journey from that terrified teen girl hidden in the basement to the woman sitting in this office has been longer and more painful than I ever imagined possible. But it's also been worth every difficult step. Every therapy session where I wanted to walk out. Every nightmare that left me gasping awake at 3 a.m.

"Thank you," I say, meaning more than just the assignment.

Siwak nods once, understanding everything I'm not saying, then heads back to his office.

I open the folder again, spreading the photos across my desk. Something about this case feels different from the others I've worked. Not just unusual. It feels...wrong. Like looking at a painting where all the proportions are slightly off but you can't quite pinpoint why.

I start with the wide shots of the clearing, trying to build a mental map of the scene. The hikers who found the boys were experienced. They didn't disturb anything, called it in immediately, waited at the trailhead for deputies. The first responders were careful too. Good scene preservation.

Then I move to the close-ups of the boys. Their positioning is too precise to be accidental. Someone arranged them this way, spent time making sure every angle was exact. But why? What does it mean?

My eyes drift to the photos of the oak trees surrounding the clearing. Ancient trees, probably centuries old, their bark thick and gnarled. The kind of trees that make you feel small, that were here long before you and, with any luck, will be here long after.

That's when I see it.

On the trunk of the largest oak, perhaps six feet up from the ground, there's a marking. At first glance, it looks like natural bark patterns, maybe damage from an animal or weather. But when I look closer, I can see the cuts are too clean, too deliberate.

It's a symbol. A carved symbol.

I pull out my magnifying glass and lean in closer. The design is intricate. It's a circle with intersecting lines, geometric shapes that form a pattern I can't quite parse. The cuts look fresh, made within the past few days based on the color of the exposed wood.

Something cold slides down my spine.

I've seen this symbol before. I know I have. But where?

I flip through more photos, looking at the other oak trees. Each one has the same symbol carved into its trunk at approximately the same height. Seven trees. Seven identical symbols. Made with precision and care by someone who knew exactly what they were doing.

The pattern of the carvings, the geometric positioning of the bodies, the peace on those boys' faces—it all feels ritualistic. Intentional.

My hands are shaking slightly as I gather the photos back into the folder. I'm trying not to spiral, so I stay unsettled.

Because somewhere in the back of my mind, buried in memories I've tried hard to forget, that symbol whispers to me. A half-remembered nightmare. A fragment of something I'm not supposed to remember.

I close my eyes and try to place it. The dark room. The concrete walls. The days that bled into weeks that bled into months. Was it there? Did I see it carved into something? Drawn on a wall?

Or is this just my trauma looking for patterns that don't exist, trying to make every new horror connect to my old one?

I open my eyes and stare at the folder. Tomorrow I'll drive to the Blue Ridge Mountains. I'll walk that clearing. I'll examine those trees. I'll find out what happened to Titus and Matthew Caine.

But tonight, I'll lie awake wondering why a symbol carved into ancient oak trees feels like a message meant specifically for me.

CHAPTER TWO

The drive to the Blue Ridge Mountains takes ninety minutes on winding roads that cut through forests heavy with snow. Emma drives while I review the case file again, memorizing details that might not be obvious at first glance. The heater works overtime against the December cold, and the radio plays soft rock that neither of us really listens to.

Supervisory Special Agent Emma Bertanelli has been my partner for three years now, though calling her a partner doesn't quite capture what she means to me. She's the closest thing I have to a friend, which isn't saying much given my track record. Her thick black curls are pulled back in a practical bun today, though a few wild strands have already escaped to frame her face. Dark eyes stay fixed on the winding road ahead, but I can see the tension in her shoulders, the way her fingers grip the steering wheel just a little too tight.

"How's Sophia doing?" I ask, glancing up from the file.

Emma's hands tighten slightly on the steering wheel. "She's good. Finally sleeping through the night most nights. Drew thinks she might be coming down with another cold, though. Daycare germs."

Her daughter is fifteen months old now, at that stage where every day brings something new. I've watched Emma navigate motherhood and this job since Sophia was born, seen her struggle with the impossible balance of being present for both. She got promoted to supervisory special agent eight months ago after reporting Daniel Brennon for assault, after enduring an internal investigation that should have been straightforward but wasn't. She's one of the best investigators I know, detail-oriented and relentless, but the cost shows in the dark circles under her eyes and the way she checks her phone every few minutes to make sure Drew hasn't called.

"And how are you doing?" I ask. "Really."

She's quiet for a moment, eyes on the road. "Some days are better than others. Therapy helps. The promotion helps. Having Brennon actually face consequences helps."

I nod. Emma reported Daniel Brennon for sexual assault eight months ago. The internal investigation was brutal, but she didn't back down. He was fired, charged, and is awaiting trial. Emma got promoted to supervisory special agent. But trauma doesn't care about justice or promotions.

"I'm glad you're on this case with me," I say.

"Where else would I be?" She glances at me with a small smile. "Besides, you need someone to keep you from going full obsessive detective mode."

"I don't do that."

"River. You literally dreamed about work."

"That was one time."

"That you told me about."

Fair point.

The landscape changes as we climb higher into the mountains. The trees grow denser, their branches heavy with snow. Everything is white and gray and silent in that way that only winter wilderness can be. Beautiful and desolate at the same time.

The trailhead parking area is already crowded with sheriff's department vehicles and the coroner's van when we arrive. Yellow crime scene tape marks the path through the woods. I can see boot prints from investigators tramping through what should be pristine evidence, but that's inevitable. You can't preserve an outdoor scene perfectly, especially not in winter.

A man in a sheriff's uniform approaches as we park. He's in his fifties, weathered face and careful eyes. The kind of cop who's seen enough to know when something is wrong on a level that goes beyond the usual bad.

"Agent Collins? Agent Bertanelli?" He extends a gloved hand. "Sheriff Tom Whitmore. Thanks for coming out so quick."

We shake hands and follow him toward the trailhead. The path is narrow, barely wide enough for two people to walk side by side. Snow crunches under our boots.

"I've worked this county for twenty-three years," Whitmore says as we walk. "Dealt with plenty of missing persons, few accidental deaths from hikers who didn't respect the terrain. But this..." He shakes his head. "This is different."

"Walk me through the discovery," Emma says, pulling out her notebook.

"Hikers found them yesterday morning around seven. Couple from Charlottesville, experienced outdoors people. They were doing a loop trail, took a detour to check out this clearing because they'd never noticed it before. That's when they saw the boys."

"They touch anything?" I ask.

"No. Called it in immediately, waited at the trailhead for my deputies. They did everything right." Whitmore pauses at a fork in the trail. "Scene's about fifteen minutes in. Fair warning, it's not like anything you've probably worked before."

The hike takes us deeper into old growth forest. These trees have been here for centuries, thick trunks and gnarled branches that create a canopy even winter can't fully penetrate. The temperature drops as we move away from the trailhead, and our breath forms clouds in the cold air.

Finally, Whitmore stops. "Just through here."

We push through a gap between two massive oak trees, and the clearing opens before us.

The first thing I notice is the silence. No birds, no wind, nothing. Just absolute quiet that feels wrong somehow, like the forest is holding its breath.

The clearing is roughly circular, maybe thirty feet across. The oak trees surrounding it are enormous, their trunks easily five feet in diameter. Seven of them, spaced evenly around the perimeter like sentinels.

The snow in the center of the clearing has been disturbed by investigators, but I can still see the outline of where the bodies were positioned. Chalk marks show their exact placement.

"Coroner took them yesterday afternoon," Whitmore says. "But we've got extensive photos and measurements."

I walk slowly around the perimeter, studying everything. The positioning was precise. Mathematical. The boys' heads pointed toward the center of the circle, their feet toward the tree line. Arms at specific angles. Everything deliberate.

"No signs of struggle?" Emma asks.

"None. No defensive wounds, no trauma. ME says it's like they just... stopped living."

I crouch near one of the chalk outlines, looking at the undisturbed snow around it. "How did someone carry two eight-year-old boys this far into the woods without leaving more tracks?"

"That's what we can't figure," Whitmore says. "There's the hiking trail, but it doesn't come within a quarter mile of here. Someone had to bushwhack through heavy forest carrying or leading two children. In winter. And we found almost nothing."

"Almost?" I stand, brushing snow from my gloves.

"There's a faint trail on the north side. Looks like someone used it recently, but the snow's covered most of it. We're bringing in trackers to see if they can follow it."

Emma is photographing the scene with her phone, getting angles the initial response team might have missed. I walk toward the nearest oak tree.

That's when I see the symbols.

In the photos they looked strange. In person, they're arresting. The carving is about six feet up the trunk, maybe six inches tall. The design is a circle with intersecting lines that form geometric patterns inside. Celtic knotwork maybe, or something older. The cuts are clean and deep, exposing pale wood beneath the dark bark.

I pull out my flashlight and examine it closely. "This is recent. Maybe a week old, based on the color."

"Same on all seven trees," Whitmore confirms. "Exact same design, same height, same depth. Whoever did this took their time."

I move to the next tree. The symbol is identical. Perfect reproduction. I circle the entire clearing, checking each oak. Seven trees. Seven perfect symbols.

Emma joins me at the fourth tree. "You recognize this design?"

"No." But that's not quite true. Something about it nags at me. A whisper of memory I can't quite grasp.

"Could be occult," she suggests. "Some kind of ritual marking."

"Or someone wants us to think it's occult." I step back, trying to see the bigger picture. "But why? What's the point of all this staging?"

The clearing, the positioning, the symbols. It's all performance. Someone created this scene deliberately, spent time making it perfect. But for what purpose?

I look up at the oak trees towering above us. The branches twist together overhead, creating patterns of their own against the white sky. These trees are old. Really old.

"Sheriff, how long have these oaks been here?"

Whitmore considers. "Forest service estimates the oldest trees in this area are around four hundred years old. These look like they're part of that original growth."

Four hundred years. These trees were saplings before this country existed, before Europeans arrived in Virginia, before any of the history I learned in school.

And someone carved symbols into them last week.

I move closer to the largest oak, the one directly north of where the boys were found. The symbol on this tree is positioned perfectly at eye level for an average adult. I trace the pattern with my gloved finger, following the lines without actually touching the carved wood.

Circle. Lines intersecting at precise angles. Smaller circles at specific points. The design has a mathematical quality to it, like it follows some kind of formula or rule.

That's when it hits me.

I have seen this before.

Not recently. Not in a case file or a textbook. But somewhere in the dark spaces of my memory, buried under years of trying to forget.

The room. The dark room where they kept me. Concrete walls and a single bulb hanging from the ceiling. I remember staring at those walls for hours, days, trying to count seconds to keep track of time. And on one wall, barely visible in the dim light, there was something scratched into the concrete.

I thought it was just random marks at the time. Damage or graffiti from whoever had been in that basement before it became my prison.

But now, looking at this symbol carved into ancient oak, I recognize the pattern.

It's the same. Not identical, but the same underlying design. The same geometric logic.

My hand drops from the tree. My breath catches.

"River?" Emma's voice sounds far away. "You okay?"

I can't answer. Can't move. The clearing spins slightly, and I have to put my hand against the oak trunk to steady myself.

Someone who knew about my captivity carved this symbol. Someone who was there, or someone who knew the people who took me.

But that's impossible. My captors were never caught.

The case went cold. The investigation turned up nothing except a scared fourteen-year-old girl with gaps in her memory and nightmares that never quite stopped.

How could this case be connected to that?

"River." Emma's hand is on my arm now. "Talk to me."

I force myself to breathe. To think like an investigator instead of a victim. Maybe I'm wrong. Maybe my mind is making connections that don't exist, seeing patterns because I'm programmed to look for them.

But I don't think so.

I look up at the oak trees surrounding the clearing. Ancient and solid and permanent. They were here centuries before my nightmare began. They'll be here centuries after I'm gone.

And someone chose them specifically to carve symbols that whisper to me across twenty years of trying to forget.

"These symbols," I say slowly, my voice not quite steady. "They're not random. They're not just occult decoration. Someone is using a very specific design. An ancient one."

"How do you know?" Whitmore asks.

I can't tell him the truth. Not yet. Not until I'm sure.

"I need to make some calls," I say instead. "Get an expert to look at these carvings. Someone who specializes in historical symbols and ancient designs."

Emma is watching me carefully. She knows something's wrong, knows I'm not telling them everything. But she doesn't push. Not in front of the sheriff.

"We should document everything before we lose the light," she says, pulling out her camera. "Get measurements, more photos, samples of the wood if forensics can do it without damaging evidence."

I nod, grateful for her practical focus. We spend the next

hour working the scene methodically, but my mind keeps returning to that symbol.

The oak trees are centuries old. The symbols carved into them are barely a week fresh. But the design itself?

That's ancient. And somehow, impossibly, it's connected to the worst two years of my life.

CHAPTER THREE

I've been photographing the scene from different angles, trying to find patterns in the positioning that might reveal something about the killer's mindset. Emma works methodically near the chalk outlines, using a small brush to clear snow away from the ground. She has more patience for this kind of detailed work than I do.

My phone buzzes in my pocket. The medical examiner's office.

"Collins," I answer, putting it on speaker so Emma can hear.

"Agent Collins, this is Dr. Elizabeth Hayes from the state ME's office." Her voice carries the professional distance of someone who spends their days with the dead. "I have preliminary findings on the Caine twins."

Emma looks up from her work, brush still in hand.
"Go ahead, Doctor."

"Both victims show no signs of external trauma. No contusions, no lacerations, no defensive wounds. Internal examination revealed no organ damage, no internal bleeding, no signs of suffocation or strangulation."

I pull a strand of hair away from my face, tucking it behind my ear. The wind has picked up. "What about toxicology?"

"That's going to take another forty-eight hours minimum. But I ran a preliminary screen for common substances. Nothing showed up. No alcohol, no standard narcotics, no carbon monoxide."

"So what killed them?" Emma asks.

Dr. Hayes is quiet for a moment. "That's what I can't tell you. Both boys were healthy, well-nourished, no pre-existing conditions. Their hearts simply stopped beating. I've seen cases like this before, but they're rare. Usually involves some kind of exotic toxin or plant-based compound that doesn't show up on standard panels."

"How long had they been dead when they were found?" I ask.

"Based on liver temperature and rigor mortis, I'd estimate eight to twelve hours. So they died sometime between seven PM and eleven PM the night before discovery."

After dark. Someone positioned those boys in that clearing at night, in December, in freezing temperatures. That takes planning and familiarity with the terrain.

"Anything else unusual?" I press.

"Their clothing was clean. No dirt, no tears, no signs of struggle or being dragged. It's like they walked into that clearing and simply lay down."

Emma and I exchange a look. Eight-year-old boys don't walk into the woods at night and arrange themselves in geometric patterns.

"Send me the full report when it's ready," I say. "And push the toxicology. I need those results as fast as you can get them."

"Will do. One more thing, Agent Collins." Dr. Hayes pauses. "I found traces of what looks like wood residue under both boys' fingernails. Fresh sawdust. Like they'd been handling carved wood recently."

I think of the symbols carved into the oak trees. "Can you analyze it?"

"Already sent samples to the lab. Should have wood type identification by tomorrow."

After we hang up, Emma goes back to her careful excavation of the snow near the eastern chalk outline. I move to the largest oak tree, the one directly north, studying the carved symbol again. In the fading afternoon light, the cuts look even deeper than I first thought. Whoever made these spent significant time on each one.

The pattern still whispers to me. That geometric precision, those intersecting lines forming shapes I can't quite name. It's not just familiar from the dark room where I was held. There's something older about it, something that predates my own trauma.

"River." Emma's voice cuts through my thoughts. "You need to see this."

I cross the clearing, stepping carefully around the chalk outlines. Emma is crouched near where Titus Caine's right hand would have been, holding something small in her gloved palm.

It's a carved wooden token, roughly the size of a silver dollar. The same symbol from the oak trees is etched into its surface with the same precision and care. Fresh sawdust still clings to some of the grooves.

"It wasn't in any of the initial reports," Emma says, standing slowly. "The snow had drifted over it."

She holds out her hand so I can see it better. The carving is remarkably detailed for something so small. Whoever made this has serious skill.

"Bag it," I say. "And check the other outline. If there's one, there might be two."

But Emma is staring at the token with an odd expression. "River, it's warm."

"What?"

"The token. It's warm to the touch."

I pull off my glove and hold out my hand. Emma transfers the token carefully, and the moment it touches my palm, I feel it. Not hot, but distinctly warm, like it's been sitting in someone's pocket.

That's impossible. The boys were found yesterday morning. This clearing has been under guard since then. Everything here should be frozen.

"Maybe it was deeper in the snow," Emma suggests. "Insulated somehow."

I turn the token over in my hand. The symbol is carved on both sides, identical geometric patterns. The warmth fades slowly as I hold it, the wood cooling to match the winter air.

We spend another twenty minutes searching the area around Matthew's outline but find nothing. Just the one token, placed near Titus's hand. One token for one twin.

By the time we finish documenting the scene, the light is failing and my hands are numb despite the gloves. The forensic techs pack up their equipment, and Emma bags the token as evidence.

The hike back to the trailhead feels longer than the hike in. The forest presses close on all sides, and twice I catch myself looking back, certain I heard something behind us. But there's never anyone there.

CHAPTER FOUR

The Caine house is a Victorian painted lady on a quiet street in a neighborhood that probably looked the same fifty years ago. Gingerbread trim, wraparound porch, mature trees in the yard casting long shadows as the sun sets. Under different circumstances, it would be charming. Today, it looks like a monument to loss.

Emma parks at the curb, and we sit for a moment, preparing ourselves. This is always the hardest part. Walking into someone's fresh grief, asking questions they don't want to answer, seeing their lives frozen at the moment everything changed.

"Ready?" Emma asks.

I nod and step out into the cold.

Warren Caine answers the door before we finish climbing the porch steps, like he's been watching for us. He's a tall man, maybe six-two, with the kind of build that suggests he works out but hasn't lately. Dark circles shadow his eyes, and his flannel shirt is buttoned wrong, one side hanging lower than the other.

"Agents?" His voice is rough, like he's been crying or yelling or both. "Sheriff Whitmore called, said you'd be coming by."

"Mr. Caine." I show him my badge. "I'm Agent Collins, this is Supervisory Special Agent Bertanelli. We're very sorry for your loss. We know this is an incredibly difficult time, but we need to ask you and your wife some questions."

He nods mechanically and steps back, letting us into a foyer that smells like coffee and something else. The sour smell of grief, of people who've stopped eating and sleeping and taking care of themselves.

The interior of the house matches the exterior Victorian charm. High ceilings, original woodwork, family photos covering every available surface. I catalog details automatically. Wedding photos, baby photos, the twins at various ages. Titus and Matthew at a pumpkin patch. At a baseball game. Blowing out candles on a birthday cake.

So many moments captured and preserved, and now no more moments coming.

"Brenda's in the living room," Warren says, leading us through a doorway to the right. "She's been... she's not herself."

The living room is formal, the kind of space that probably doesn't get used much. Antique furniture, lace curtains, and a fireplace with the ashes of a recent fire. Brenda Caine sits in a wingback chair near the window, her hands folded in her lap, staring at nothing.

She's younger than her husband, maybe late thirties, with light brown hair pulled back in a severe bun. She's dressed carefully in dark slacks and a sweater, makeup applied with precision. Everything about her appearance is controlled, composed. Only her eyes give her away, they're empty in a way that makes my stomach turn.

I've seen a lot of grief in this job. There's the raw, immediate kind that Warren is showing, all tears and disbelief and desperate hope that this is somehow a mistake. Then there's the shutdown kind, where the mind simply can't process what's happened and retreats somewhere safe until it's ready.

Brenda's grief is neither of those. It's something else entirely. Something that feels wrong.

"Mrs. Caine?" I keep my voice gentle as I take the seat across from her. Emma settles on the sofa beside Warren, pulling out her notebook. "Thank you for seeing us. We know how difficult this must be."

Brenda's eyes shift to me slowly, like she's moving through water. "You're the FBI agents."

"Yes, ma'am. We're leading the investigation into your sons' deaths."

"They're with the stars now." Her voice is calm, almost serene. "Warren doesn't understand, but I do. They're exactly where they're meant to be."

Warren makes a strangled sound, his hands clenching into fists on his knees. "Brenda, please. Don't say things like that."

"It's the truth." She looks at him with something that might be pity. "You think this is tragedy, but it's transformation. Our boys were chosen for something greater than we could give them."

The hair on the back of my neck stands up. I glance at Emma, who's gone very still, her pen frozen above her notebook. This isn't the response of a grieving mother. This is something else entirely.

"Mrs. Caine," I say carefully, "what do you mean by chosen?"

"I mean they were special. Both of them, from the moment they were born. Twins carry double souls. They can bridge what others cannot." She speaks with absolute certainty.

I tuck a loose strand of hair behind my ear, buying myself a moment to think. Double souls. Bridge what others cannot. The language feels ritualistic, like she's quoting from something specific.

"Brenda's been reading a lot of spiritual books," Warren says quickly, his voice desperate to explain. "Since we moved here, she's been exploring different beliefs. Meditation, crystals, that kind of thing. It's just how she's processing."

But that's not what this sounds like. This sounds practiced. Rehearsed. Like she's been preparing these words for some time.

"Mrs. Caine, can you tell us about the day your sons disappeared?" I ask, pivoting away to something more concrete. "What were they doing before they went into the woods?"

"Playing." Her tone shifts slightly, becoming more present. "They were always playing outside. We have five acres here, backing right up to the national forest. The boys loved exploring, following deer trails, climbing trees. I never worried about them out there."

"Why not?" Emma asks.

"Because they knew the woods. And the woods knew them." Brenda's smile is small and strange. "They had a guardian there. Someone who watched over them, who taught them about the stars."

Warren's head snaps up. "What are you talking about?"

"The star man." Brenda looks at her husband like he's being deliberately obtuse. "The boys told us about him a week ago, Warren. Don't you remember? They came home so excited, talking about the nice man who knew all the constellations, who told them they were special. That they had important work to do."

"I thought they were making up stories," Warren says, his voice rising. "Kids have imaginary friends. I didn't think—"

"He wasn't imaginary." Brenda turns back to me. "He was real. He saw what they were, what they could become. He understood their purpose in ways we never could."

My pulse quickens. A man in the woods, talking to eight-year-old boys about stars and purpose. Teaching them, grooming them, telling them they're special. The pattern is sickeningly familiar.

"Did your sons describe this man?" I ask. "What he looked like, what he was wearing?"

"They said he was tall. That he had kind eyes. That he knew their names without being told." Brenda's smile widens slightly. "That's how we know he was meant to find them. He was guided to our boys."

"Guided by what?" Emma's voice is sharp.

"By the old powers. The ones that came before churches and laws and all the limitations people put on what's sacred." Brenda leans forward, suddenly animated. "There are older truths, Agent Bertanelli. Practices that have been forgotten but never truly lost. My boys were part of something ancient, something that matters more than our small lives and small griefs."

Warren stands abruptly, his chair scraping against the hardwood floor. "Stop it, Brenda. Just stop. Our sons are dead. They didn't transform, they didn't bridge anything.

They're gone, and you're sitting here talking like this is some kind of blessing."

"You don't understand," Brenda says simply. "You've always been too afraid to see past what you think you know."

I stand as well, my hand moving instinctively toward my weapon. Not because I think Brenda is dangerous, exactly, but because everything about this conversation has shifted into territory I don't recognize. The calm in her voice when she talks about her dead children. The certainty that their deaths served some higher purpose.

The fact that she knew there was a man in the woods talking to her sons, and she didn't see that as a threat.

"Mr. and Mrs. Caine," I say, keeping my voice level, "we're going to need you both to come down to the FBI field office tomorrow for formal statements. There's a lot more we need to discuss."

"Of course." Brenda stands gracefully, smoothing her sweater. "I'm happy to help however I can. The truth needs to be told, after all."

"What truth?" Warren looks between his wife and me, confusion and fear warring on his face. "What is she talking about?"

But Brenda just smiles that small, serene smile and walks out of the room, leaving the three of us staring after her.

Emma and I exchange a look. We've both heard enough to know that Brenda Caine isn't just a grieving mother processing trauma through spiritual exploration. She's involved in something, believes in something, that directly connects to her sons' deaths.

And the man in the woods, the one who knew the boys' names, is he our killer? I know it with the same certainty I knew something was wrong when I first saw those symbols carved into ancient oak trees.

"Mr. Caine," I say quietly, "we need you to tell us everything you know about your wife's spiritual activities. Every book she's read, every group she's joined, every person she's met through these interests. Everything."

He nods, sinking back into his chair. "I'll tell you whatever you need. I just want to understand what happened to my boys."

But as Emma and I leave the Victorian house and step back into the cold December evening, I'm afraid Warren Caine is going to learn things about his wife he never imagined. Things that will make her a stranger to him.

Emma starts the engine, but neither of us moves. We sit in the growing darkness, processing what we've just heard.

A man who knows constellations. Who tells children they're special. Who grooms them with kindness and knowledge and the promise of important work.

And a mother who possibly let it happen. Who believed her sons were chosen for something greater than their small lives.

The carved symbols. The wooden token. The precise positioning of two small bodies under winter stars.

Everything is pointing to this being a ritual murder and the mother knowing something about it.

CHAPTER FIVE

I dream of the woman first. Always the woman.
Her voice is kind when she leans out the car window, apologetic and a little embarrassed. She's lost, she says. Just needs directions. The afternoon is gray, threatening rain, and I'm twelve years old walking home from the bus stop. Taking the long way because I got a C- on my math test and I'm not ready to face my mother yet.

"I just need to find Riverside Drive," the woman says. She has red lipstick, I remember that detail with perfect clarity. Too red for a Tuesday afternoon. "Can you help me, sweetie?"

In the dream, like in real life, I point the way. Two blocks down, then left at the church.

"I'm terrible with directions," she laughs, and her laugh sounds genuine, warm. "Would you mind just showing me? I'll drive you right back, I promise. It'll take two minutes."

The door is already open. The interior smells like vanilla and something else, something chemical I can't identify. I climb in because she seems nice. Because adults are supposed to be trusted. Because I'm twelve and I don't yet understand that monsters wear friendly faces.

The door locks with a soft click.

"Good girl," she says, and her voice changes. Goes flat and cold. "You're going to be very good for us, aren't you?"

I try to open the door. The handle doesn't work. I scream but she's already driving, windows up, radio playing loud enough to drown me out. We're on the highway before I stop screaming, my throat raw, my hands shaking.

The dream shifts, the way dreams do. Now I'm in the dark room.

Concrete walls. A single bulb hanging from the ceiling, dim and flickering. A metal-frame bed with a thin mattress. A bucket in the corner that I try not to look at. The door is heavy steel, bolted from the outside. I've tried it a hundred times in those first days. A thousand times. It never opens.

The walls have marks on them. Scratches. Tallies from whoever was here before me. And something else. A symbol carved into the concrete near the floor, barely visible in the bad light. A circle with intersecting lines. Geometric shapes that form a pattern I don't understand.

I trace it with my finger sometimes, in the dream and in memory. Trying to make sense of it.

Footsteps echo from somewhere above. Heavy boots on concrete. A man's footsteps, and they're coming closer.

The door opens. He's backlit, a dark shape without features. He doesn't speak right away. Just stands there, watching me huddle in the corner. I'm wearing the same clothes I was wearing when she took me. They're dirty now. I haven't had a proper bath in days. Weeks. I've lost count.

"Come here," he says finally. His voice is low, measured. Not angry. Somehow that makes it worse.

I don't move. I've learned that moving too quickly makes things worse.

He crosses the room in three strides and picks up my left foot. I'm wearing the sneakers my dad bought me for my birthday. Pink and white, with laces I haven't learned to tie properly yet. They're always coming undone.

"You need to learn to do this right," he says, and his hands are quick and efficient as he ties my laces. Not a regular bow. Something more complex. A knot that loops and crosses in a specific pattern. "Pay attention. This is important."

In the dream, I watch his hands form the pattern. Loop, cross, pull through. Again and again until both shoes are tied in identical complex knots.

"These bindings matter," he says, and there's something in his voice that sounds like teaching. Like he's a patient instructor and I'm a student who needs to understand. "Everything connects. Everything serves the crossing."

"What crossing?" My voice is small, scared.

"The one you were meant for." He stands, looks down at me. "The woman chose you. Saw something in you. But you have to be prepared first. You have to learn."

The dream fragments. Time passes in broken pieces. Days bleeding into weeks. The woman brings food sometimes, speaks in that flat voice. The man comes to check the knots on my shoes, to make sure I'm learning the pattern. They talk about me like I'm not there, like I'm a project they're working on together.

"She's not ready yet," the woman says one day.

"She will be," the man replies. "The crossing requires patience."

Crossing. They keep saying that word. Crossing. Like I'm

supposed to understand what it means. Like it explains why I'm here in this concrete room with symbols carved into the walls and my shoes tied in knots that won't come undone.

The dream shifts again. I'm older now, fourteen. I've been here so long. Too long. But something has changed. They've gotten careless, or I've gotten smarter. The door isn't quite latched one day when the woman brings breakfast. She's distracted, arguing with someone on her phone.

I wait until she's gone. Until the footsteps fade. Then I push the door open and run.

The rest is confusion. Stairs. More concrete hallways. A basement in a building I don't recognize. Outside is cold and bright and I'm running in my pink sneakers with their strange knots, running until someone finds me. Until police come. Until I'm safe.

But I never feel safe again.

I wake gasping, my heart hammering against my ribs like it's trying to escape my chest. The room is dark and unfamiliar for a terrible moment. Wrong walls, wrong ceiling, wrong everything.

Then strong arms wrap around me and I remember where I am.

"River." Aiden's voice is sleep-rough but alert. "Hey, I've got you. You're safe."

I'm in his apartment. In his bed. The sheets are tangled around my legs and I'm drenched in sweat despite the cool air. My hands are shaking and I can't quite catch my breath.

"Sorry," I manage. "I'm sorry."

"Don't." His arms tighten slightly, grounding me without restraining me. He's learned how to hold me after nightmares. Firm enough to feel real but loose enough that I don't feel trapped. "You don't apologize for this. Ever."

I focus on breathing. On the present moment. Aiden's apartment smells like coffee and the lavender laundry detergent he uses. The digital clock on his nightstand reads 3:47 AM. Through the window I can see the lights of Charlottesville, proof that I'm not in a concrete basement. That I escaped. That I'm twenty years and hundreds of miles away from that room.

Aiden doesn't ask questions right away. He just holds me while my breathing slows, while the nightmare's grip loosens. His chest rises and falls against my back in a steady rhythm I can match. After a while, he reaches for the glass of water he keeps on the nightstand and hands it to me.

I drink, grateful. My throat is raw. Was I screaming? I don't remember.

"The case," I say finally, because he'll understand without me needing to explain more. "The symbols. They're triggering things."

Aiden shifts so he can see my face better. Even in the dim light from the window, I can make out his features. Dark curly hair standing up in all directions, exactly like it does in the morning. He's not wearing his glasses. Without them he looks younger than thirty-four, less like the skilled neurologist who spends his days diagnosing complex brain disorders and more like the person he might have been if his sister hadn't died. If trauma hadn't shaped him the way it shaped me.

"Do you want to talk about it?" he asks.

I should say no. I've spent most of my adult life not talking about it, keeping those two years locked away in a place I rarely access. But Aiden is different. He doesn't push, doesn't demand, doesn't treat my trauma like something he needs to fix. His sister's death taught him that some wounds don't heal, they just become part of who you are.

"The symbols carved into the trees," I say slowly. "I've seen them before. Or something like them. In the place where they kept me."

His arms tighten fractionally. "The concrete room?"

I nod. He knows some of this story. Not all of it. I've told him bits and pieces over the three months we've been together. About the woman with red lipstick. About the basement. About running until I found help. But I've never told him about the symbols on the wall, about the strange knots, about the word they kept using.

Crossing.

"There were marks on the walls," I continue. "I thought they were just scratches at first. Graffiti, maybe. But they were deliberate. The same kind of geometric pattern that's carved into those oak trees."

Aiden is a neurologist, trained to see patterns in brain scans, to diagnose problems from subtle symptoms. I watch him process this information, making connections.

"You think whoever took you is connected to this case?"

"I don't know. Maybe. Or maybe it's bigger than that. Maybe there's a network, people who use these symbols." The possibility makes me feel sick. Twenty years of thinking my captors were just two individuals. Two people who took me for reasons I never understood. The idea that they were part of something larger is almost worse.

"What else do you remember?" Aiden asks gently. "From the dream, I mean. Sometimes dreams surface things our conscious mind suppresses."

He would have made a good therapist. That was his plan before medical school, before he watched his sister struggle with addiction and PTSD and realized he wanted to understand the physical mechanisms of trauma. How it rewires the brain. How pain becomes permanently encoded in neural pathways.

"The way they tied my shoes," I say. The detail feels stupid, insignificant compared to everything else. But it's stuck with me for twenty years. "The man taught me a specific knot. Made me practice it. Said the bindings mattered, that everything had to be connected for the crossing."

"The crossing." Aiden repeats the phrase carefully. "What does that mean?"

"I don't know. They said it all the time. 'She's not ready for the crossing.' 'The crossing requires patience.' I never understood what they meant."

I realize I'm shaking again. Aiden pulls the blanket up around my shoulders, creates a cocoon of warmth and safety. His apartment is small but comfortable. A one-bedroom in a converted house near the hospital where he works. Books everywhere, medical journals stacked on surfaces, a bike in the corner he rides to work when weather permits. It's lived-in in a way my apartment isn't. Like an actual person exists here, not just someone who sleeps between shifts.

"River." His voice has changed, gone careful in a way that makes me look at him. "You were talking in your sleep. Before you woke up."

"What did I say?"

"You kept repeating something. 'The crossing. They wanted me for the crossing.'" He pauses, studying my face. "You've never mentioned that phrase before."

Because I'd buried it. Pushed it down with everything

else from those two years. But the case has dredged it up. The symbols, the ritualistic positioning of the Caine twins, Brenda talking about her sons being chosen for something greater. It's all connected to that word I haven't let myself think about in decades.

Crossing.

"I need to find out what it means," I say. "Not just for this case. For me. I need to know what they wanted from me."

Aiden shifts so we're facing each other, both of us sitting up now. His hand finds mine under the blanket. His fingers are long, steady. Surgeon's hands, though he chose diagnosis over surgery. Chose understanding over intervention.

"Whatever you need," he says. "I'm here. But River, promise me you'll be careful. If your case is connected to your own abduction, that means whoever took you might still be out there."

I know. The thought has been circling my mind since I saw those symbols carved into ancient oak trees. My captors were never caught. The case went cold. I gave every detail I could remember to investigators but it wasn't enough. The basement could have been anywhere. The woman's car was never found. The man's face was always backlit, always in shadow. I escaped but they were never held accountable.

What if they've been doing this for twenty years? What if there are other victims, other children taken for this mysterious crossing?

What if Titus and Matthew Caine died for the same purpose I was taken?

"I should go," I say, starting to untangle myself from the blankets. "It's late. You have work in the morning."

"River." Aiden doesn't let go of my hand. "It's almost four AM. Stay. Please."

I hesitate. My instinct is always to leave, to retreat to my own space where I can process things alone. But I'm exhausted and Aiden's bed is warm and the nightmare is still too close to the surface. Going home means being alone with it.

"Okay," I say finally.

We lie back down, Aiden's arm around me, my head on his chest. I can hear his heartbeat, steady and regular. He probably won't fall back asleep. He'll lie here until his alarm goes off, making sure I'm okay. That's who he is. Someone who stays even when staying is uncomfortable.

"Tell me about your day tomorrow," I say, because I need to think about something normal. Something that has nothing to do with dead children or carved symbols or the word crossing.

"Consult on a seizure patient first thing," he says, his voice rumbling through his chest. "Then rounds on the stroke unit. Meeting with the department chair about the new imaging equipment we're trying to get funded. Lunch will probably be vending machine coffee and whatever leftovers are in the break room fridge."

I smile despite everything. This is the life he chose. Long hours, complex cases, bureaucratic battles over equipment. He loves it the way I love my work. Not because it's easy but because it matters.

"What about you?" he asks.

"Interview the Caine parents formally at the field office. Wait for toxicology results. Research those symbols." And maybe, though I don't say it out loud, start looking through my own case file. The one I haven't opened in years because it hurts too much to see my twelve-year-old face staring out from missing persons posters. To read the investigator's notes about how I was "remarkably composed" during interviews. How I "showed little emotion" when describing my captivity.

They didn't understand that I'd already learned to bury things deep. That showing emotion meant being vulnerable, and vulnerability meant getting hurt.

Aiden's breathing slows gradually, and I realize he's falling back asleep despite my assumption. Good. He works too hard, long shifts where people's lives depend on his ability to spot problems other doctors miss. He needs rest.

I lie awake watching the sky slowly lighten outside his window. Dawn comes late in December, and even when it arrives it's gray and cold. But it comes. That's something I learned in that concrete room. No matter how dark it gets, morning always comes eventually.

My phone buzzes on the nightstand. A text from Emma.
Can't sleep either. Coffee at 6?
I text back: *See you there.*

Carefully, I slide out of Aiden's arms and gather my clothes from where they're scattered on the floor. He stirs but doesn't wake. I leave a note on the kitchen counter next to the coffee maker where I know he'll see it.

Thank you for being patient with my broken pieces. - R

Outside, the December morning is bitter cold. I drive through empty streets back to my apartment to shower and change. In an hour I'll meet Emma and we'll go over everything we know about the Caine case. We'll build timelines and suspect lists and try to make sense of two boys dead in a clearing marked with ancient symbols.

But right now, alone in my car, I let myself think about the phrase I spoke in my sleep.

The crossing. They wanted me for the crossing.

Whatever it means, whatever purpose those two people had for me twenty years ago, I'm going to find out. Not just to solve this case.

But because I need to understand why I was taken. Why I was kept. And why, after two years of preparation, they let me escape.

Or maybe I didn't escape at all. Maybe I was released.

The thought follows me home like a shadow, dark and cold and impossible to shake.

CHAPTER SIX

Gerald Ford Elementary smells like every school I've ever been in. Floor wax, cafeteria food lingering from yesterday's lunch, and that particular scent of construction paper and pencil shavings that must be universal to childhood education. The hallway walls are covered with student artwork, handprint pumpkins still up from October even though it's December now.

Emma and I sign in at the front office. The secretary, a woman in her sixties with reading glasses on a beaded chain, looks at our badges and her face crumples slightly.

"About the Caine boys," she says, not a question. "Principal Morrison is expecting you."

We follow her down a hallway lined with small lockers painted bright blue. Through classroom windows I can see teachers at whiteboards, students bent over worksheets. Normal school day routines continuing because they have to, even when two chairs sit empty in second-grade classrooms.

Principal Emily Morrison meets us in a conference room

that doubles as a teacher's lounge. There's a kitchenette in one corner, motivational posters on the walls, a bulletin board covered with staff schedules. She's younger than I expected, maybe early forties, wearing slacks and a cardigan that looks professionally pressed but comfortable.

"Agents." She shakes our hands. "I've asked Titus and Matthew's teachers to make themselves available. Whatever you need."

"We appreciate that," I say, pulling out my notebook. "We're trying to build a complete picture of who these boys were. Their routines, their friendships, anything that might help us understand what happened."

Morrison's eyes are red-rimmed behind her glasses. "They were wonderful children. Both of them. This whole school is devastated."

The first teacher we interview is Patricia Wells, who had Titus in her second-grade class. She's in her fifties, with gray hair pulled back in a practical bun. When she sits down across from us, her hands shake slightly as she folds them on the table.

"Titus was sunshine," she says simply. "That's the only way I can describe him. He'd walk into class every morning with this huge smile, ready to tell me about something he saw on the way to school. A bird's nest, an interesting rock, once he brought in a cicada shell he found stuck to a tree."

Emma takes notes while I listen, watching Wells' face. I see the grief that is written there.

"He made friends easily?" I ask.

"Very easily. He was the kind of child who included everyone. If someone was sitting alone at lunch, Titus would invite them to his table. If someone dropped their pencil box, he'd help pick everything up." She pauses, swallowing hard. "He was just... kind. Naturally kind in a way you can't really teach."

"What about academically?"

"Bright. Not a straight-A student, but solid. Math came easily to him. Reading took more effort, but he never gave up. He had this determination." Wells pulls a tissue from her pocket, dabs at her eyes. "I'm sorry."

"Take your time," Emma says gently.

"His science project last month was on constellations. He built this mobile of the solar system and gave a presentation about how ancient people used stars to navigate. He was so excited about it." Her voice breaks. "He talked about wanting to be an astronaut when he grew up."

Something cold touches the back of my neck. Constellations. The star man Brenda mentioned.

"Did he say where he learned about astronomy?" I ask carefully.

Wells thinks about it. "He mentioned learning things from books at home, but also... he said someone had been teaching him about the night sky. I assumed he meant his father."

But Warren Caine said the boys talked about meeting someone in the woods. Someone who knew all the constellations.

Matthew's teacher, Robert Kim, is younger, maybe early thirties. He teaches the other second-grade class and speaks about Matthew with the same clear affection Wells showed for Titus.

"Matthew was quieter than his brother," Kim says. "But not shy. Just... observant. He'd sit back and watch before he participated in something new. He was the kid who noticed everything."

"Like what?" Emma asks.

"Details other children missed. If I changed the classroom seating arrangement, Matthew would be the one to comment on it. If someone was having a bad day, he'd pick up on it before I did sometimes. He was remarkably empathetic for his age."

Kim pulls out a folder and slides it across the table. Inside are drawings Matthew made during art time. They're detailed, careful. A forest scene with individual leaves on trees. A portrait of what must be his family.

"He loved to draw," Kim continues. "Especially nature scenes. He'd spend his whole recess sitting under a tree sketching if we let him."

"Did he ever draw anything unusual?" I ask. "Or mention meeting anyone new?"

Kim considers this. "Actually, yes. About two weeks ago he drew a picture of a man standing in the woods at night. When I asked him about it, he said he and Titus had met someone who taught them about nocturnal animals. About how owls hunt and why deer move differently after dark."

My pen stills on the page. "Did he describe this person?"

"Just that he was tall and knew a lot about the woods. Matthew seemed excited about it. He said the man told him he had a gift for observation." Kim's expression darkens. "Should I have reported that? I thought it sounded like someone from the nature center or a family friend."

"You couldn't have known," Emma says, but I can see her jaw tightening.

We spend another hour interviewing support staff. The librarian remembers both boys checking out books about space and forest ecology. The gym teacher says they were well-coordinated, loved outdoor activities, often asked to play capture the flag instead of basketball. The lunch lady recalls Matthew always saying please and thank you, Titus asking about her grandchildren.

Everyone loved these boys. No red flags, no behavioral concerns, no signs of trouble at home or with peers.

By the time we finish at the school, it's past noon. Emma and I sit in her car in the parking lot, reviewing notes.

"Two well-adjusted, happy kids," Emma says. "Good students, good friends. Loved by their teachers. No indication of problems."

"Except someone was grooming them while teaching them about the stars," I say.

Emma starts the engine but doesn't put the car in gear yet. "The nature education angle is interesting. Both teachers mentioned the boys were excited about outdoor learning."

"Let's talk to the neighbors next," I suggest. "See what they know about the family's routines."

THE CAINE HOUSE sits at the end of a quiet street that backs up to national forest. The neighboring houses are spaced far apart, separated by mature trees. Privacy was clearly a priority for people who bought here.

We start with the house directly to the right of the Caines'. An elderly woman named Margaret Foster answers the door in a quilted vest, reading glasses pushed up on her head. She invites us into a living room that smells like lavender and old books.

"Lovely family," she says, settling into an armchair. "The

boys would wave to me every morning when they waited for the school bus. Such polite children."

"Did you ever see them playing in the woods behind the houses?" I ask.

"Oh, all the time. They were little adventurers. They'd come back with interesting things to show their mother. Pine cones, leaves, once a shed snake skin that made Brenda squeal." Foster smiles at the memory, then her expression falls. "I still can't believe they're gone."

"Did you ever notice anyone else in the woods?" Emma asks. "Maybe someone the boys were talking to?"

Foster thinks about this, her fingers tapping against the arm of her chair. "Now that you mention it, about a month ago I saw the boys standing at the edge of the tree line talking to someone. I couldn't see who it was clearly, the trees were too thick. But they seemed animated, excited about something."

"Did you mention this to their parents?"

"No. The woods are public land. People hike through there all the time. I didn't think anything of it." Her hand moves to her mouth. "Should I have?"

"You had no reason to be concerned," I assure her, though my stomach is knotting.

We interview two more neighbors. One mentions seeing a parked car on the access road that runs along the forest edge a few times over the past month. Dark sedan, couldn't make out the model. Another says she'd seen the boys heading into the woods on Saturday mornings, which was unusual because they typically slept late on weekends.

Saturday mornings. Regular schedule. Easy to predict, easy to plan around.

Back in the car, Emma pulls out her phone. "I'm going to

check if there are any organized activities in that forest. Nature centers, hiking groups, educational programs."

She searches while I stare at the Caine house. The tire swing hanging motionless. The sandbox covered with snow. The cheerful blue trim that now looks garish against all this grief.

"Found something," Emma says, turning her screen toward me. "Greenwood Legacy Foundation. They run environmental education programs for families. Says here they do weekend nature walks, teach kids about local ecosystems, wildlife identification, that kind of thing."

"Are they based nearby?"

Emma scrolls. "Office in downtown Charlottesville. Programs held at various locations including Shenandoah National Forest. They work with schools too, providing supplemental science education." She looks up at me. "Their Saturday morning program is called 'Junior Naturalists.' For kids ages six to twelve."

The age range includes the Caine twins perfectly.

"Let me see their staff page," I say.

Emma navigates to it. Photos of smiling instructors in hiking gear. Bios highlighting degrees in biology, environmental science, outdoor education. It all looks legitimate and professional. It's exactly the kind of program parents would trust.

And then I see a name that makes my breath catch.

The program director is listed as Eleanor Vance. PhD in mythology and folklore, extensive background in environmental education, dedicated to "reconnecting families with ancient wisdom and natural cycles."

That is exactly the same kind of language Brenda used when talking about her sons being chosen.

"Emma," I say quietly. "Look at this bio."

She reads it, and I watch her expression shift from curiosity to alarm.

"Call the field office," I tell her. "I want everything we can find on Greenwood Legacy Foundation and Eleanor Vance. Financial records, tax filings, program rosters, everything."

Emma's already dialing. While she talks to whoever's answering at the office, I screenshot the webpage. Eleanor Vance's professional photo shows a woman in her late forties with an easy smile, wearing a fleece vest over a turtleneck. She looks approachable, trustworthy. Like someone you'd be happy to leave your children with on a Saturday morning.

"Apparently, both Titus and Matthew attended a nature program every Saturday morning," Emma says hanging up.

I pull up the program calendar on my phone. The last Saturday session before the boys died was nine days ago. The topic was "Winter Solstice Traditions and Celestial Navigation."

My hands are steady as I take screenshots, but inside I'm already connecting the dots. The symbols carved into oak trees. The precise positioning under the stars.

If this organization had anything to do with their deaths, it's not just one person hurting two children. It's systemic and hidden in plain sight.

Emma ends her call. "Garrett's pulling everything now. Says we should have preliminary financials within an hour."

"We need to visit their office," I say. "Today."

"Agreed. But River..." Emma's looking at me carefully. "Are you thinking what I'm thinking?"

"That the person who killed Titus and Matthew Caine had regular, supervised access to them through a program their parents thought was safe?" I meet her eyes. "Yes. That's exactly what I'm thinking."

My phone buzzes. A text from Siwak: *Toxicology preliminary back. Need you at office ASAP.*

"Change of plans," I tell Emma. "Office first, then Greenwood Legacy Foundation."

As she drives, I can't stop thinking about those Saturday mornings and about two boys excited to learn about nature. I also can't stop thinking about how predators don't alway lurk in the shadows.

CHAPTER SEVEN

Warren Caine hasn't slept in three days.

He sits at the kitchen table watching dawn lighten the windows, the same way he's watched every dawn since they found his boys. The coffee in his mug has gone cold. He doesn't remember pouring it. Time moves strangely now, lurching forward and backward without warning.

The house is too quiet. That's what kills him. No footsteps thundering down the stairs. No argument over who gets the bathroom first. No cereal boxes rattling, no backpacks being stuffed with homework folders and lunch boxes. Just silence pressing against his ears until he wants to scream.

Brenda is upstairs sleeping. Or pretending to sleep. She's gotten good at pretending lately.

His hands shake as he lifts the mug. The coffee tastes like dirt. Everything tastes like crap now. Food, water, the air itself. Nothing sits right in his stomach. The doctor tried to give him something to help him rest, but Warren refused.

Sleep means dreams, and dreams mean seeing Titus and Matthew in that clearing the way the FBI agent described it. Arranged like dolls. Peaceful. Dead.

He sets the mug down hard enough that it cracks against the table. The sound is sharp, satisfying. He wants to break something. Wants to put his fist through a wall or throw every dish in the kitchen against the floor. But that would wake Brenda, and he can't face her right now. Can't look at her calm face and hear her talk about transformation and chosen ones and the boys being where they're meant to be.

His wife is insane. That's the only explanation. Grief has broken something fundamental in her brain. Except.

Except.

Warren rubs his eyes with the heels of his hands. The problem is that Brenda started changing before the boys died. He's been trying not to think about it, trying to chalk it up to his own guilt and horror twisting his memories. But sitting here in the gray morning light, he can't lie to himself anymore.

It started about a year ago. Small things at first. She stopped watching television with him at night, said the noise disturbed her new meditation practice. She started buying books about energy healing and sacred geometry and ancient traditions. Started using phrases like "old wisdom" and "natural cycles" that made him uncomfortable in a way he couldn't name.

He'd thought it was a phase. Middle-aged woman searching for meaning, right? Plenty of people got into yoga or Buddhism or whatever. It seemed harmless. She was happy, or at least she seemed happy. More centered, she called it. More aligned with her true purpose.

The red flags were everywhere and he'd just ignored them.

She'd been the one who found Greenwood Legacy Foundation. Came home one day excited about this nature program for kids, said it would be good for Titus and Matthew to learn about the environment. Warren had looked at the website, seen the professional photos and educational mission statement, figured why not. The boys loved being outdoors. It seemed perfect.

They'd gone to the first Saturday session together, all four of them. Met Eleanor Vance, the program director, who had a PhD and spoke passionately about reconnecting children with the natural world. She seemed impressive. Knowledgeable. The other families there looked normal. Other parents were making the same choice they were making.

After that first session, Brenda started going alone with the boys. Said Warren worked too hard during the week, he should sleep in on Saturdays. He'd been grateful. Let himself enjoy those quiet mornings with coffee and the newspaper.

Now he wonders what happened during those Saturday sessions he didn't attend.

The FBI agents had asked about Brenda's spiritual interests. He'd tried to explain them away, make them sound normal. But one of the agents, the one with the careful eyes and mousy brown hair, she'd looked at him like she knew he was lying. Not to her. To himself.

Upstairs, floorboards creak. Brenda is awake.

Warren's chest tightens. He doesn't know this woman anymore. The person sleeping in his bed, the mother of his dead children, she's a stranger wearing his wife's face.

Yesterday during the FBI interview, she'd talked about the boys being chosen. About double souls and bridging and transformation. She'd smiled when she said it. *Smiled.*

What kind of mother smiles when her children are dead?

The kind who wanted them dead, a voice whispers in his head. The kind who let it happen.

No. No, he can't think that. Brenda loved those boys. She made them Halloween costumes by hand and volunteered in their classrooms and kept every drawing they ever made. She threw elaborate birthday parties and read them stories every night and sang to them when they were sick.

But she'd also talked about them being special. About their twins having gifts other children didn't have. About them being meant for something greater than an ordinary life.

He'd thought she meant they'd grow up to be scientists or artists or something. Successful. Fulfilled.

Not whatever *this* is.

Warren's phone sits on the table next to his broken coffee mug. He should call his brother in Ohio, let his family know about the funeral arrangements. Should check in with his office, tell them he needs more time. Should eat something even though the thought of food makes him want to vomit.

Instead, he sits frozen, watching light creep across the tile.

The boys loved this kitchen. Titus would do homework at this table, tongue sticking out in concentration. Matthew would draw pictures while Brenda cooked dinner, his pencil making soft scratching sounds against paper. They'd had a good life here.

When did it stop being normal?

Brenda appears in the doorway. She's wearing a long nightgown, her hair loose around her shoulders. She looks ethereal in the morning light. Beautiful and terrifying.

"You're up early," she says.

"Couldn't sleep."

She moves to the coffee maker, pours herself a cup. Her hands are steady. No shaking, no trembling. She's been sleeping fine, apparently. Eating fine. Functioning like nothing happened.

"The FBI agents are coming back today," Warren says. "They want formal statements."

"I know." Brenda sips her coffee, looking out the window at their backyard. At the woods beyond where their sons used to play. "I'm ready to tell them everything."

Something in her voice makes Warren's skin prickle. "Everything?"

"About the program. About what Eleanor taught them. About their purpose." She turns to look at him, and her eyes are distant. Serene. "It's time people understood."

"Understood what?" His voice cracks. "Brenda, our sons are dead. What is there to understand?"

"That death isn't an ending. That some souls are meant for greater passages. That Titus and Matthew were bridges to something beyond our limited perception." She speaks like she's reciting from a script. Like these aren't her own words.

Warren stands so fast his chair scrapes against the floor. "Stop. Just stop talking like that. You sound insane."

"You've always been afraid of things you can't see." No anger in her voice, just pity. "That's why you could never understand what our sons were becoming."

"They were becoming third-graders! They were becoming kids who liked Star Wars and soccer and reading chapter books!" His hands are fists now, shaking at his sides. "They weren't becoming anything else because they're dead, Brenda. Someone killed them."

"Someone prepared them," she corrects gently. "Someone helped them fulfill their purpose."

He can't breathe. The kitchen is too small, the walls pressing in. His wife is insane. His sons are dead. And somehow these two facts are connected in ways he's only beginning to understand.

"I'm calling my lawyer," Warren says. His voice sounds far away, like it belongs to someone else. "I think you need help. Professional help."

"I have all the help I need." Brenda sets down her coffee mug with a soft click. "The foundation. Eleanor. The others who understand. They're my family now."

"I'm your family. I was your family. Those boys were your family."

"They still are. They're just in a different place now. Doing important work."

Warren backs toward the doorway. He needs to get away from her before he says something he can't take back. Or does something worse. His whole body is shaking with rage and grief and a creeping horror he doesn't know how to name.

"I'm going to tell the FBI everything," he says. "About the foundation. About Eleanor Vance. About how you've been acting. All of it."

Brenda just nods, unbothered. "Tell them whatever you need to tell them. The truth doesn't change based on your understanding of it."

He leaves her standing in the kitchen. Takes the stairs two at a time, goes into the bathroom and locks the door. Sits on the closed toilet seat with his head in his hands and tries not to fall apart completely.

His phone buzzes in his pocket. Probably his brother checking in. Warren pulls it out, ready to ignore the call.

But it's not a call. It's a text message from an unknown number.

They're with the stars now. As was promised. Be at peace.

Warren stares at the screen. Reads it again. Then again.

As was promised.

His hands start shaking so hard he almost drops the phone. Who sent this? Who would send this? He scrolls up but there's no message history with this number. This is the first text from whoever this is.

As was promised.

Brenda's voice drifts up from downstairs, humming something. A melody he doesn't recognize.

Warren looks at the text again. The words blur through tears he didn't realize were falling.

Someone promised that his sons would die. Someone made a plan. And somehow, impossibly, Brenda knew about it. Maybe she more than knew about it. Maybe she agreed to it. Did she help?

He needs to call the FBI agents and show them this message. He needs to tell them about Brenda's strange calmness, her talk of purpose and bridges and transformation.

But his hands won't stop shaking enough to dial. And somewhere in the back of his mind, a terrible question is forming.

If Brenda knew what was going to happen to the boys, if

she believed in their "purpose" enough to let it happen, what else is she capable of? What else has already been set in motion?

Warren saves the screenshot of the text message. Then he opens his phone's browser and searches for hotels nearby. He can't stay here. Not anymore. Not with her.

CHAPTER EIGHT

The conference room on the third floor has better lighting than my desk, which is why Emma and I claimed it the moment we got back to the field office. The table is covered with printouts—crime scene photos, close-ups of the oak tree carvings, the wooden token found near Titus Caine's hand. Everything arranged in careful rows like pieces of a puzzle we're trying to solve through sheer organization.

My eyes burn from staring at the symbols for the past two hours. I've traced the patterns so many times my finger has an indent from the pen I was using. Circle with intersecting lines. Smaller circles at specific points.

"The wood analysis came back," Emma says, reading from her laptop. "The token and the tree carvings are both white oak. Same species as the trees in the clearing."

"So our killer carved the token from one of those ancient trees."

"Or from another white oak in the area. The forest is full of them." Emma clicks through more files. "But the symbolism is intentional. Using wood from a centuries-old tree to mark an eight-year-old victim."

I pull one of the close-up photos closer. The carving is remarkably clean, each line cut with precision. "This took time. And skill. You don't learn to carve like this overnight."

"Garrett tracked down three local woodworkers who do custom carving. Two have solid alibis for the night the boys died, one is seventy-eight years old and uses a wheelchair." Emma closes her laptop with a frustrated sigh. "Dead end."

My phone buzzes. A text from Siwak: *Dr. Tavares is here. Conference room C.*

"The anthropologist," I tell Emma, already gathering the photos. "Let's see if she can tell us what these symbols mean."

Conference room C is smaller, windowless. Dr. Helena Tavares is waiting when we arrive, and she's not what I expected. Most forensic anthropologists I've met are either fresh-faced academics or weathered field researchers. Tavares is somewhere in between—late forties maybe, with dark hair streaked with gray pulled back in a practical braid. She's wearing jeans and a blazer over a faded Smithsonian Museum t-shirt. Reading glasses hang from a beaded chain around her neck.

"Agents Collins and Bertanelli?" She stands to shake our hands. Her grip is firm, her palms calloused. "Helena Tavares. I understand you have some interesting symbols for me to look at."

"Interesting is one word for them," I say, spreading the photos across the table. "Disturbing is another."

Tavares pulls on her reading glasses and leans over the images. She's quiet for a long moment, her finger tracing the air above one of the tree carvings without touching the photo itself.

"Where did you find these?" she asks finally.

"Crime scene. Two eight-year-old victims found in the Blue Ridge Mountains, positioned in a clearing surrounded by seven oak trees. Each tree had this symbol carved into it."

"And this?" Tavares picks up the photo of the wooden token.

"Found near one victim's hand. Same symbol, carved into white oak."

Tavares sets the photo down carefully, like it might bite. She moves to another image, then another, studying each one with the kind of focused intensity I recognize. She's not just looking at them. She's reading them.

"This is sophisticated work," she says. "The execution is modern. It has clean cuts made with a sharp blade, but the symbology is ancient. Very ancient."

Emma pulls out her notebook. "Can you be more specific?"

"The core design is proto-Indo-European. The circle represents cosmic order, the boundary between worlds. The intersecting lines are paths of transition." Tavares traces the pattern with her finger. "But layered on top of that are Celtic and Norse influences. These smaller circles here? They mark cardinal directions but also celestial bodies. The way they're positioned suggests winter solstice alignment."

My chest tightens. Winter solstice. The boys died in December, but the symbolism points to the darkest time of year. Death and rebirth. Transformation.

"What about these marks?" I point to small notches along some of the lines. "Are they decorative?"

"No. Nothing about this is decorative." Tavares pulls out

her phone and takes several photos of our crime scene images. "These notches are counting marks. Seven of them in a specific sequence. They're measuring something."

"Measuring what?" Emma asks.

"Days, possibly. Or ritual steps. Hard to say without more context." Tavares sits back, removing her glasses. "Where did you say you found these symbols?"

"Blue Ridge Mountains. Clearing with seven ancient oak trees."

"Oak is sacred in multiple traditions. Seven is a mystical number—days of the week, classical planets, stages of transformation." She's speaking faster now, making connections. "The victims were children?"

"Twin boys. Eight years old."

Something shifts in Tavares' expression. "Twins. Of course. Double souls, liminal beings, perfect for threshold work."

The phrase hits me like cold water. Double souls. Brenda Caine used almost the exact same words.

"Threshold work?" I keep my voice steady. "What does that mean?"

"The symbols tell a story," Tavares says, standing to examine the photos from a different angle. "It's a ritual sequence. Preparation, purification, transformation, passage. The positioning of the symbols on the trees, the way they relate to each other spatially—it's a map for moving between states of being."

"Between life and death," Emma says quietly.

"Between this world and whatever comes next. Every major religious tradition has some version of it. The Greeks had psychopomps, guides for the dead. Norse mythology had Bifrost, the rainbow bridge. Celtic druids performed rituals at thin places where the veil between worlds grew transparent." Tavares taps one of the photos. "This is someone invoking very old practices. Someone who understands not just the symbols but their function."

I think about the man in my captivity, teaching me to tie my shoes with a complex knot. *These bindings matter. Everything connects. Everything serves the crossing.*

"What if the ritual wasn't about guiding the dead?" I ask. "What if it was about using them for something? Using their deaths to accomplish something?"

Tavares meets my eyes. "Then you're talking about sacrifice. Which is the oldest ritual of all."

The room feels colder. Emma is very still beside me, her pen frozen over her notebook.

"Human sacrifice," Emma says. "You're saying these symbols are instructions for human sacrifice."

"I'm saying they describe a process of transformation through death. Whether that's metaphorical or literal depends on who's interpreting them." Tavares gathers the photos into a stack, aligning their edges with precision. "There are groups that study these practices academically. Neo-pagans, reconstructionists, scholars of ancient religion. Most of them would be horrified by actual violence. But occasionally you get someone who takes it too far. Someone who decides that understanding isn't enough—they need to practice."

"Do you know anyone like that?" I ask. "Anyone in this area who has that kind of knowledge?"

"No one I'd suspect of murder. But I can make some calls, ask around the academic community. Someone this skilled in ancient symbols likely has formal education or deep self-study. They'd need access to primary sources, archaeological reports, museum collections."

I pull out my phone and show her the Greenwood Legacy Foundation website, Eleanor Vance's bio displayed. "What about her?"

Tavares reads it, her expression neutral. "PhD in mythology and folklore from UVA. That would give her the background. But environmental education is a far cry from ritual murder."

"She ran Saturday nature programs for children," Emma says. "Including our victims. Used language about 'ancient wisdom' and 'natural cycles.'"

"That's not uncommon in environmental education. Lots of programs draw on indigenous practices and traditional ecological knowledge." But Tavares is frowning now, looking at Eleanor Vance's photo more carefully. "Still, the combination of expertise and access is concerning."

I take back my phone and pull up another photo—the one of all seven trees arranged in the clearing. "Can you tell us anything else about the layout? Why seven trees, why that specific positioning?"

Tavares studies it for a long moment. "Seven is the number of completion in many traditions. The positioning creates a temenos—sacred space set apart from the ordinary world. It's a container for transformation. Whatever happened in that clearing, the killer believed they were creating conditions for passage."

"The crossing," I say quietly.

Both Emma and Tavares look at me.

"That's what someone might call it," Tavares says slowly. "A crossing. Movement from one state to another. Why?"

I can't tell her about my own captivity. Not yet. Not

without more evidence connecting the cases. "Just something that came up in interviews."

Tavares doesn't look convinced, but she doesn't push. Instead, she picks up the full spread of crime scene photos—wide shots showing all seven trees, the chalk outlines, the surrounding forest.

She goes very still.

"Dr. Tavares?" Emma prompts.

Tavares sets the photos down carefully. Her face has lost color, her hands not quite steady now.

"Where exactly in the Blue Ridge was this clearing?" Her voice is tight.

"About fifteen miles northwest of Charlottesville. Near Riprap Trail access."

"What's the tree formation? I need precise measurements."

Emma pulls out the forensic report. "Circular clearing approximately thirty feet in diameter. Seven oaks forming a ring with roughly even spacing. Forty-two to forty-four feet between tree centers."

Tavares closes her eyes briefly. When she opens them, she's looking at me with something like dread.

"I've seen these exact symbols before," she says. "In a case file from 1994. I consulted on it early in my career, right after I finished my doctorate."

The room seems to tilt. 1994. Thirty-one years ago.

"What case?" Emma asks, already pulling out her laptop.

"Two children found dead in the Appalachian Mountains. A brother and sister, ages nine and eleven. They were found in a clearing surrounded by oak trees with these same symbols carved into the bark." Tavares taps the photos.

"Same geometric pattern. Same positioning. Same winter solstice orientation."

My mouth has gone dry. "Were the children positioned in any specific way?"

"In a circle. Arms at specific angles, like hands on a clock. The investigating agents thought it was ritualistic, brought me in to analyze the symbols. But we never found the killer. The case went cold." Tavares looks at each of us in turn. "The lead investigator kept working it for years after everyone else moved on. I remember because he'd call me every winter solstice, asking if I'd found any new information about the symbols."

"Do you remember his name?" I ask.

"Agent Thomas Mercer. FBI. He retired about five years ago." Tavares picks up one of the photos again, her hands steadier now. "If these symbols are showing up again after thirty years, either someone is copying that old case, or..."

"Or the person who killed those children in 1994 is still active," Emma finishes.

The silence that follows is heavy with implications. A killer working for three decades. Multiple victims over multiple years. All of them children. All of them arranged in clearings marked with ancient symbols of transformation and sacrifice.

All of them part of the crossing.

"I need everything you have on that 1994 case," I say. "Reports, photos, witness statements, all of it."

"I'll have to track down my old files. It's been a long time." Tavares is already pulling out her phone. "But I remember some details. The children were siblings, not twins. They attended some kind of outdoor education program run by a local nature group. And there was a photograph taken at one of their events—a group shot of instructors and families. The FBI was never able to identify everyone in that photo, but there was a woman whose face was partially obscured. They tried to enhance it but the technology wasn't good enough back then."

My heart is pounding. "Do you still have that photograph?"

"It should be in my files. I'll look for it tonight and send you whatever I find." Tavares gathers her things, but she's moving slowly, reluctance in every gesture. "Agent Collins, if this is the same killer, they've been at this for over thirty years. That's a long time to perfect a technique. A long time to build a network or following. You're not just dealing with one person anymore. You might be dealing with a movement."

After she leaves, Emma and I sit in silence. The photos are still spread across the table, the symbols seeming to pulse in the fluorescent light.

"1994," Emma says finally. "Agent Mercer. We need to find him."

"And we need to see that photograph. If there's a woman in it who was involved in an outdoor education program thirty years ago, and Eleanor Vance is running similar programs now..." I don't finish the thought. Don't need to.

Emma's already searching databases on her laptop. "Thomas Mercer. Retired 2019 after thirty-five years with the Bureau. Last known address is Fredericksburg, Virginia."

"Call him. Set up a meeting. I want to talk to him about that 1994 case." I start gathering the photos, organizing them back into files. "And get everything you can from the archives. If Mercer kept working the case, there should be mountains of follow-up reports."

"River." Emma's voice makes me look up. "If this killer has been active since 1994, and your abduction was..." She trails off, but I know what she's thinking.

My abduction was in 2003. Nine years after the 1994 murders. Right in the middle of what might be a thirty-year killing spree.

"I know," I say quietly. "Believe me, I know."

But I don't tell her about the symbols carved into my concrete prison wall. About the knots and the crossing and the preparations that never reached completion. Because if I'm right, if my captors were part of this same network, then I wasn't just a random victim.

I was chosen. Prepared. Meant for something.

And somehow, I got away before they could finish what they started.

The question is: did they ever stop looking for me?

CHAPTER NINE

My sister, Leslie's, house looks the same from the outside. Perfect suburban scene with its manicured lawn, seasonal wreath on the door, warm lights glowing through the windows. If I didn't know better, I'd think nothing had changed since my last visit.

But I do know better.

"Shoes off, please," Leslie says as I step inside, her voice carrying that forced brightness that means she's barely holding it together. "Bennett just tracked mud through the kitchen."

The interior is exactly as I remember it. High ceilings, sage green La Cornue stove in the massive kitchen, perfectly coordinated backsplash, pale pink enameled cookware arranged just so. Everything thought out to the last detail. The house that Leslie worked so hard to make perfect.

The house she's now maintaining alone.

"Aunt River!" My nephew appears in the hallway, six years old and gangly in dinosaur pajama pants even though it's only five-thirty. "Look what I made at school!"

He's clutching a piece of construction paper covered in crayon drawings. I crouch down to his level, accepting the offering. "Let me see, buddy."

Before I can examine it properly, my niece toddles into view. Ava is four, all blonde curls and sticky fingers. She crashes into my legs.

"River! River! I gots a new baby doll!"

"You got a new baby doll," Leslie corrects automatically, following her daughter out. My sister looks exhausted. Her blonde hair is in a messy ponytail, no makeup, yoga pants that have seen better days. This is a version of Leslie I rarely see—the one without the careful presentation, without the Instagram-ready aesthetic.

I pick up Ava, settling her on my hip while she babbles about her doll's name, which is apparently Princess Sparkle Unicorn. Bennett dances around us, still trying to show me his drawing.

"In a minute, Bennett," I tell him. "Let me say hi to your mom first."

Leslie attempts a smile but it doesn't reach her eyes. "Dinner's almost ready. Just pasta and sauce from a jar. Nothing fancy."

This is a change. This is a woman who used to make everything from scratch, who coordinated her cookware with her backsplash. The small surrenders of someone barely keeping it together.

"Sounds perfect," I say.

I follow her into the kitchen while Ava clings to me like a koala. The familiar space smells like marinara and garlic bread. Normal. Comforting. It's completely at odds with the tension radiating off my sister.

"Can you set the table?" Leslie asks, pulling plates from

the cabinet. "I've been so scattered lately I can't remember if I even have napkins."

I locate everything, setting the table one-handed while Ava plays with my hair. Bennett has moved on to building something with blocks in the family room, his drawing temporarily forgotten on the counter.

"How are you doing?" I ask quietly. "Really?"

Leslie's shoulders sag. She sets down the plates carefully, gripping the edge of the counter. "I'm managing. One day at a time. All the clichés people say because there aren't words for how much this sucks."

Two months ago Chris moved out, according to what Siwak told me. Two months of Leslie navigating this house alone, maintaining the perfect facade while everything crumbles inside.

"The kids still think he's on a business trip," Leslie continues, pulling garlic bread from the oven. "We agreed not to tell them until we figured out the details. Custody, division of assets, all of it. Bennett asks when Daddy's coming home every single night."

Guilt sits heavy in my chest. I saw Chris at the hospital with another woman last fall. Saw the way he touched her back, the intimacy between them. And I didn't say anything to Leslie. Didn't warn her.

"Leslie," I start, but she shakes her head.

"Don't. I know that look. Whatever you're about to apologize for, don't."

"I should have told you what I saw."

She goes very still, her back to me. "You saw him with her."

It's not a question. I set Ava down, who immediately runs off, and move closer to my sister.

"At the hospital. Last fall. I was interviewing a patient, and I saw Chris in the parking garage with a woman. The way he was with her..." I trail off. "I thought about telling you every day. But I didn't know for sure, and I didn't want to hurt you if I was wrong."

Leslie turns around. Her eyes are wet but no tears fall. "You weren't wrong. Her name is Amanda. She does sound healing or energy work or some bullshit. They met at one of those meditation retreats Chris started going to last year."

"How did you find out?" I ask.

"Credit card statements. A hotel in Richmond on a weekend he said he was at a work conference. When I confronted him, he didn't even try to deny it." Leslie laughs, but it's bitter. "He said Amanda understands him in ways I never could. That she's on the same spiritual journey. That he needs to be authentic to his true self."

"That's crap."

"That's what I said. Less politely." She wipes her eyes with the back of her hand. "I told him to get out. He packed a bag that night. We told the kids he had an extended business trip while we 'worked things out.'" She makes air quotes with her fingers. "But we're not working anything out. I want a divorce. I just don't want to traumatize the kids more than necessary."

I can picture it. Leslie in full fury, the woman I grew up with who never backed down from a fight, who became a lawyer because she loved winning arguments. That woman has been buried under years of perfect-wife-and-mother performance, but she's still in there.

"I'm proud of you," I say.

She looks at me, surprised. "For what? Failing at marriage?"

"For knowing when to walk away. For protecting yourself and the kids." I lean against the counter. "That takes strength."

Leslie's face crumples. I pull her into a hug, letting her cry into my shoulder while Bennett and Ava play obliviously in the next room. She shakes with the kind of grief that comes from losing not just a relationship but a whole imagined future.

"I'm so stupid," she says into my shirt. "All the signs were there. The late nights. The new interest in spirituality. The distance. I just kept telling myself it was a phase."

"You're not stupid. And you're not the problem. He chose to cheat. That's on him."

She pulls back, wiping her face with her sleeve. "The worst part is I still love him. How messed up is that?"

"That's not messed up. That's human."

Bennett appears in the doorway. "Mommy, are you sad?"

Leslie composes herself instantly, switching into mom mode. "I'm okay, honey. Just talking to Aunt River about grown-up stuff. Are you hungry?"

"Starving!" He throws his arms wide for emphasis.

We eat dinner at the long table in the formal dining room, the one Leslie usually reserves for holidays. Bennett chats about school, about his friend who can read chapter books, about the class hamster who escaped. Ava mostly plays with her pasta, making sauce patterns on her plate.

It's chaotic and messy and normal. The sounds of family filling this too-big house where one parent is conspicuously absent.

After dinner, Leslie bathes the kids while I clean up in her beautiful kitchen. I find solace in the mundane comfort of loading the dishwasher and wiping down counters.

By the time the kids are in pajamas, it's past seven. Leslie sets them up in the family room with a cartoon while we have coffee.

"How's your case going?" she asks.

"The twin boys are dead. Found them two days ago." I wrap my hands around my mug. "The mother is involved somehow. She talks about them being chosen, about their deaths serving a higher purpose."

Leslie looks sick. "That's insane."

"That's what I thought. But the more we investigate, the more we find. There's an environmental education program that might be a cover for recruitment." I pause. "And Chris's name showed up. Donor lists for the foundation running the nature programs."

She goes very still. "What?"

"Multiple donations over the past eighteen months. I'm not saying he's involved in anything criminal, but the foundation is definitely connected to the murders."

Leslie sets down her mug carefully. "He never mentioned donating to any foundation."

"I wanted to tell you first. I don't want you blindsided again."

"Thank you." She meets my eyes. "For telling me this time."

The guilt eases slightly.

Bennett wanders into the kitchen, dragging his feet. "I'm not tired."

"Nice try, kiddo," Leslie says. "It's bedtime."

"But I wanted to show Aunt River my picture!"

He runs back to the family room and returns with the drawing he tried to show me earlier. I take it, expecting dinosaurs or spaceships.

Instead, I'm looking at a forest scene. Trees drawn with careful detail. And on several of the trees, there are marks. Symbols.

My blood goes cold.

"That's beautiful, Bennett," I manage. "Where did you learn to draw trees like this?"

"From the nice lady at the nature place!" He beams. "She showed us how to look at tree bark up close. Some trees have patterns on them."

Leslie frowns. "They went on a field trip last month to some environmental place."

"For school. Mrs. Patterson said it was ed-u-ca-tion-al." He sounds out the word carefully. "The nice lady taught us about the forest and showed us trees with special marks. She said they tell stories if you know how to read them."

I force myself to breathe normally. "Do you remember the lady's name?"

"Miss Eleanor. She was really nice. She gave us all cookies shaped like leaves."

The room tilts. Eleanor Vance. Running programs for Gerald Ford Elementary, where the Caine twins went to school. And apparently Bennett's school too.

"Did Miss Eleanor teach you anything else?" I ask, keeping my voice casual.

"She said some kids are special. That they can see things other people can't see." Bennett yawns. "She said if we're really quiet in the forest, we can hear the old voices."

"That's really interesting, buddy," I say. "Can I keep this drawing? I'd love to put it on my fridge."

"Really?" His face lights up. "Okay!"

Leslie hustles the kids off to bed. I sit alone in her perfect kitchen, staring at Bennett's drawing. The symbols aren't exact matches—a six-year-old's interpretation, simplified. But the basic structure is there. Circles. Intersecting lines.

Leslie returns ten minutes later and looks at me, surprised. "What's going on?" She asks.

"I think that Bennett was with the woman who had something to do with the murder of those boys."

Her mouth drops open and she grows pale.

I pull out my phone. "I need to call Emma. We need every school Greenwood Legacy has worked with."

Leslie sinks into a chair. "Chris took them to a Greenwood family event last fall. Before he moved out. Some family wellness workshop. I didn't go—I had a headache. He took them without me."

"I need to talk to him," I say. "Where's he staying?"

"With Amanda." Leslie's hands shake as she pulls out her phone, sends me the address. "River, if he knew what these people were doing, if he exposed our kids..."

"I'll find out what he knows."

She wraps her arms around herself. "What if Eleanor tries to contact Bennett? What if she targets him?"

"Has anyone from Greenwood reached out since the field trip?"

"I don't know." Fear naked on her face. "They could have our information. Our address."

I move beside her. "Tomorrow I'll have security check the house. We'll make sure you're safe. And I'll talk to Bennett's teacher about that field trip."

"I want to keep them home from school."

"That might be smart. At least until we know the extent of Greenwood's school involvement."

From upstairs, Ava starts singing about princesses. Innocent. Oblivious.

"I'm scared," Leslie says quietly.

"It's going to be okay. I will do everything in my power to protect Bennett and Ava."

She nods, but I can tell that she doesn't exactly believe me.

"I need to go," I tell her. "Follow up on this tonight."

At the door, she grabs my hand. "Be careful."

"I will."

"River." Her grip tightens. "Thank you." She pulls me into a fierce hug. "I love you."

"I love you too."

I'm in my car when Emma texts: *Got Mercer's contact. Meeting tomorrow. Tavares sent the 1994 file—you need to see these photos.*

I forward Bennett's drawing. *Greenwood ran a field trip for my nephew's school last month.*

Emma's response: *Jesus. Is Bennett okay?*

For now. But we need every school they've worked with.

I stare at the drawing on my passenger seat. A six-year-old boy who learned about special tree marks from a nice lady who gave him cookies.

A nice lady who might be grooming children for ritual sacrifice.

CHAPTER TEN

Dr. Helena Tavares arrives at the FBI field office at nine the next morning carrying a worn leather messenger bag and a cardboard file box that looks like it's survived multiple moves. She's dressed the same as before—practical jeans, blazer over a museum t-shirt, reading glasses on a beaded chain. But there's a tension in her shoulders that wasn't there two days ago.

Emma and I meet her in the same conference room where we first discussed the symbols. The table is already covered with our current case materials—photos of the Caine twins, the oak tree carvings, the wooden token. Tavares sets her box down at the opposite end, like she's deliberately keeping the past and present separated.

"I haven't looked at these files in over a decade," she says, pulling manila folders from the box. "After Mercer retired, no one else showed much interest in the case. Eventually I archived everything in my home office and tried to forget about it."

"But you couldn't," I say.

She meets my eyes. "No. You don't forget cases like this. The children were Jennifer and Michael Hartley. I still remember their names."

Emma has her notebook ready, pen poised. I pull one of the chairs closer to Tavares, giving her space to spread out the materials.

The first thing she removes is a crime scene photo. Even after thirty years, even faded and slightly yellowed, the image is arresting. Two children lying in a clearing surrounded by trees. A girl with dark braids wearing a purple jacket. A boy in jeans and a striped shirt. Both positioned with the same geometric precision we saw with the Caine twins.

"Jennifer was eleven. Michael was nine." Tavares's voice is steady but quiet. "They disappeared on December nineteenth, 1994, after attending a Saturday nature program in the Monongahela National Forest in West Virginia. Their bodies were found two days later by a park ranger doing routine patrol."

I pick up the photo, studying the details. The positioning is nearly identical to our current case. Arms at specific angles, bodies forming part of a larger pattern. Peaceful expressions on their faces, like they're sleeping.

"Cause of death?" Emma asks.

"Unknown. Just like your current victims." Tavares pulls out the autopsy report, pages yellowed but still legible. "No external trauma, no signs of struggle, no obvious toxicology hits on the standard panels of the time. The medical examiner suspected some kind of plant-based compound but couldn't identify it with 1994 technology."

The parallels are impossible to ignore. I set down the first photo and reach for another. This one shows the clearing from above, seven oak trees forming a near-perfect circle. On each trunk, carved symbols.

My hands go cold. The symbols are identical to the ones we found on the Caine case. Not similar. Identical. The same geometric pattern, the same precision, the same positioning at adult eye level.

"How far apart were these trees?" I ask, my voice not quite steady.

Tavares consults the case file. "Forty-three feet between centers. The clearing was approximately thirty feet in diameter."

"The same measurements as our current scene," Emma says, checking her notes. "Forty-two to forty-four feet between trees, thirty-foot clearing."

Tavares nods slowly. "Whoever's doing this now is following the exact same template from 1994. Either they were directly involved in the original murders, or they have detailed knowledge of that case."

I flip through more photos. Wide shots of the forest. Close-ups of the carved symbols. Evidence markers placed around small items found at the scene. And then I see it—a photo of a wooden token, nearly identical to the one we found near Titus Caine's hand.

"They found a token too," I say, holding up the image.

"Near Jennifer's right hand. Same white oak, same symbol carved on both sides. Same approximate size." Tavares pulls out an evidence bag containing the actual token, preserved for three decades. "This was never released to the media. Very few people outside the investigation team knew about it."

Emma leans forward. "Which means our current killer

either worked the 1994 case or has inside knowledge from someone who did."

The implications are staggering. We're not just looking at a copycat. We're looking at someone with direct access to sealed case files, someone who knows details that were deliberately kept from the public.

"Tell us about the investigation," I say. "How did it unfold?"

Tavares settles into her chair, organizing the files in front of her. "The children's parents reported them missing when they didn't return from the nature program. The program director claimed the kids had been picked up by their parents at the designated time. But the parents never picked them up. Someone else took them."

"Who was running the program?" Emma asks.

"A local environmental education group called Mountain Heritage Foundation. They ran weekend programs for families, taught wilderness skills, local ecology, that kind of thing. It was well-regarded in the community. Parents trusted them."

Just like parents trust Greenwood Legacy Foundation now.

"The FBI got involved immediately because it was a potential abduction across state lines," Tavares continues. "Agent Thomas Mercer was assigned as lead investigator. He interviewed everyone associated with the foundation—instructors, volunteers, other families. But everyone had alibis for the time the children were taken."

"What about the person who claimed to pick them up?" I ask.

"That's where it got complicated. The program director, a woman named Margaret Ashford, insisted she saw the children leave with a man who identified himself as their uncle. But when shown photos of the children's actual relatives, she couldn't identify which one it was. Her description was vague—tall, average build, probably in his forties. Could have been anyone."

Emma's pen scratches across her notebook. "Did Mercer think she was lying?"

"He wasn't sure. She seemed genuinely shaken by what happened. But there were inconsistencies in her story. Small things that didn't quite line up." Tavares pulls out a typed interview transcript. "Three months into the investigation, Margaret Ashford disappeared. Left her apartment, left her job, left no forwarding address. Mercer tried to track her down but she'd vanished completely."

The room feels colder. I reach for another file, this one containing witness statements and investigative notes in neat handwriting. Mercer's notes, I assume.

"What else did Mercer find?" I ask.

"He discovered that several families who participated in the Mountain Heritage programs reported their children talking about a 'special teacher' who told them things about the forest. Old stories, ancient practices. Some parents thought it was charming—traditional folklore being passed down. Others found it odd but didn't think much of it."

My chest tightens. The same pattern. Children being taught about old ways, about being special, about having gifts others don't have. Grooming disguised as education.

"Did he identify this special teacher?" Emma asks.

Tavares pulls out another document, this one a list of program instructors and volunteers. "There were dozens of people involved with the foundation over the years. Mercer interviewed most of them. But several names on the volunteer lists couldn't be verified. People who'd worked one or two events, then disappeared. Fake names, probably."

I scan the list, my eyes catching on the dates. Programs running every Saturday from March through November. Family workshops. Summer camps. Years of access to children, years of opportunity.

"Mercer kept investigating long after the case officially went cold," Tavares says. "Every few months he'd call me, asking if I'd found any new information about the symbols. He became somewhat obsessed with it. His colleagues thought he needed to let it go, but he couldn't."

"Because he knew the killer was still out there," I say quietly.

"Because he knew it would happen again." Tavares pulls out a folder marked "SUSPECTS - ACTIVE." "Six months into the investigation, Mercer identified a person of interest. Someone with connections to the Mountain Heritage Foundation, someone with knowledge of ancient rituals and symbology."

Emma and I both lean forward.

"The suspect's name was redacted in most of the official reports," Tavares continues, flipping through pages. "But in Mercer's personal notes, which he shared with me years later, he referred to this person as being connected to a group called The Hollow Circle."

"The Hollow Circle," I repeat. The name sends ice through my veins. "What is that?"

"Mercer never found out exactly. His notes suggest it was some kind of organization or network, people who believed in ancient practices related to seasonal cycles and transformation rituals. He traced references to similar groups going back decades—different names, different locations, but similar beliefs."

Tavares pulls out a photocopy of Mercer's handwritten notes. The writing is cramped but legible, filled with circled phrases and connecting arrows.

Hollow Circle - operating since at least 1970s? Multiple sightings reported in Appalachian region. Members use nature education programs as cover for recruitment. Target children they believe have "gifts." Margaret Ashford had donor list showing contributions from HC-affiliated individuals. List disappeared when she did.

Primary suspect fled before warrant could be executed. Last seen heading west. Believed to be in contact with other HC members. CHILDREN AT RISK.

"Who was the primary suspect?" I ask, my pulse quickening.

Tavares flips to another page of notes. "Mercer never got a chance to bring him in. By the time they had enough evidence for a warrant, the suspect had disappeared. No forwarding address, no paper trail. Gone."

"But Mercer had a name," Emma says.

"He had a name. But no photo on file, no fingerprints, no concrete proof of identity. The man had used multiple aliases over the years. Mercer suspected he was still operating under a new identity somewhere else."

The implications are staggering. A suspect who disappeared in 1995, who could have been active for decades before that, who might still be operating now. Someone skilled at creating new identities, at infiltrating communities, at building trust while preparing children for something horrific.

"What was the name Mercer had?" I ask, though part of me doesn't want to know.

Tavares turns the page of Mercer's notes. At the bottom, heavily underlined, is a single name.

Primary suspect: Individual known as "The Shepherd" in Hollow Circle communications. Real identity unknown.

The Shepherd.

The name hits me like a physical blow. I'm back in that dark room, listening to the man and woman talk about my purpose, about the crossing, about preparations that needed to be made. The man's voice, patient and measured: *The Shepherd will be pleased with your progress.*

Emma is watching me carefully. "River? You okay?"

I force myself to breathe. To stay present. "The Shepherd. Did Mercer find any other references to that name?"

Tavares flips through more notes. "Several. He traced mentions of The Shepherd going back to the 1970s. Always in connection with missing children cases that went unsolved. Always in areas where nature education programs operated. Mercer believed The Shepherd was the leader or organizer of The Hollow Circle. Someone who'd been orchestrating these rituals for decades."

"And he's still out there," Emma says quietly. "Still operating. Still killing children."

"If the symbols and positioning in your current case match the 1994 murders exactly," Tavares says, "then either The Shepherd is still active, or someone trained by him is continuing his work."

I think about Eleanor Vance. Her PhD in mythology and folklore. Her environmental education programs. Her access to hundreds of children over the years. The way she talked about ancient wisdom and natural cycles.

Is she The Shepherd? Or is she working for him?

"I need to talk to Mercer," I say, standing. "Today if possible."

"I already set it up," Emma says, checking her phone. "He's expecting us at two o'clock at his home in Richmond. I told him we're working a case that might be connected to his 1994 investigation."

Tavares carefully gathers her files back into the box. "Be prepared. Mercer spent thirty years of his career on this case. It consumed him. When I last spoke to him five years ago, he was still convinced The Hollow Circle was operating, still believed children were at risk."

"He was right," I say.

She nods slowly. "I know. And that's the worst part. He spent three decades trying to warn people, trying to find proof, trying to stop them. And no one listened."

After Tavares leaves, Emma and I sit in silence, surrounded by evidence from two cases separated by thirty years but connected by the same horrifying pattern.

"The Shepherd," Emma says finally. "You think Eleanor Vance is working for him?"

"Or she's him. The Shepherd could be a title, not a person."

I pull out my phone and text Garrett: *Need deep background check on Eleanor Vance. Everything before her PhD. Employment history, known associates, any gaps in her timeline. Priority.*

His response is immediate: *Already running it. Will have preliminary by end of day.*

I look at the photos spread across the table. Jennifer and

Michael Hartley, dead for thirty years. Titus and Matthew Caine, dead for days. And somewhere, The Shepherd is identifying his next victims.

My nephew drew pictures of symbols taught to him by a nice lady who gave him cookies.

"We need to move fast," I tell Emma. "If The Hollow Circle has been operating since the seventies, if they've been doing this for fifty years, they have systems in place. They know how to disappear when law enforcement gets close."

"Then we don't give them time to disappear." Emma gathers her notes. "We talk to Mercer, we find out everything he knows about The Shepherd and The Hollow Circle. Then we bring in Eleanor Vance for questioning before she realizes we're onto her."

My phone buzzes. A text from an unknown number: *Agent Collins, this is Thomas Mercer. Helena Tavares gave me your contact. I've been waiting thirty years for someone to take this case seriously. Come prepared. What I have to show you will change everything you think you know.*

I show the text to Emma. She reads it, her expression grim.

I think about my own captivity. About escaping before they could finish what they started.

Nine years after the 1994 murders. Twenty-two years before the Caine twins.

Right in the middle of The Shepherd's timeline.

"Let's go to Richmond," I say. "Let's find out what Mercer knows."

CHAPTER ELEVEN

Thomas Mercer's house sits on a quiet street in Richmond's West End, a modest brick ranch that looks like it was built in the seventies and hasn't changed much since. The lawn is neatly maintained, the shutters freshly painted.

Emma parks at the curb and we sit for a moment, watching the house. A wind chime hangs from the porch, making soft metallic sounds in the December breeze.

"You ready for this?" Emma asks.

I think about the network called The Hollow Circle that's been operating for fifty years. "No. But let's go anyway."

Mercer answers the door before we finish climbing the porch steps. He's tall, maybe six-two, with white hair and the kind of lean build that comes from restless energy rather than exercise. Seventy-four years old according to Emma's research, but his eyes are sharp and alert.

"Agents Collins and Bertanelli." His handshake is firm, his voice carrying the trace of a Boston accent worn smooth by decades in Virginia. "Come in. I've been preparing."

The living room is not exactly what I expected. Every wall is covered with bulletin boards, cork and fabric, pinned with photographs and maps and news clippings. Red string connects different elements, creating webs of association that span decades. File boxes are stacked in corners. A folding table holds open case files, their pages yellowed with age.

This isn't a living room. It's a command center for a man who never stopped working a case that officially closed thirty years ago.

"Sorry for the mess," Mercer says, though he doesn't sound sorry. "I don't get many visitors. Most people think I'm crazy." He gestures to a worn sofa. "Please, sit."

We settle onto the couch while Mercer takes a chair across from us, positioning himself in front of the largest bulletin board. Behind him, I can see photos of Jennifer and Michael Hartley at various ages. School pictures. Family photos. Frozen in time before everything ended.

"Dr. Tavares said you're working a case with similar elements to the Hartley murders," Mercer says. "Tell me what you've found."

Emma pulls out her tablet, showing him photos of the Caine crime scene. Mercer's expression doesn't change, but his hands tighten on the arms of his chair.

"Same symbols," he says quietly. "Same positioning. How old were the victims?"

"Eight. Twin boys."

"Twins." He closes his eyes briefly. "Of course. The Hartleys were siblings but not twins. I always wondered if that mattered to them. If they were looking for something more specific."

"Them?" I ask.

"The Hollow Circle. The Shepherd. Whatever you want to call it." Mercer stands and moves to one of the bulletin boards, touching a section covered with handwritten notes. "This isn't one person working alone. It never was. This is an organization with structure, with beliefs, with specific requirements for their rituals."

He turns to face us. "Tell me about the toxicology."

"Preliminary screens came back negative," Emma says. "No standard substances. But the ME suspects plant-based compounds that don't show up on typical panels."

"Just like the Hartleys." Mercer pulls a file from a stack, opens it without looking. He knows exactly where everything is. "We ran every test available in 1994. Found nothing. The children simply stopped living. No trauma, no poison we could identify, no explanation."

I lean forward. "But you had a theory."

"I had more than a theory. I had a suspect." Mercer's voice hardens. "Six months into the investigation, I identified a man who'd been volunteering with the Mountain Heritage Foundation. He used the name David Brenner, though I'm certain that wasn't his real identity. He ran special sessions on weekends—nature walks where he taught children about 'the old ways.' Parents thought it was folklore. Traditional stories."

"But it was recruitment," I say.

"Indoctrination. He was teaching them his beliefs, identifying which children were receptive, which ones could be manipulated." Mercer pulls out another file. "I interviewed dozens of families. Some of the children talked about Mr. Brenner telling them they were special. That they could see things others couldn't. That they had important work to do."

The same language Eleanor Vance used with Bennett. The same pattern repeating across decades.

"What happened when you tried to bring him in?" Emma asks.

"He disappeared." Mercer's jaw tightens. "We were building a case, gathering evidence. I was maybe two weeks from getting a warrant. Then one day he didn't show up for his volunteer shift. Didn't show up anywhere. His apartment was cleared out, his car abandoned at a bus station. He vanished like he'd never existed."

"You think someone warned him," I say.

"I *know* someone warned him. Someone with access to our investigation, someone who knew exactly how close we were." Mercer moves to another board, this one covered with photos of various people. "I investigated everyone connected to the case. The Mountain Heritage Foundation staff, local law enforcement, even some of my own colleagues. But I never found the leak."

He taps one photo, a woman in her forties with kind eyes. "Margaret Ashford, the program director. She disappeared three months after Brenner did. Last seen withdrawing her entire savings from a bank in Charleston. No trace of her after that."

"You think she was part of The Hollow Circle," Emma says.

"I think The Hollow Circle was everywhere I looked, but I couldn't prove it. People with clean backgrounds, respectable jobs, community ties. All of them connected through these nature programs, these spiritual wellness groups."

Mercer returns to his chair, suddenly looking every one of his seventy-four years. "The case destroyed me. I couldn't let it go. My wife left me. My colleagues thought I was obsessed. The Bureau forced me into early retirement in 2009, said I needed to take care of my mental health." He laughs, bitter. "But I wasn't crazy. Everything I suspected was true. And now you're here, fifteen years later, telling me it's happened again."

"It's happened more than once," I say quietly. "We think The Hollow Circle has been operating continuously since at least the seventies. Maybe longer."

Mercer nods slowly, like I've confirmed something he's always known. "The Shepherd. Did Tavares tell you about him?"

"She said he was your primary suspect. That you believed he was the leader."

"The Shepherd isn't just the leader. He's the architect of all of this. The one who decides which children are chosen, when the crossings happen, how the rituals are performed." Mercer stands again, moving to a file cabinet. "I collected references to The Shepherd going back decades. Different locations, different names, but always the same pattern. Children disappearing after involvement with nature programs. Bodies found in clearings with oak trees. Symbols carved into bark."

He pulls out a thick folder, pages spilling from the edges. "I was never able to identify him. Never got a real name, never got a clear photo. He's like a ghost. But I know he's real, and I know he's still out there."

Emma and I exchange a glance. Everything Mercer is saying aligns with what we've found. It's all connected to The Shepherd, to this network that's been hiding in plain sight.

"You said you didn't have a clear photo," I say. "But you had something."

Mercer's expression shifts, becomes more guarded. "One photo. From 1994. Taken at a Mountain Heritage Foundation event two months before the Hartley children disappeared."

He opens the folder and carefully removes a photograph protected in a plastic sleeve. It's a group shot, maybe twenty people gathered in front of a wooden building. Adults and children, all smiling for the camera.

"This was taken at their fall harvest festival," Mercer says, holding the photo but not yet showing it to us. "I didn't notice what I'm about to show you until months after the murders. I was going through background materials, looking at everything again, and I saw it."

He turns the photo toward us.

The image is slightly faded, the colors washed out by age. In the foreground, families pose with carved pumpkins and hay bales. But in the background, partially obscured by other people, two figures stand slightly apart from the group.

A man, tall and lean, his face turned away from the camera. Only his profile is visible, not enough to make an identification.

And behind him, a woman. Younger, maybe in her thirties. Blonde hair pulled back. She's looking directly at the camera with an expression that's hard to read. Not smiling, exactly. Something else.

Something calculating.

Mercer points to the woman with a pen. "We never identified her. She wasn't on any staff lists, wasn't registered as a parent or volunteer. When I showed this photo to people who were there that day, no one remembered seeing her. It's like she was a ghost."

I take the photo from him, bringing it closer. My hands are steady even though my heart is racing.

The woman is younger here than she would be now. Thirty years younger. But the bone structure is the same. The way she holds herself. The eyes that look kind until you realize they're assessing, measuring, deciding.

"I've never forgotten that face," Mercer says. "Thirty years later, I could still draw it from memory. I always believed she was important. That if I could identify her, I could crack this whole thing open."

I can't speak. Can't move. The photo trembles slightly in my hands.

Because I know this woman.

Not from case files or investigation photos or criminal databases.

I know her because I've seen her face in my nightmares for twenty years.

The woman with blonde hair and kind eyes who leaned out of a rust-colored sedan and asked a twelve-year-old girl for directions. Who promised it would only take two minutes. Who locked the door with a soft click and drove away while I screamed.

The woman who kept me in a dark room for two years, who fed me from trays and spoke in that flat, emotionless voice. Who talked about the crossing and preparations and getting me ready for something I never understood.

Nine years after this photo was taken, she abducted me.

"Agent Collins?" Mercer's voice sounds far away. "Are you all right?"

Emma is watching me, her expression shifting from concern to alarm. "River? What is it?"

I force myself to look up from the photo, to meet Mercer's eyes.

"I know who she is," I say, my voice not quite steady. "Not her name. But I know her face."

Mercer goes very still. "How?"

"She abducted me off a street corner and held me captive for two years."

The silence that follows is absolute.

"She's my kidnapper," I continue, the words coming easier now. "The woman who took me when I was twelve. Who kept me in a basement and talked about the crossing and prepared me for something that never happened because I escaped."

I set the photo down on the table between us, my hand finally shaking.

"She's still out there. And she's been working for The Shepherd all along."

CHAPTER TWELVE

The drive back to Charlottesville takes two hours due to all of the traffic, but I barely register the passing landscape. Emma drives in silence while I stare at a photocopy of the 1994 image clutched in my hands. The woman's face, frozen in time three decades ago, stares back at me with that same calculating expression I remember from a rust-colored sedan.

"We need to open your case file," Emma says finally. "Cross-reference with the Hartley murders. Look for connections."

"I know."

"River." She glances at me. "This changes everything. Your abduction might not have been random. If she was part of The Hollow Circle in 1994, if she was working with The Shepherd—"

"I said I know." My voice comes out sharper than intended.

Emma's hands tighten on the steering wheel but she doesn't push. We drive another ten miles before I can speak again.

"I was twelve years old," I say quietly. "Walking home from school. She asked for directions and I got in her car because adults are supposed to be safe. Because I wanted to be helpful. What if she chose me specifically?"

"Then you survived something you were never supposed to survive." Emma's voice is firm. "Whatever they wanted from you, they didn't get it. You escaped. You won."

But it doesn't feel like winning. It feels like a countdown I didn't know was running.

The FBI field office feels different when we walk in. Like the walls have moved closer. Every face in the hallway could be someone connected to The Hollow Circle, someone watching, reporting back. I force myself to breathe normally and head straight for the conference room where Garrett has been compiling research.

He's surrounded by open laptops, printouts covering every surface. When he sees us, he stands quickly. "I've got the preliminary information on The Hollow Circle. It's not what I expected."

Emma and I take seats while Garrett pulls up files on the main screen. "The Hollow Circle isn't a traditional cult with centralized leadership and a compound. It's more like a decentralized network. Think of it as a belief system that spreads person to person, community to community. Some members know each other. Most don't."

"How do they organize?" I ask.

"Small cells, usually around environmental or spiritual wellness organizations. Nature centers, meditation groups, alternative education programs. Most members believe they're part of a movement focused on reconnecting with pre-Christian traditions and environmental consciousness.

They don't realize there's an inner circle with darker intentions."

Garrett clicks through slides showing various organizations. Community gardens in Oregon. A folk music festival in Vermont. A wilderness therapy program in Colorado. All of them showing subtle variations of the same symbol we found carved into oak trees.

"How many members are we talking about?" Emma asks.

"Hard to say. I've identified at least two hundred individuals across fifteen states with confirmed connections to Hollow Circle activities. But most of them appear to be peripheral—attending events, making small donations, participating in workshops. They're searching for meaning, not planning ritual sacrifices."

"What about the inner circle?" I lean forward, studying the faces on screen. "The true believers."

"Much smaller. Maybe twenty to thirty people who appear to understand the full ideology. They're the ones who use phrases like 'the old ways' and 'necessary cycles.' They're recruited carefully over years." Garrett pulls up a new document. "Here's where it gets interesting. Many of them are prominent community members. Teachers, nonprofit directors, small business owners. People with access to children and families."

My stomach turns. The perfect cover. Respected positions, trusted roles. Who would suspect the beloved nature program director of grooming children for ritual sacrifice?

"Have you found any connection between current members and the 1994 case?" Emma asks.

"Working on it. But The Hollow Circle has been active for decades under different names. Sometimes they're called The Old Path. Sometimes The Returning. Sometimes just The Circle. Same symbols, same basic beliefs, different packaging."

I think about Eleanor Vance and her PhD in mythology. About how academic research can be a cover for obsession. About how knowledge of ancient practices could be twisted into justification for horror.

"What about The Shepherd?" I ask. "Any confirmed identities?"

Garrett shakes his head. "Everyone refers to him as The Shepherd or The Teacher. A few older members mention meeting someone by that title in the seventies or eighties. Descriptions vary—tall, charismatic, knowledgeable about pre-Christian rituals. But no names, no photos except the partial image from Mercer's file."

"He's been operating for fifty years without anyone identifying him." Emma's frustration is evident. "How is that possible?"

"Because he's patient. He plants seeds and disappears. Lets others do the actual work while he remains hidden." Garrett pulls up another file. "But he makes mistakes. Financial transactions leave trails. Donor lists connect people. And we're starting to map the network."

He displays a complex web of connections, lines linking various organizations and individuals. My eyes follow the threads, trying to understand the scope.

"This donor list," Garrett says, zooming in on one section. "It's from a Hollow Circle fundraising event two years ago. Held at a private estate in Virginia, supposedly for environmental causes. But the money went to fund programs that we now know Eleanor Vance was running."

The names on the list blur as I scan them. Thirty people

who contributed anywhere from five hundred to ten thousand dollars. I'm looking for patterns, for anyone I might recognize.

Then I see it.

Third from the bottom. Christopher Raskin. $2,500 donation.

The room tilts slightly. Emma catches my expression, moves closer to look at the screen.

"No," she says quietly. "River, that can't be—"

"Christopher Raskin." I point to the name with a hand that's remarkably steady. "My brother-in-law. Leslie's husband."

Garrett looks between us, confused. "You know this person?"

"He's family." The word tastes bitter. "He's been married to my sister for years. They have two kids. He's a financial consultant. He volunteers at their church." Except he hasn't been volunteering at church lately, has he? He's been attending meditation retreats. Men's spiritual groups. Growing distant from Leslie while becoming obsessed with something he wouldn't explain.

Emma is already pulling up more information. "When did he start having problems in his marriage?"

"Leslie said about a year ago. He became secretive, stayed out late, pulled away emotionally." The timeline slots into place with sickening clarity. "That's when he must have gotten involved with The Hollow Circle."

"Or when they recruited him." Emma's voice is grim.

Garrett pulls up more recent activity. "Christopher Raskin appears on multiple donor lists over the past eighteen months. Small contributions, nothing that would raise flags individually. But together it shows sustained involvement. And he attended at least four Hollow Circle events that we've identified."

"Including any run by Greenwood Legacy Foundation?" I ask.

Garrett checks another database. "Yes. Two family workshops last fall. One was specifically about 'reconnecting children with ancient wisdom through nature.'"

My nephew's drawing flashes through my mind. Trees with symbols. Miss Eleanor who gave him cookies and talked about special children who could see things others couldn't. Chris took Bennett and Ava to those events. Put them in Eleanor Vance's presence.

"I need to talk to Leslie." I stand, my chair scraping against the floor. "She needs to know what Chris has been involved in. She needs to protect the kids."

"River, wait." Emma catches my arm. "We need to approach this carefully. If we confront Chris directly, he might warn the others. We could lose our chance to bring down the entire network."

"My sister's children have been exposed to a woman who believes in ritual sacrifice." My voice is harder than I intend. "I'm not waiting."

"I'm not saying wait. I'm saying be strategic." Emma's grip on my arm tightens. "Talk to Leslie, absolutely. But don't let her confront Chris yet. Not until we understand the full extent of his involvement."

She's right. I hate that she's right, but she is. If Chris is connected to Eleanor Vance, if he's part of the inner circle, alerting him could destroy the investigation. Could give The Shepherd time to disappear again.

"Okay." I force myself to think like an agent instead of an

aunt. "I'll talk to Leslie tonight. Get information about Chris's activities without tipping him off. Find out what he's said about these groups, who he's introduced to the family, what events the kids attended."

"And we'll continue mapping The Hollow Circle network." Garrett is already pulling up new files. "Cross-reference Chris's known associates, track his movements, identify other members he might be connected to."

Emma releases my arm. "We're going to figure this out. But River, you need to compartmentalize. I know that's asking a lot given everything you just learned about your own case, but—"

"I can do it." I cut her off. Not because I'm confident but because I have to be. The Caine twins are dead. Children are in danger. My personal trauma has to wait.

But as I gather my things to leave, I can't help thinking about the woman in that 1994 photo. About The Shepherd standing in the shadows behind her. About a network that's been operating for fifty years, recruiting believers, targeting children.

About my brother-in-law's name on a donor list for an organization that killed two eight-year-old boys.

I pull out my phone and text Leslie: *Need to talk tonight. Important. Can I come by after the kids are in bed?*

Her response is immediate: *Is everything okay?*

I stare at the message. Everything is decidedly not okay. Her husband is connected to a ritual sacrifice network. Her children have been in the presence of people who believe in using kids as "bridges to the old gods." And I'm about to destroy what's left of her crumbling marriage by revealing just how deep Chris's betrayal goes.

We'll talk tonight, I type back. *See you at eight.*

Emma is watching me from across the room. "You going to be okay?"

"No." The honesty surprises both of us. "But I'm going to do my job anyway."

Because that's what I've always done. Compartmentalize the trauma, focus on the case, save the next victim. Even when the case involves my own family. Even when the trauma is mine.

I look at the photocopy of the 1994 image still clutched in my hand. The woman who took me stares back, frozen in time but still hunting. Still serving The Shepherd. Still part of a network I'm only beginning to understand.

And my brother-in-law is on the donor list.

CHAPTER THIRTEEN

The community center sits in a modest neighborhood on the east side of Charlottesville, the kind of place that hosts bake sales and yoga classes and neighborhood association meetings. Nothing about it screams danger. Nothing about it suggests ritual sacrifice. That's the point, I suppose.

Emma's car is already parked half a block down when I arrive at six-thirty. I slide into the passenger seat, bringing the cold December air with me.

"Talked to Leslie last night," I say, pulling a folded pamphlet from my jacket pocket. "She gave me this."

Emma takes it, unfolding the glossy tri-fold carefully. The cover shows a serene forest scene, sunlight filtering through trees. Beneath it, elegant text reads: "Greenwood Legacy Foundation: Reconnecting Families with Ancient Wisdom."

And there, embossed in the corner, is the symbol. The same geometric pattern carved into oak trees where two children died. Circle with intersecting lines, smaller circles at precise points. The symbol that's been haunting my dreams since I saw it in that clearing.

"Jesus," Emma breathes. "He had this in his house?"

"Leslie found it when she was packing up his things after he moved out. Said she thought it was just another meditation retreat pamphlet. Didn't think anything of it until I asked about his activities last night."

Emma turns the pamphlet over, scanning the contents. Programs for families. Nature walks. Seasonal celebrations. All of it presented with beautiful photography and language about environmental stewardship and spiritual growth. Nothing that would raise alarm bells for parents looking to enrich their children's lives.

"It's brilliant," Emma says quietly. "Hiding in plain sight. Look legitimate. Get nonprofit status and community awards. Who would suspect?"

"That's why they've lasted fifty years." I take the pamphlet back, studying Eleanor Vance's photo on the inside panel. She's smiling warmly, surrounded by children on a nature hike. The caption identifies her as Founder and Executive Director. PhD in Mythology and Folklore. Dedicated to helping families reconnect with the natural world.

"The gathering starts at seven," Emma says, checking her watch. "According to their public calendar, it's a 'Winter Solstice Celebration Planning Meeting.' Open to all members and interested community members."

We settled in to watch. The community center has large windows facing the street, and we have a clear view of the main entrance and the parking lot. Emma has a camera with a telephoto lens positioned on the dashboard, ready to document everyone who enters.

The first arrivals come at six-fifty. A couple in their forties, dressed casually, carrying reusable shopping bags. They look like every other middle-class couple in Charlottesville. Maybe they teach at the university. Maybe they work in tech. Nothing about them suggests danger.

More people arrive in clusters. Young families with children. Older couples holding hands. A group of women who hug each other in the parking lot before entering together. I watch their faces through the telephoto lens—they're smiling, relaxed, eager. These are people seeking community and meaning. Not monsters.

"How many of them know?" I ask quietly. "How many understand what the inner circle actually does?"

"Most of them probably don't." Emma adjusts the camera angle. "That's how these networks operate. The outer circle provides cover and legitimacy. The inner circle does the actual work."

By seven-fifteen, at least forty people have entered the building. Through the windows, I can see them gathered in what looks like a large multipurpose room. Someone is setting up chairs in a circle. Someone else is fixing the seasonal decorations—pine boughs, candles, small sculptures made of twisted wood.

Eleanor Vance appears at seven-twenty. I recognize her immediately from her photos, though she's more magnetic in person. Late forties, dark hair pulled back in a loose bun, wearing flowing clothes that suggest artistic sensibility without being costume-like. She moves through the room greeting people, touching shoulders, laughing. Everyone gravitates toward her.

"She's good," Emma murmurs, snapping photos.

"Charismatic without being overwhelming. Warm without being intrusive."

I watch Eleanor hug a young mother whose child clings to her leg. Watch her crouch down to speak to the child at eye level, making him smile. This is someone parents trust with their kids. Someone who seems genuinely invested in their wellbeing.

That's what makes her dangerous.

The meeting begins at seven-thirty. Through the windows, we can see Eleanor standing in the center of the circle, speaking. I wish we had audio. Everyone appears engaged, nodding, occasionally asking questions. It looks like any community organization planning an event. Bake sale logistics. Volunteer coordination. Nothing sinister.

"This is the public face," I say. "The part they want everyone to see."

"So where's the private face?"

A van pulls into the parking lot at seven-fifty. It's plain white, no markings. The driver doesn't park near the main entrance. Instead, the van continues around the side of the building toward what appears to be a service entrance.

Emma and I exchange a glance. She's already adjusting the camera angle.

Three people emerge from the van. Two men and a woman, all dressed in dark clothing. They don't head toward the main entrance. They disappear around the back of the building.

"There's another entrance," Emma says, pulling up building plans on her tablet. "There's a service entrance and loading dock on the east side. Leads to a basement level that's used for storage and maintenance."

"Or private meetings the general membership doesn't know about."

We watch carefully. At eight o'clock, two more people arrive separately and head around back. One is a woman in her fifties carrying what looks like a large fabric bag. The other is a younger man, maybe early thirties, walking with purpose.

The public meeting in the main room continues. Eleanor is still visible through the windows, leading what appears to be a planning discussion. But I'm willing to bet there's another meeting happening somewhere below us. A gathering of the true believers.

"Should we try to get closer?" Emma asks. "Maybe position ourselves near the back entrance?"

"Too risky. If they're security conscious, they'll have someone watching." I keep my eyes on the building. "Let's document everyone who uses that entrance. We can run faces later, build a list of inner circle members."

At eight-fifteen, a sedan pulls into the lot. Expensive, dark blue, well-maintained. It parks near the back and a single occupant emerges.

My breath catches.

Even at this distance, even in dim parking lot lighting, I recognize him. The way he moves. The set of his shoulders. The efficient way he locks his car and surveys the lot before walking.

Christopher Raskin. My brother-in-law. The father of my nephew and niece.

"That's him," I say, my voice flat. "That's Chris."

Emma raises the camera, capturing several shots as Chris walks past the main entrance without looking at it. He knows exactly where he's going. No hesitation, no checking for directions. He's been here before.

He disappears around the corner toward the back entrance.

My hands clench into fists on my lap. Chris isn't attending the public meeting.

He's going to the private meeting. The one in the basement. The gathering of people who understand what Greenwood Legacy Foundation really does.

"River." Emma lowers the camera, her voice careful. "We need to be smart about this. We can't confront him yet."

"I know."

"If we tip him off, he'll warn the others. Eleanor Vance could disappear. The whole network could scatter."

"I said I know." But knowing doesn't make it easier. Doesn't make me less furious that my sister's husband, the man who held Bennett and Ava as infants, who coached their soccer games and read them bedtime stories, is walking into a meeting with people who believe children are bridges to old gods.

We sit in tense silence for another twenty minutes. The public meeting in the main room begins to wrap up. People emerge in groups, chatting and laughing, heading to their cars. Normal people having a normal evening. They drive away without knowing what's really happening.

But the vehicles that parked near the back entrance don't leave.

At nine-thirty, my phone buzzes. A text from Leslie: *Is Chris in some kind of trouble? You seemed really worried last night.*

I stare at the message. How do I answer that? Yes, your husband is involved with people who killed two children?

Yes, he took Bennett and Ava to events run by a woman who believes in (and possibly does) ritual sacrifice? Yes, he just walked into a private meeting I'm not allowed to interrupt because it might blow our investigation?

Still looking into it, I type back. *Will know more soon.*

It's not enough. It's nowhere near enough. But it's all I can give her right now.

Emma shifts in her seat. "Movement."

The back entrance opens. One by one, the inner circle members emerge. They move quickly, efficiently, heading to their vehicles without lingering or conversation. Whatever happened in that basement meeting, they're done now.

Chris exits fourth. I watch him through the camera lens as he walks to his car. His expression is hard to read at this distance, but his body language suggests tension. Maybe even conflict. He sits in his car for a full minute before starting the engine.

"Follow him?" Emma asks.

"No. We know where he's staying." With Amanda, his mistress who does sound healing and energy work. "Let's document the rest of them."

We photograph license plates and faces as the remaining members disperse. Seven people total who entered through the back. Seven people who are part of something the public membership doesn't see.

When the last car pulls away, Emma and I sit in the darkened surveillance vehicle processing what we just witnessed.

"He's not peripheral," I say finally. "Chris isn't just a donor who attended a few events. He knows about the private meetings."

"Which means he might know about the Caine twins. About the rituals. About Eleanor Vance's true beliefs."

The possibility makes me feel sick. What does Chris really know? He still took Bennett and Ava to Greenwood events. Still exposed them to Eleanor Vance. Still donated money to fund programs that were grooming children for sacrifice. But did he know *that*?

"We need to bring him in for questioning," I say. "Soon."

"Agreed. But carefully. We present it as routine follow-up on his donation history. Don't let him know we're onto anything until we have him in an interview room." Emma starts the engine. "And River? When we do interview him, you can't be in the room."

"Like hell I can't."

"You're too close to this. He's family. Any defense attorney would use that to challenge anything he says." She pulls away from the curb. "I'll conduct the interview. You can watch from observation."

I want to argue. Want to insist that I have every right to question the man who endangered my sister's children. But Emma is right. I'm too close. Too invested. Too likely to let my anger show in ways that could compromise the case.

"Fine," I say. "But we do it tomorrow. I'm not giving him time to prepare or coordinate with the others."

"Tomorrow." Emma's jaw is set. "First thing in the morning."

As we drive back toward the field office, I think about Chris sitting in that basement meeting. Learning things. Planning things.

And tomorrow, I'm going to watch through one-way glass while Emma asks him exactly how deep his involvement goes.

While I find out if my brother-in-law is just a fool who got in over his head, or something much worse.

CHAPTER FOURTEEN

The conference room on the third floor is packed by eight the next morning. Our entire task force plus additional agents from Crimes Against Children, Violent Crimes, and Behavioral Analysis. Siwak stands at the head of the table looking like he hasn't slept in a while.

Emma and I take seats near the front. I'm running on four hours of rest and too much coffee, my mind still replaying last night's surveillance. Chris disappearing through that back entrance. The inner circle gathering while the public meeting provided cover upstairs.

"Thank you all for coming on such short notice," Siwak begins, his voice carrying the weight of bad news. "We have a development. At six-forty this morning, I received a call from the Maryland field office."

He pulls up a photo on the main screen. Two boys, identical twins, grinning at the camera. They're wearing matching blue shirts, arms around each other's shoulders. Eight years old, maybe. Dark skin, bright eyes, the kind of joy that should last a lifetime.

My chest tightens.

"Liam and Noah Okafor," Siwak continues. "Age eight. Reported missing yesterday evening by their parents after they failed to return home from a special outdoor education event at Patapsco Valley State Park in Maryland."

The room goes very quiet. Everyone understands what this means.

"Maryland State Police initiated an immediate search. K-9 units, helicopter, the full response. They found the boys' backpacks near a trailhead but no other trace." Siwak pulls up a map showing the park location. "The parents were cooperative, devastated. Father is a software engineer, mother is a nurse. Nigerian immigrants, been in the U.S. for twelve years. Model citizens. No custody issues, no family conflicts. By all accounts, devoted parents."

Garrett raises his hand. "What was the outdoor education event?"

"That's where it gets relevant to our case." Siwak pulls up another document. "The event was advertised as a special winter nature program focusing on wildlife tracking and forest ecology. About fifteen children attended with various parents and guardians. The program ran from two to four PM. At four-fifteen, when parents were collecting their kids, the Okafor twins were nowhere to be found."

"Who organized the program?" I ask, though I already know the answer. Can feel it settling like lead in my stomach.

"Local environmental education group. We're still confirming details, but initial reports suggest it may be affiliated with organizations in Virginia." Siwak's eyes meet mine. "Maryland FBI is requesting our assistance given our current investigation into the Caine murders."

Emma leans forward. "Timeline. When exactly did the boys disappear?"

"Last seen at approximately three-forty-five PM. One of the program instructors noticed them near a marked trail but assumed they were with their parents. When the program ended at four and parents started collecting kids, the twins were gone."

I pull up my own timeline on my tablet. "The Caine twins' bodies were discovered seventy-two hours ago. We've been investigating openly since then. Press coverage started yesterday morning."

"Right." Siwak's expression is grim. "Which means whoever took the Okafor boys grabbed them before news of the Caine murders became public. Before they knew we'd found the bodies and started investigating."

The implications ripple through the room. Agents exchange glances, some pulling out phones to check news coverage, others reviewing case files.

"He already had his next victims selected," someone says from the back of the room.

"More than selected." I stand, moving to the screen. "The Caine twins died between seven and eleven PM on the night they were taken. Their bodies were arranged in that clearing, positioned precisely. Symbols carved into seven trees. A wooden token placed near one victim. That took hours of work. Careful, methodical preparation."

I pull up crime scene photos, the oak trees marked with those geometric symbols. "He did all of this knowing we would find them eventually. Knowing it would trigger an investigation. And he didn't care because he already had Liam and Noah Okafor."

Emma stands beside me. "The Okafor boys disappeared

at three-forty-five PM yesterday. The first news coverage of the Caine case didn't hit local media until eight AM yesterday. He grabbed them almost sixteen hours before he could have known we were investigating."

"So he's not reacting to pressure," Garrett says slowly. "He's following a predetermined schedule."

"Exactly." The word tastes bitter. "This isn't opportunistic. It's planned. Systematic."

Siwak pulls up a calendar. "The Caine twins died six days ago. The Okafor twins disappeared yesterday. Both cases involve eight-year-old male twins. Both involve outdoor education programs. Both near wooded areas with difficult terrain."

"Winter solstice is in nine days," I say quietly. Everyone turns to look at me. "In pre-Christian traditions, the winter solstice was significant for ritual sacrifice. The longest night of the year. A liminal time when the veil between worlds was believed to be thinnest."

"You think he's building toward the solstice?" Siwak asks.

"Dr. Tavares mentioned it when analyzing the symbols. They're oriented for winter solstice alignment. And if this is connected to The Hollow Circle and their beliefs about ancient practices..." I trail off, but everyone can fill in the blanks.

Emma pulls up her notes. "The 1994 case. The Hartley children. When did they die?"

I already know the answer. "December nineteenth through twenty-first. The winter solstice."

The silence that follows is heavy with understanding. Thirty years apart, the same pattern. The same timing. The same belief system driving someone to kill children.

"We need to coordinate with Maryland immediately,"

Siwak says. "River, Emma, you'll head the joint investigation. Garrett, pull everything we have on similar cases around winter solstice dates going back as far as records allow. If this is a pattern, I want to see it."

"What about The Hollow Circle?" Emma asks. "We identified seven people attending that inner circle meeting last night, including Christopher Raskin. Should we bring them in?"

Siwak considers this. "Not yet. If we move too fast, we might scatter the network before we understand its full scope. But I want surveillance on all seven. Twenty-four hour coverage. Anyone makes a move, I want to know about it."

"Eleanor Vance?" I ask.

"Her too. In fact, she's priority one. If the Okafor boys disappeared from an event organized by a group affiliated with Greenwood Legacy Foundation, she's directly connected to both cases."

I think about Eleanor standing in that community center last night, warm and charismatic, surrounded by people who trust her with their children. How many other programs is she running? How many other families has she targeted?

"We should get warrants," I say. "For Greenwood's records. Donor lists, program rosters, staff information. Everything."

"Already in progress," Siwak confirms. "Judge Reynolds is reviewing the warrants now. We should have them by noon."

An agent from Behavioral Analysis raises her hand. "The escalation concerns me. Two sets of twins in less than a week. That's extremely accelerated for this type of offender.

Usually there's more time between victims, more careful planning."

"Unless he's building toward something specific," Emma says. "A ritual that requires multiple sacrifices. Multiple 'bridges' as The Hollow Circle calls them."

I pull up the map Dr. Tavares found in Eleanor Vance's home office. Seven locations marked in the Blue Ridge Mountains. One where the Caine twins died. Six remaining.

"Seven locations. Seven rituals. We've only stopped one." I look at Siwak. "What if the Okafor boys aren't the last? What if he's planning seven separate sacrifices leading up to the solstice?"

The room erupts in low conversation. Seven sets of twins. Fourteen children. The scope is staggering.

Siwak holds up a hand for quiet. "We're getting ahead of ourselves. Right now we have two confirmed cases and two missing boys who might still be alive. That's our focus. We find Liam and Noah Okafor. We build our case against Eleanor Vance and The Hollow Circle. We prevent any additional victims."

He assigns teams. Maryland coordination. Surveillance operations. Warrant execution. Research into historical patterns. Everyone has a role. Everyone moves with the urgency of knowing two children are missing and time is running out.

As the meeting breaks up, Emma and I gather our materials. We need to be on the road to Maryland within the hour.

"River." Siwak calls me back. "A word."

I wait while the room empties. Siwak closes the door, his expression grave.

"Your brother-in-law is part of this investigation," he says. "That's a problem."

"I know. Emma will handle any direct interaction with him. I'll maintain professional distance."

"It's more than that." Siwak sits on the edge of the conference table. "If Christopher Raskin is involved in The Hollow Circle, if he has knowledge of these crimes, his connection to you could be used by defense attorneys to challenge the entire investigation. They'll claim we targeted him because of family relationships. That you had personal motivations."

"I didn't even know he was involved until yesterday."

"I know that. You know that. But in court, it'll look different." He rubs his forehead. "I'm not removing you from the case. You're the best investigator I have. But I need you to be careful. Document everything. Keep your interactions with Chris minimal and always with witnesses present."

"Understood."

"And River?" He meets my eyes. "If this gets too personal, if you can't maintain objectivity, you need to tell me. No shame in it. This case is already complicated enough without family dynamics."

I want to argue that I can handle it, that I'm professional enough to separate personal from investigative. But the truth is I spent last night watching my brother-in-law enter a meeting with people who believe in child sacrifice. I spent the drive home wondering how much he knows, what he's exposed my nephew and niece to, whether Leslie is safe.

"I'll tell you if it becomes a problem," I say finally.

Siwak nods, dismissing me. I'm almost to the door when he speaks again.

"The woman from the 1994 photo. The one you

identified as your abductor. We're working on identifying her through facial recognition and cross-referencing with known associates of The Hollow Circle. If we find her, if she's connected to the current cases, you'll need to recuse yourself from that aspect of the investigation."

My hand tightens on the door handle. "I understand."

"Do you? Because from what Tavares told me, this woman held you captive for two years. Drugged you with the same compounds we found in the Caine twins' systems. Prepared you for some kind of ritual that never happened because you escaped. If she's involved now, if The Shepherd is still out there orchestrating this, your entire abduction case becomes part of this investigation."

I turn to face him. "Then we'll handle it appropriately. But sir, with respect, my personal history with this network might be an asset. I understand how they think. I know how they operate. I can use that."

"Or it could cloud your judgment." His voice softens. "I'm not trying to sideline you, River. I'm trying to protect you and this investigation. These people hurt you once. I won't let them hurt you again."

The concern in his voice almost breaks through my professional walls. Almost makes me acknowledge how terrifying it is to realize my abduction might have been part of something larger. That The Shepherd has been out there all along, watching, waiting, positioning pieces on a board I didn't know I was playing on.

But I can't afford to fall apart. Not when children are still at risk.

"I appreciate that, sir. But I'm okay. I can do this."

He studies me for a long moment, then nods. "Get to Maryland. Find those boys."

I meet Emma in the parking garage. She's already loaded our go-bags and equipment into the SUV. The drive to Maryland will take two hours, giving us time to review everything we know about the Okafor case.

As I slide into the passenger seat, Emma starts the engine. "You okay? Siwak looked serious."

"He's worried about the Chris situation. About my connection to the 1994 case." I buckle my seatbelt. "Thinks it might compromise the investigation."

"Will it?"

The honest answer is I don't know. How can I be objective when my own captivity might be part of this pattern? When my brother-in-law is attending secret meetings with the same network that held me prisoner?

"I won't let it," I say instead.

Emma pulls out of the garage into gray December morning light. The sky threatens snow, matching my mood.

"The timeline bothers me," I say, pulling up my notes. "The Caine twins died six days ago. The killer spent hours positioning their bodies, carving symbols, arranging everything precisely. Then he just... waited. Waited for us to find them. And while we were discovering his crime scene, he was already moving on his next victims."

"He's confident," Emma says. "Believes he won't be caught."

"Or he doesn't care if he is." I stare out the window at passing suburbs. "If he's building toward the winter solstice, if this is about completing some kind of ritual cycle, then his timeline matters more than evading capture. He'll finish what he started regardless of law enforcement."

"Then we stop him before the solstice." Emma's jaw sets.

"We find the Okafor boys. We arrest Eleanor Vance. We dismantle The Hollow Circle."

I want to share her confidence. Want to believe we can interrupt a network that's been operating for fifty years. But I keep thinking about Agent Mercer, obsessed with the 1994 case for three decades, never able to identify The Shepherd or stop the killings.

What makes us think we'll succeed where he failed?

My phone buzzes. It's a text from Leslie: *Chris didn't come home last night. Not answering calls. I'm worried.*

I stare at the message. Chris was at that meeting until nine-thirty. Where did he go after? Who did he meet with?

We'll find him, I text back.

It's not a lie, exactly. We have surveillance on him. But what we'll discover when we do might destroy what's left of Leslie's world.

"He's not reacting to our investigation," I say aloud, the realization crystallizing. "He planned this. The Caine twins were just the beginning. He's accelerating toward something."

Emma glances at me. "The winter solstice."

"Nine days away. If he's planning seven rituals, seven sets of twins, he's running out of time. He'll move faster now. Take more risks. Get desperate."

"Which means more children at risk."

"Or it means he will make mistakes and get sloppy. Maybe that will give us an opening."

CHAPTER FIFTEEN

The Maryland FBI field office is in Baltimore, but the Okafor family lives in Ellicott City, closer to where their sons disappeared. We bypass the office and drive straight to the family's home, a modest split-level in a neighborhood that looks like it was built in the eighties. Basketball hoops in driveways. Minivans in garages. The kind of place where families put down roots.

Emma parks behind a Maryland State Police cruiser. Through the front window, I can see movement inside the house. Lots of people. The weight of a community rallying around a family in crisis.

"Let me do most of the talking," Emma says as we approach the door. "They've been interviewed multiple times already. They're exhausted and terrified. We need them to trust us."

The door opens before we can knock. A woman in her early thirties, wearing a church volunteer shirt, her eyes red from crying.

We show our credentials. She steps aside to let us enter.

The living room is full of people. I count at least a dozen adults, maybe more in other rooms. Church members, probably. Family friends. The kind of support system that shows up in a crisis. Coffee and food cover every surface. Someone has set up a prayer corner with candles and photos of the twins.

A man rises from the couch when he sees us. Late thirties, tall, exhausted. Joseph Okafor. The boys' father.

"Agents," he says, his accent carrying the musical tones of Nigerian English. "Thank you for coming. The Maryland agents said you're working a similar case in Virginia."

"We are." Emma's voice is gentle. "Is there somewhere private we could talk?"

Joseph leads us to a small home office, closing the door on the well-meaning crowd. A woman joins us—Ngozi Okafor, the mother. She's smaller than her husband, wearing scrubs like she came straight from the hospital. Her hands tremble as she sits.

"Tell us about yesterday," Emma says. "Everything you remember."

Ngozi speaks first, her words rushing together. "The boys were so excited. They love nature, love being outside. When we saw the advertisement for the special winter program, we thought it would be perfect. Educational. Safe. Other families were going."

"What advertisement?" I ask.

Joseph pulls out his phone, scrolling to a saved image. It's a flyer, professionally designed. "Winter Wildlife Tracking Program—Special Event for Young Naturalists." Below that, details about the program, the location, the time. And at the bottom, in small print: "Presented in partnership with Greenwood Legacy Foundation."

My chest tightens. Emma and I exchange a glance.

"Had your sons attended any Greenwood programs before?" Emma asks carefully.

"Once," Ngozi says. "Last fall. A Saturday morning nature walk. They had such a wonderful time. Talked about it for weeks. The instructor was so kind, so patient with the children. The boys loved her."

"Do you remember the instructor's name?"

"Eleanor. Eleanor Vance." Ngozi's voice breaks. "She was wonderful with them. She told us Liam and Noah had a special connection to nature. That twins often have gifts others don't see. She said they reminded her of children in old stories, the ones who could walk between worlds."

The phrasing sends ice through my veins. Children who walk between worlds. Bridges to the old powers. The same language from Dr. Tavares's analysis, from Eleanor's academic papers, from the beliefs of The Hollow Circle.

"Did Eleanor Vance run yesterday's program?" I ask.

"No." Joseph shakes his head. "There were two instructors we didn't recognize. A man and a woman, both younger. They said Eleanor had trained them, that she sent them specifically because the program was designed for children with 'special sensitivities.'"

"Do you remember their names?"

"Michael and Sarah. I didn't get last names." Joseph's frustration is evident. "I should have asked. Should have gotten more information. But it seemed legitimate. There were other families, other children. How could I know?"

Because predators are good at seeming legitimate. Because they hide behind nonprofit status and community awards and smiling faces. Because they spend years building trust specifically so parents won't question them.

"Tell me about yesterday afternoon," Emma says. "What time did you arrive at the park?"

"One-forty-five. The program started at two." Ngozi pulls a tissue from her pocket, gripping it like a lifeline. "We stayed for the first thirty minutes. They divided the children into groups for different activities. Liam and Noah were in the wildlife tracking group. They were learning how to identify animal prints in the snow."

"Then what?"

"The instructors said parents could leave if they wanted. That they'd bring the children back to the main parking area at four o'clock." Joseph's voice roughens. "We trusted them. Other parents were leaving too. It seemed safe."

Emma makes notes, her expression neutral. No judgment. Just gathering facts.

"We went home. It's only twenty minutes from the park. We planned to pick them up at four." Ngozi's hands twist the tissue. "But when we got back, when all the parents were there, the boys were gone. The instructors looked confused. Said they'd seen Liam and Noah near the marked trail just a few minutes earlier. Said they must have wandered ahead to the parking lot."

"But they weren't there," Joseph finishes. "They were nowhere. We searched. Everyone searched. The instructors, the other parents, we covered every marked trail. Called their names until we were hoarse. The police came with dogs. Helicopters. Nothing."

I lean forward slightly. "These instructors—Michael and Sarah. Did they seem concerned when the boys went missing?"

"Yes. Very concerned." Ngozi hesitates. "But also... I don't know. Something felt wrong. They kept saying the boys would turn up, that children wander but they always come back. They seemed too calm."

"Did you get contact information for them?"

"The police took it. But when they tried to follow up last night, both phone numbers were disconnected. The email addresses bounced back." Joseph's fists clench. "They were fake. The instructors were fake. Everything was a trap and we walked right into it."

Emma asks more questions. Timeline details. Description of the instructors. Other families present. The specific location in the park where the boys were last seen. Ngozi and Joseph answer everything, their desperation to help is evident in every word.

When we finish, Emma gives them her card. "We're going to find your sons. I know you've heard that from everyone, but I mean it. We have a strong team, solid leads, and we're not stopping until they're home."

"The other case in Virginia," Joseph says as we stand to leave. "The similar one. Did those children...?"

He can't finish the question. Emma and I don't answer. We can't tell them the Caine twins are dead. Can't take away their hope even though the statistics are grim.

"We're doing everything possible," Emma says instead.

Outside, the December air feels sharp after the suffocating warmth of the house. I breathe deeply, trying to clear my head.

"Greenwood Legacy Foundation," I say once we're back in the SUV. "Eleanor Vance probably trained these instructors. She identified the Okafor twins as special. She set this up."

"But she wasn't there personally. She's insulating herself.

Using others to do the actual abduction." Emma starts driving. "Smart. Keeps her hands clean."

"We need to talk to the other families who were at that event. Get descriptions of Michael and Sarah. Find out who else was there, who might have been watching."

"Already on it. Maryland agents are interviewing everyone." Emma pulls up her tablet, checking messages. "But River, look at the timeline. The Okafor boys were taken at approximately three-forty-five PM yesterday. That's almost twenty hours ago. If the pattern holds, if this follows the same ritual structure as the Caine twins..."

"We might already be too late to save them." The words taste like ash.

We drive toward Patapsco Valley State Park in heavy silence. The park is massive, thousands of acres of forest and trails. Maryland State Police have established a command post near the main parking area where the program took place.

A detective meets us when we arrive. "Agents Bertanelli and Collins? Detective Brody. We've got K-9 units still searching, but the trail went cold about half a mile into the woods. The dogs picked up the boys' scent heading east on a marked trail, then lost it near a service road."

"Someone drove them out," Emma says.

"That's our theory. The service road connects to a highway access about two miles from here. If they had a vehicle waiting, the boys could be anywhere by now."

I walk the area where the program took place. It's a large clearing with picnic tables and informational signboards about local wildlife. Educational and wholesome. Exactly the kind of place parents would feel safe leaving their children.

At the edge of the clearing, where the marked trail enters the forest, I notice something. Fresh wood shavings scattered near the base of a large oak tree.

I crouch down, examining them carefully. They're pale, recently cut. I look up at the tree trunk.

There, at about six feet height, someone has started to carve a symbol. It's not complete—just the beginning of a circle with one intersecting line. But I recognize the pattern immediately.

"Emma." My voice is tight.

She joins me, sees what I'm seeing. "Jesus."

"They were here. Whoever took the Okafor boys was here early, marking the location. Preparing the site." I pull out evidence bags, carefully collecting the wood shavings. "This connects directly to the Caine crime scene. Same methodology. Same symbols."

Detective Brody looks confused. "What symbols?"

Emma shows him photos from the Caine case. The carved oak trees. The geometric patterns. He goes pale.

"We need to process this entire area as a crime scene," Emma says. "Everything. I want every family interviewed again, every detail documented. Someone saw something."

While Brody coordinates with his team, I photograph the partially carved symbol from multiple angles. The cut is fresh, probably made within the last few days. Someone came to this park, selected this specific tree, began the ritual marking.

Eleanor Vance might not have been here yesterday, but her influence was. Her teachings, her beliefs, her carefully trained followers.

My phone rings. Garrett.

"River, I've been going through Greenwood Legacy

Foundation's public records. They've run programs in five different states over the past three years. Hundreds of events. Thousands of children." He sounds shaken. "But there's a pattern. In each location, within six months of Greenwood programs starting, there were reports of missing children. Not all twins. Some were siblings, some single children. Most cases went cold."

"How many children total?"

"Twenty-three missing over three years across five states. Not all of them were attributed to the same perpetrator because the cases were handled by different jurisdictions. But River, if Greenwood is the common factor, if Eleanor Vance has been doing this for years..."

Twenty-three children. The number sits like lead in my stomach.

"Send me everything," I say. "Every case file, every location, every connection to Greenwood. We need to see the full pattern."

After I hang up, I find Emma coordinating with the search teams. "We need to talk to Eleanor Vance. Now. Not as a person of interest. As a suspect."

"Agreed. But we need to be smart about it. If we come at her too hard and can't make charges stick, she'll lawyer up and we might get nothing."

"We have to make it work." I pull up the evidence we've gathered. "She's connected to both abduction sites. Her foundation ran the programs both sets of twins attended. She personally identified these children as special. The symbols carved at this location match the ones from our crime scene. We have enough for a search warrant at minimum."

Emma considers this. "Let's head back to Virginia.

Interview Eleanor formally. Execute warrants on Greenwood offices and her home. Search everything."

"What about the Okafor boys? We just leave Maryland to handle the search?"

"We coordinate. But River, if someone from this network has them, they won't be keeping them at a random location. Whoever's doing this plans carefully. Location matters to them." Emma pulls up a map of the region. "The clearing where the Caine twins died wasn't random. They'll use somewhere significant. Somewhere that fits their ritual pattern."

It's a gamble. The boys could be anywhere. But Emma's right—this network operates on symbolism and ancient practices. They wouldn't deviate from careful planning. We find the network's key players, we have a chance of finding Liam and Noah alive.

If they're still alive.

As we drive back toward Virginia, my phone buzzes with a text from Siwak: *Warrants approved. Teams executing at Greenwood headquarters and Eleanor Vance's residence now.*

It's happening. Three days after finding the Caine twins dead in that clearing, we're finally moving against the person responsible.

But in the back of my mind, I keep hearing Mercer's voice from yesterday. The Shepherd always stays hidden. Always uses others to do the work. Always remains one step ahead.

Eleanor Vance might be the face of Greenwood Legacy Foundation. But is she the architect? Or is she just another follower, another true believer serving someone who's been orchestrating these horrors for fifty years?

"The parents mentioned Eleanor said twins have gifts," I

tell Emma. "That they can walk between worlds. That's not general new age language. That's specific. From her academic research on pre-Christian sacrifice rituals."

"What if she's been preparing for this for years? Maybe her whole career." Emma navigates highway traffic. "What if the PhD wasn't a curiosity, but instruction. Learning the old practices so she could revive them."

"Or so she could teach them to others." I think about The Hollow Circle. The network of believers spread across multiple states. "What if Eleanor is training the next generation of believers? Creating a network that will outlive her?"

"Then we're not just stopping one person. We're dismantling an ideology."

My phone buzzes again. This time it's a text from an unknown number: *They're with the stars now. As was promised. The cycle continues. - A Friend*

I stare at the message, my hands going cold.

Emma glances over. "What is it?"

I show her the text. Her expression darkens.

"Warren Caine received a similar message," I say, remembering. "Right after his sons died. 'They're with the stars now. As was promised. Be at peace.'"

"Someone is watching. Tracking the investigation. Sending messages." Emma's jaw sets. "Forward that to our tech team. Have them trace it."

I do, and though I'm hopeful, I'm not sure if we'll find anything useful. Still, someone could make a mistake and this would be a big break.

But the message itself is revealing. Someone knows the Okafor boys are dead or soon will be. Someone knows about the investigation, knows we're closing in. And they're not worried.

They're promising the cycle will continue.

As we cross back into Virginia, I watch the winter landscape pass by. Gray sky, bare trees, the kind of cold that seeps into bones. Nine days until winter solstice. If Eleanor is planning seven rituals, seven sets of twins, we've already lost two sets.

How many more children will disappear before we stop this?

And what happens on the solstice if we don't?

CHAPTER SIXTEEN

Greenwood Legacy Foundation occupies a renovated Victorian house on the outskirts of Charlottesville, the kind of building that screams respectability and community values. Wide porch, fresh paint, a tasteful sign out front featuring their logo—a stylized tree with intertwining branches forming a circle.

The same symbol carved into oak trees where children died.

By the time Emma and I arrive, the search is already underway. FBI vehicles line the street. Agents move in and out carrying boxes of files. Crime scene techs photograph everything.

Garrett meets us at the door. "We've got a lot. Financial records, program rosters going back eight years, personnel files, donor lists. They kept meticulous records."

"Where is she?" I ask.

"Not here. Agents went to her home address first. She wasn't there either. Car's gone. We've issued a Be on the

Lookout." He leads us inside, past rooms being systematically searched. "But here's what we found."

He takes us to Eleanor's office on the second floor. It's exactly what you'd expect from an academic turned nonprofit director. Bookshelves lined with texts on mythology, folklore, environmental education. Framed degrees on the walls. Photos of smiling children on nature walks.

But on her desk, spread out like she was working on it recently, is a hand-drawn organizational chart. Names and dates and connections. At the top: "The Returning—Phase III Implementation."

I lean over the chart, studying the structure. It's not a traditional hierarchy. It's more like a web, with Eleanor at one node and connections branching out to dozens of other names. Some I recognize from last night's surveillance. Others are new.

And there, in small handwriting at the bottom: "C. Raskin—Family Access Point, Bridge to RC."

RC. River Collins.

Emma sees it the same time I do. "He was recruited specifically to get close to you. This was targeted."

"We need to find him. Now." I pull out my phone. "Get surveillance on him immediately. If Eleanor has disappeared, she might contact him."

Garrett is already typing on his tablet. "We had surveillance on his location since this morning. According to the last check-in, he's at his temporary residence with Amanda Fletcher."

"Bring him in. I want him in an interview room within the hour."

"River—" Emma starts.

"I know. I'll watch from observation. But we need to know what he knows. If Eleanor recruited him to access me, he might know where she is. Might know what she's planning next."

Garrett makes the call while I continue examining Eleanor's office. There's something organized about her documentation that bothers me. She's not trying to hide her connections. She's documenting them. Like this is research, not conspiracy.

In a file cabinet, I find years of notes on individual children who attended programs. Detailed observations about their behavior, their receptiveness to "alternative thinking," their family situations. Red flags for any child protection agency. Evidence of systematic grooming.

And there, in a file marked "Special Circumstances," I find profiles on five sets of twins who attended programs in the last year. The Caine twins are there. So are the Okafor twins. But there are three more sets I don't recognize.

"Emma." I hold up the files. "Six more potential targets. We need to contact these families immediately."

She reviews the names quickly. "Two are local. One family moved to Tennessee six months ago."

"Contact them anyway. Warn them. If Eleanor is working toward seven rituals, she's already identified her victims."

A tech agent enters carrying a laptop. "We found this in a locked desk drawer. Password protected, but we got in. You need to see what's on it."

The laptop contains folders organized by year. Inside each folder: detailed planning documents for programs, but also notes on "promising candidates" and "successful transformations." The language is coded, but the intent is clear.

And there's correspondence. Emails to addresses that appear to be pseudonyms. Discussing "the old practices" and "necessary cycles" and "preparing bridges for the crossing."

One email chain makes my blood run cold. It's from three years ago, shortly after a high-profile case I worked made national news. Eleanor is writing to someone identified only as "Shepherd":

"I've identified a potential connection. Christopher R., local businessman, married with children. More importantly, he's family to RC—the bridge that was never completed. The one you've been tracking. I believe I can recruit him through spiritual wellness programs. He's searching for meaning, vulnerable to alternative thinking. If successful, this provides the access point we've been seeking."

The response, from Shepherd:

"Proceed carefully. RC is valuable but also dangerous. She escaped once. She knows more than she realizes. When the time comes for her return to the crossing, it must be done properly. Continue cultivating the family connection. Be patient. The old gods reward patience."

I step back from the laptop, my hands shaking. Emma steadies me with a hand on my shoulder.

"He's been tracking you," she says quietly. "Since your escape. Maybe before. You weren't random, River. You never were."

The room feels too small. Too close. Everything I've believed about my abduction—wrong place, wrong time, random victim—shatters. I was chosen. Targeted. Marked by someone who calls himself The Shepherd and has been orchestrating these horrors for decades.

And Chris. My brother-in-law, father to my nephew and niece, married to my sister—he was recruited specifically to provide access to me.

"I need air." I head for the hallway, down the stairs, out to the porch. The December cold hits my face like a slap.

Emma follows but gives me space. Just stands nearby while I process.

"Why?" I ask finally. "Why target me specifically? I was twelve years old."

"You were a child. You were chosen for the ritual they never completed. The crossing they prepared you for." Emma's voice is gentle but firm. "When you escaped, you became unfinished business. Maybe that made you more valuable. Maybe their belief system says uncompleted rituals create debt that must be repaid."

"So this whole time, while I've been building a career, living my life, thinking I was free—he's been watching. Planning. Positioning people around me."

"And now we know. Which means we can use it." Emma moves to stand in front of me. "You're not their victim anymore, River. You're the agent investigating them. You have resources they don't expect."

She's right. I know she's right. But it doesn't stop the feeling that my entire life has been an illusion. That I've been trapped in The Shepherd's web without realizing it.

My phone buzzes. Garrett: *Christopher Raskin is en route to field office. ETA thirty minutes.*

Time to get answers.

THE FBI FIELD office interview room is deliberately bland. Gray walls, metal table, uncomfortable chairs. A camera in the corner documenting everything. One-way glass on the wall.

I stand on the observation side with Garrett and Siwak, watching as agents escort Chris into the room. He looks confused, worried, but not terrified. Not yet.

Emma enters a moment later, carrying a folder. She's good at this—calm, professional, approachable. She sits across from Chris and introduces herself formally for the recording.

"Mr. Raskin, thank you for coming in. I'm Special Agent Emma Bertanelli. This is a voluntary interview regarding your connection to Greenwood Legacy Foundation and The Hollow Circle. You're not under arrest. You're free to leave at any time. Do you understand?"

"Yes." Chris's voice is steady. "But I don't understand what this is about. My lawyer said—"

"You're welcome to have your lawyer present. But right now, we're just having a conversation. Trying to understand your involvement with certain organizations." Emma opens the folder, pulls out the first document. "You donated $2,500 to The Hollow Circle two years ago. Can you tell me about that?"

Chris shifts in his seat. "It was a fundraiser. For environmental causes. I attended with a colleague from work who was involved in spiritual wellness groups. It seemed worthwhile."

"And you continued to make donations. Multiple times over the next eighteen months."

"I believed in what they were doing. Helping people reconnect with nature. Finding meaning outside of materialistic culture." He's defensive now. "It's not illegal to donate to nonprofits."

"No, it's not." Emma's tone remains neutral. "Tell me about how you got involved with these groups."

Chris explains about feeling empty in his marriage and career. About attending a meditation retreat where he met Amanda. About Eleanor Vance's programs seeming to offer something deeper than traditional therapy or religion.

"Eleanor specifically recruited you," Emma says. It's not a question.

"She... she approached me at a fundraiser about two years ago. We talked about spirituality and finding purpose. She mentioned her foundation, suggested I attend some programs."

"Did she ask about your family?"

"Yes. Standard getting-to-know-you conversation. I mentioned I had kids, a wife, a sister-in-law who works for the FBI."

Emma slides a document across the table. It's the email between Eleanor and The Shepherd. "She was very interested in your sister-in-law specifically. In FBI Agent River Collins."

Chris reads the email. His face goes pale. "I don't... I didn't know about this."

"Eleanor recruited you to gain access to Agent Collins. You were what she called a 'family access point.'"

"No." Chris shakes his head. "No, I got involved because I was searching for meaning. Because I needed something."

"But you told Eleanor about River." Emma's voice sharpens slightly. "You gave her information about River's... history."

"It came up in conversation. Eleanor was interested in

trauma and healing. I mentioned River had experienced something terrible as a child but had overcome it."

"So, you told her about her kidnapping?"

"Yes, but I only did that because her survival was an inspiration."

I watch from behind the glass, my fists clenched. Chris handed them information about me without realizing what they'd do with it.

Emma continues pressing. "You took your children to Greenwood events. Bennett and Ava attended programs run by Eleanor Vance."

"Yes. Family workshops. Nature education. They were legitimate programs."

"Were they? Because children who attended those programs are dead, Mr. Raskin. Twin boys found in a clearing with symbols carved around them. The same symbols that appear in Greenwood materials."

Chris's eyes widen. "What? No. No, those programs were about environmental education. About mythology and folklore. Eleanor wouldn't—"

"Eleanor Vance is a suspect in multiple child abductions and homicides. The programs you attended, the organization you donated to, they're part of a network called The Hollow Circle. A network that believes in ritual sacrifice."

"That's insane." Chris stands, agitated. "I attended meditation sessions. Discussion groups about ancient practices. It was academic. Philosophical. No one talked about hurting children."

"Did you attend meetings at the community center?" Emma asks. "Private meetings, separate from the public gatherings?"

Chris hesitates.

"Yes," he finally admits. "Sometimes there were smaller groups. More focused discussions about pre-Christian traditions and seasonal cycles. But it was historical analysis. Cultural education."

"What did they teach in those meetings?"

"About how modern society has lost connection to natural rhythms. How ancient cultures understood cycles of death and renewal. How certain traditions have been suppressed by organized religion." Chris sits back down. "It resonated with me. I felt like I'd found something meaningful."

Emma slides another document across—notes from Eleanor's files identifying "promising candidates" for inner circle recruitment. Chris's name is there with detailed observations about his receptiveness to alternative thinking.

"You were being groomed," Emma says bluntly. "Carefully cultivated over two years to bring you deeper into the organization. They identified you as someone who could be manipulated. And they used you to get information about Agent Collins."

Chris stares at the document, his hands shaking. "I didn't know. I swear I didn't know any of this."

"But you suspected something was wrong," Emma presses. "That's why your marriage fell apart. That's why Leslie said you became obsessed and secretive."

"I..." Chris struggles with the words. "I knew something felt off. Some of the things Eleanor said about children being special, about twins having gifts—it made me uncomfortable. But I told myself I was misunderstanding. That it was metaphorical."

"Was it metaphorical when Eleanor specifically asked

about Agent Collins? When she wanted to know details about her schedule, her cases, her personal life?"

Chris closes his eyes. "She asked questions. I thought she was just curious. Making conversation. I didn't realize..."

"That you were being used to gather intelligence on a federal agent. Intelligence that could be used to target her." Emma's voice is hard now. "You exposed your family to dangerous people. You took your children to events run by someone who grooms kids for ritual sacrifice. And you gave information about Agent Collins to a network that has been tracking her since her abduction twenty years ago."

The silence that follows is heavy. Chris sits with his head in his hands, the weight of realization crushing him.

"I didn't know," he whispers. "I need you to believe me. I didn't know what they were really doing."

Emma lets him sit with it for a moment before continuing. "Eleanor Vance has disappeared. Two more children are missing—twin boys, eight years old. If you know anything about where she might be, where she might take victims, you need to tell me now."

"I don't know where she is."

"Think. Meetings you attended. Conversations you overheard. Locations that were mentioned."

Chris thinks, his brow furrowed. "There were discussions about significant sites. Places where ancient peoples performed rituals. Eleanor was obsessed with locations that had historical significance for pre-Christian cultures."

"Be specific."

"She talked about the Blue Ridge Mountains. About how certain clearings still held power from practices performed there centuries ago. About archaeological sites that mainstream science dismissed but were actually ceremonial locations."

"Did she mention specific locations?"

"No. But she had maps. Detailed maps with markings. I saw them once during a meeting. Seven locations marked in red."

Emma and I exchange a look through the glass. The same map we found in Eleanor's office.

"When was this meeting?" Emma asks.

"Three weeks ago. Maybe a month. It was one of the inner circle gatherings." Chris looks up. "She said something about the winter solstice. About how this year was important. That the cycle would complete."

"Complete how?"

"She didn't explain. Just said that years of preparation were coming to fruition. That bridges would be built. That the old gods would finally receive what was owed."

The phrase hits me like a physical blow. What was owed. Like there's debt to be paid.

Emma continues questioning for another thirty minutes, extracting every detail Chris can remember. Names of other inner circle members. Dates of meetings. Conversations he overheard. It paints a picture of systematic indoctrination, of a network that reveals its true nature gradually to avoid scaring away potential recruits.

Finally, Emma stands. "We'll need you to remain available for further questioning. Don't leave the area. Don't contact anyone from Greenwood or The Hollow Circle. If Eleanor Vance tries to reach you, you notify us immediately."

"Am I being charged with anything?"

"We're still investigating. Don't leave the area. Don't

contact anyone from Greenwood or The Hollow Circle. If Eleanor Vance tries to reach you, you notify us immediately."

Chris nods, his face ashen. "Can I... can I see River? I need to apologize. Need to explain—"

"No," Emma says firmly. "Agent Collins is lead investigator on this case. Any contact between you would be inappropriate."

After Chris is escorted out, I join Emma in the interview room. We stand in silence for a moment, processing.

"I don't think he knew anything," Emma says finally. "About the murders, about the true nature of the inner circle. He was a fool, but not a monster."

"He still gave them information about me. Exposed Bennett and Ava to Eleanor Vance."

"I know. And he'll live with that." Emma gathers her files. "But he gave us useful information. Confirmed the seven locations. Confirmed the winter solstice timeline. That's something."

My phone rings. Siwak.

"River, we've got something from Eleanor's computer. A calendar entry for tonight. Location coordinates in the Blue Ridge Mountains." His voice is tense. "One of the seven marked locations. We think she's planning another ritual. Tonight."

Tonight. Less than forty-eight hours after the Okafor boys were taken.

"Coordinate tactical teams," I say. "Emma and I are heading there now."

As we rush to the parking garage, I can't stop thinking about what Chris revealed. Eleanor asked about me. Specifically. Wanted to know my schedule, my cases, my life.

Because The Shepherd has been tracking me since I escaped twenty years ago.

Because I'm unfinished business.

Because in their belief system, I'm a bridge that was never completed. And bridges are meant to be crossed.

The question is: what happens when The Shepherd decides it's finally time to finish what was started?

CHAPTER SEVENTEEN

Garrett has Eleanor Vance's academic history spread across three monitors by the time Emma and I return from the Chris interview. Journal articles, conference presentations, her dissertation, faculty evaluations. The digital paper trail of a woman who spent fifteen years in academia before walking away.

"University of Virginia," Garrett says, not looking up from his screens. "PhD in Folklore and Mythology, completed 2008. Dissertation titled 'Sacrifice and Transformation in Pre-Christian European Ritual Practice.' Graduated with honors, immediately hired as assistant professor."

I pull up a chair, scanning the publications list. Eleanor was prolific. Twenty-three peer-reviewed articles in seven years. Books chapters. Conference keynotes. A rising star in her field.

"What was her focus?" Emma asks.

"Primarily Germanic and Celtic traditions. Seasonal rituals, offerings to gods, the role of children in religious practices." Garrett clicks through to a publication from 2011. "This one got a lot of attention in academic circles. 'The Child as Sacred Intermediary: Examining Evidence of Juvenile Sacrifice in Iron Age Europe.'"

The title makes my skin crawl. Emma leans closer, reading over my shoulder.

The abstract is dense with academic language, but the core argument is clear: certain pre-Christian cultures believed children—particularly those with unusual qualities—could serve as bridges between the mortal world and divine realm. Their deaths weren't viewed as murder but as transformation. As necessary sacrifice to maintain cosmic balance.

"She's not just studying this," I say quietly. "She's arguing for it. Explaining the logic behind it."

"Academic research," Garrett says. "Supposed to be objective analysis of historical practices. But look at her language choices."

He highlights several passages. Words like "profound spiritual technology" and "sophisticated understanding of cyclical renewal" and "unfortunately maligned by Christian historians." The supposedly neutral academic tone can't quite hide Eleanor's reverence for the practices she's describing.

"She believes in this," Emma says. "Not as history. As truth."

I scroll through more publications. They follow a progression. Early work is standard academic analysis—careful, measured, properly skeptical. But around 2013, something shifts. The language becomes more passionate. Arguments become more provocative. Eleanor starts challenging mainstream interpretations, suggesting modern society has lost something vital by abandoning ancient practices.

"Here." Garrett pulls up a 2015 article. "This is where it gets really concerning."

The title: "Willing Sacrifice in Pre-Christian Europe: The Child as Bridge Between Worlds."

I open the full text, my hands steady despite the sick feeling in my stomach. The abstract is remarkably direct:

"This paper examines archaeological and textual evidence for voluntary participation of juveniles in ritual sacrifice practices across pre-Christian Europe. Particular attention is paid to the selection criteria for sacrificial candidates, with emphasis on twins, triplets, and children born during liminal periods (solstices, equinoxes). Evidence suggests these children were not victims but honored participants in ceremonies designed to maintain cosmic order. Modern ethical frameworks, while understandable, prevent us from recognizing the sophisticated spiritual technology these practices represented. The paper argues for renewed scholarly attention to the belief systems underlying these practices, rather than dismissing them through contemporary moral judgment."

"Sophisticated spiritual technology," Emma reads aloud. "She's calling child sacrifice technology."

"And defending it as honored participation rather than murder." I skim the full article. It's thoroughly researched, extensively footnoted, academically rigorous. It's also a manifesto disguised as scholarship.

Eleanor argues that twins were particularly valued because they represented duality—two souls, two bodies, existing in perfect balance. During liminal times like solstices, when the boundary between worlds grew thin, twin children could serve as portals. Their sacrifice wasn't cruelty but sacred duty.

"Did anyone challenge this?" I ask. "Other academics, peer reviewers?"

"Oh yeah." Garrett pulls up responses. "The article generated significant controversy. Three scholars wrote rebuttals. The journal editor added a disclaimer. But Eleanor defended her work. Said she was simply presenting evidence without modern bias."

"What happened after this?"

"Her tenure review in 2016 was contentious. The university had concerns about her research direction and her teaching." Garrett finds the relevant documents. "Students complained that she was promoting dangerous ideologies in her courses. That she spoke about ancient practices with admiration rather than critical distance."

I read the student complaints. They're surprisingly specific. Eleanor talking about how modern society has "lost touch with necessary cycles of death and renewal." Suggesting that ancient peoples "understood truths we've forgotten." Making students uncomfortable with her reverence for practices most scholars condemned.

"She was denied tenure," Garrett continues. "But here's the interesting part—she didn't fight it. Didn't appeal. Just left academia in spring 2017. Six months later, Greenwood Legacy Foundation was created."

"She was done trying to convince academics," Emma says. "She was ready to put theory into practice."

I pull up Greenwood's founding documents. Eleanor is listed as founder and executive director. The mission statement talks about environmental education and reconnecting families with nature. Perfect cover.

"Has she published anything since leaving academia?" I ask.

"Not in peer-reviewed journals. But she has a blog." Garrett pulls it up. "Personal essays about spirituality, nature, traditional wisdom. Posted sporadically over the past eight years."

The blog is carefully written. Nothing explicitly criminal. But reading between the lines, Eleanor's beliefs are clear. She talks about "cycles that must be honored" and "debts that must be paid" and "children who carry special gifts."

One post from two years ago makes me pause:

"I've been asked why I left academia. The answer is simple: some truths cannot be fully understood through scholarship alone. They must be experienced. They must be lived. Ancient peoples knew this. They didn't separate theory from practice, belief from action. In our modern world, we've lost that integration. My work now is to help people—especially children—reconnect with older ways of knowing. Not through books, but through direct experience with the natural world and its eternal patterns."

"That's when she started intensifying Greenwood programs," Garrett notes. "Two years ago. More events, more locations, specific focus on children she identified as 'sensitive' or 'gifted.'"

Emma leans back in her chair. "She spent fifteen years building academic credentials. Establishing herself as an expert. Learning everything about ancient sacrifice practices. Then she walked away and started recruiting."

"Not recruiting," I say quietly. "Preparing. She's not just gathering followers. She's enacting the practices she studied. Everything she learned academically, she's now applying."

I think about the Caine twins positioned in that clearing.

The precise geometric arrangement. The symbols carved with mathematical accuracy. The wooden token made from ancient oak. Every detail drawn from Eleanor's research. Her dissertation made real.

"What about her lecture?" Emma asks. "Garrett mentioned controversial remarks that contributed to her tenure denial."

Garrett searches his files. "November 2015. Guest lecture at a conference on European archaeology. Someone recorded it." He pulls up an audio file. "Want to hear the relevant section?"

I nod. He plays it.

Eleanor's voice is clear, confident, compelling. She's discussing seasonal rituals when she goes off-script:

"We look at these practices through a lens of horror. Child sacrifice seems monstrous to us. But what if we're wrong? What if those ancient peoples understood something we've lost? Modern society celebrates life without acknowledging death's necessity. We see ending as tragedy, never as transformation. But nature operates on cycles of death and renewal. Forests burn to regenerate. Animals die to feed others. Perhaps these ancient practices weren't barbaric. Perhaps they were humanity's attempt to align with nature's fundamental truth: that death isn't an enemy, but a necessary part of cosmic order."

There's a pause in the recording. You can hear the audience shifting, uncomfortable.

"I'm not advocating for revival of these practices," Eleanor continues quickly. *"I'm simply suggesting we approach them with intellectual honesty rather than reflexive condemnation. If we're going to understand pre-Christian spirituality, we must be willing to consider that their worldview, while different from ours, had its own internal logic. Its own truth."*

The recording ends. The room is quiet.

"She was lying," I say. "That disclaimer at the end about not advocating revival. She was already planning it."

Emma pulls up the timeline. "This lecture was November 2015. Her controversial paper was published six months later. Tenure denied spring 2017. Greenwood Legacy Foundation incorporated fall 2017."

"She knew she was going to lose her academic position," I realize. "The lecture was her burning bridges. Testing how far she could push before they expelled her. Once she knew academia wouldn't tolerate her views, she moved on to implementation."

Garrett pulls up another document. "Her personnel file from UVA includes a psychological evaluation conducted during her tenure review. The counselor noted: 'Dr. Vance exhibits unusual certainty regarding her research subjects. Shows difficulty separating academic analysis from personal belief. When challenged on ethical implications of her work, becomes defensive and suggests critics lack understanding of historical context.'"

"They saw warning signs," Emma says. "They just didn't realize what she was planning."

I stand, moving to the window. Outside, Charlottesville goes about its normal Tuesday afternoon. People going to work, picking up kids, living ordinary lives. None of them knowing that a woman with a PhD and years of academic credibility has been methodically planning ritual sacrifice of children.

"We need everything," I tell Garrett. "Every article she published, every lecture she gave, every course she taught. I want to understand exactly what she believes. Because that will tell us what she's planning next."

"Already compiling it." Garrett's fingers fly across the keyboard. "But River, there's a lot here. Fifteen years of academic work. Hundreds of pages."

"Then we prioritize. Focus on anything about twins, about winter solstice, about specific rituals. Anything that might tell us where she's holding the Okafor boys."

My phone buzzes. Siwak: *Eleanor's home search underway. Initial reports show extensive personal library. Team is photographing everything.*

Eleanor's entire academic career was preparation for this. The dissertation, the publications, the lectures. She wasn't stumbling into these beliefs. She spent fifteen years learning ancient practices, understanding their logic, building expertise. All while hiding behind academic legitimacy.

And now she's putting that knowledge into action.

CHAPTER EIGHTEEN

Aiden's apartment smells like garlic and rosemary when I arrive at nine-thirty. He's at the stove, stirring something in a large pot, still wearing his scrubs from the hospital. When he sees me, his expression shifts from concentration to concern.

"You look exhausted," he says.

"Long day." I drop my bag by the door, shed my jacket. "What are you making?"

"Soup. Minestrone. Thought you might need actual food instead of whatever you've been surviving on." He gestures to the couch. "Sit. It'll be ready in ten minutes."

I sink into his couch, letting the warmth and normalcy of his space wash over me. The apartment is small but comfortable. Books everywhere. A telescope by the window. Photos of his family on the shelves. Normal things. Safe things.

Aiden brings me a glass of water, sits beside me. "Want to talk about it?"

Where do I even start? With my brother-in-law being

recruited to provide access to me? With discovering my abduction was targeted, not random? With children dying while Eleanor Vance calmly cites academic research to justify murder?

"Eleanor Vance has a PhD," I say finally. "From a prestigious university. She spent fifteen years researching child sacrifice in pre-Christian Europe. Then she left academia and started putting her research into practice."

Aiden's hand finds mine. "She's the one running the foundation?"

"She's the one grooming children. Identifying twins as special. Teaching them about ancient practices disguised as nature education." I close my eyes. "She looks so normal, Aiden. Like someone you'd want running your kid's summer camp. Warm, articulate, passionate about environmental education. Parents trust her completely."

"That's how these people operate. They don't look like monsters."

"I know. I know that intellectually. But seeing it..." I trail off. "A nine-year-old girl is in the hospital right now. Poisoned with plant compounds after attending one of Eleanor's events. The Caine twins are dead. The Okafor twins are missing. And Eleanor just finished writing a paper about how child sacrifice was actually sophisticated spiritual technology."

Aiden is quiet for a moment, his thumb tracing circles on my hand. "You're spiraling."

"I'm working a case."

"River." His voice is gentle but firm. "I've watched you consume yourself with cases before. But this one is different. This one is personal in ways that scare me."

I pull my hand away, stand up. "Of course it's personal. Children are dying."

"That's not what I mean." He follows me to the window. "You said your abduction might be connected to this case. That's huge. And I'm worried about what that means for you. You're not just investigating a network—you're investigating the people who might have targeted you when you were twelve."

"Which means I understand them better than anyone else on the team."

"Or it means you're too close to see clearly." Aiden moves to stand beside me. "I'm not saying you should step away. I know you won't. But you need to take care of yourself. You're not sleeping. You're barely eating. When's the last time you took a full breath?"

The question catches me off guard. When was the last time I felt like I could breathe? Before finding the Caine twins? Before seeing my nephew's drawing? Before realizing my entire life has been shadowed by a predator I didn't know was watching?

"I have to stop them," I say quietly. "If I don't, more children die. It's that simple."

"Nothing is that simple. River, you can't save everyone. You know that, right? You can do everything right, work every angle, follow every lead, and sometimes people still die. Sometimes evil wins."

"Not this time."

"You can't guarantee that." His voice is kind but unflinching. "You're human. You have limits. And if you burn yourself out trying to be everywhere at once, trying to prevent every tragedy, you'll end up unable to help anyone."

I want to argue. Want to insist I'm fine, I can handle it,

I've dealt with worse. But the truth is I'm exhausted. I'm terrified. And I'm starting to understand just how deeply I've been targeted.

"I keep thinking about what you said once," I tell him. "About how evil isn't always obvious. Sometimes it wears scrubs and has a medical degree and knows exactly where to cut to cause maximum damage."

"I was talking about my ex-girlfriend," Aiden says with a slight smile. "The cardiologist who cheated on me with another surgeon."

Despite everything, I almost laugh. "Okay, bad example. But the principle holds. Eleanor Vance has been published in peer-reviewed journals. She runs a nonprofit with 501(c)(3 status. Parents love her. Kids love her. She's everything you'd want in an educator."

"Except she's teaching children to accept their own deaths as transformation."

"Exactly." I turn to face him. "That's what terrifies me, Aiden. It's not monsters in dark alleys. It's people with credentials and community awards who smile while they poison children. How do you protect against that? How do you warn people when the danger looks so benign?"

Before Aiden can answer, his phone rings. He glances at the screen, frowns. "It's the hospital. I'm not on call tonight."

"Answer it."

He does, moving to the kitchen. I can only hear his side of the conversation, but his expression changes quickly from confusion to alarm.

"When did she come in? What are her symptoms?" Pause. "Pupils fixed and dilated? For how long?" Longer pause. "I'm on my way."

He ends the call, already moving toward the bedroom

for fresh scrubs. "I have to go to the hospital. There's a child in the ER with unusual symptoms. They want me to consult."

"What kind of symptoms?"

"Severe lethargy, dissociation, fixed and dilated pupils. They can't get her to respond to stimuli." He emerges with his hospital ID and keys. "The parents are frantic. They said she was fine until this evening, then suddenly collapsed."

My chest tightens. "How old?"

"Nine."

"Aiden." I'm already grabbing my jacket. "Ask them if she attended any nature programs recently. Specifically ask about Greenwood Legacy Foundation."

He stops, understanding dawning on his face. "You think this is related?"

"Fixed pupils, dissociation, sudden onset after being fine? That matches what the Caine twins' autopsy suggested. And we have another child showing similar symptoms after attending a Greenwood event." I'm heading for the door. "I'm coming with you."

We drive to the hospital in tense silence. Aiden navigates traffic while I text Emma: *Child at UVA Medical Center with symptoms matching possible poisoning. Age 9. Checking for Greenwood connection.*

Her response is immediate: *On my way.*

The ER is chaos when we arrive. Aiden flashes his ID and we're waved through. A nurse intercepts us near the pediatric bay.

"Dr. Watkins, she's in Bay 4. Parents are with her. We've got her on supportive care but her neuro status hasn't changed. Tox screen is pending but the symptoms are unusual."

"I need to speak with the parents first," Aiden says, his doctor voice calm and authoritative. "Agent Collins is FBI. She may have information relevant to the case."

The nurse's eyes widen slightly but she nods, leading us to Bay 4.

Inside, a girl lies motionless on the bed. Small, dark hair, her face peaceful despite the IV lines and monitors. Her parents hover nearby—father standing rigid, mother clutching her daughter's hand.

Aiden introduces himself, explains he's been called to consult. I hang back, letting him establish rapport.

"Can you tell me what happened tonight?" Aiden asks gently.

The mother speaks, her voice breaking. "She was fine all day. Playing with her brother, doing homework. Then after dinner she said she felt tired. I thought maybe she was coming down with something. But then she just... collapsed. We couldn't wake her up."

"Any recent illnesses? New medications? Exposure to chemicals or plants?"

"No. Nothing. She's healthy. She's never..." The mother can't finish.

"What about activities?" I step forward, showing my credentials. "Has she attended any outdoor programs or events recently?"

The father looks confused. "Why would that matter?"

"Please. It's important."

"She went on a field trip last weekend," the mother says. "Some kind of nature walk. Her school organized it. She was so excited."

My heart sinks. "Do you remember what organization ran the program?"

"Some foundation. Environmental education. Greenwood something."

"Greenwood Legacy Foundation."

"Yes. That's it." The mother looks between Aiden and me. "Why? What does that have to do with this?"

Aiden catches my eye. The answer is clear in his expression: everything.

CHAPTER NINETEEN

The raid on Eleanor Vance's home happens at dawn. I'm there with Emma, part of the twelve-agent team that descends on the modest craftsman bungalow in a quiet Charlottesville neighborhood. Nothing about the house screams danger. It has a well-maintained garden, a bird feeder, a welcome mat.

The kind of place where a respected person would live.

"FBI! Search warrant!" The breach team announces our presence, though we already know Eleanor isn't here. Her car hasn't been at this address in two days. But houses hold secrets. And we're hoping Eleanor's will tell us where she's gone.

I follow Emma inside once the house is cleared. The interior matches the exterior—tasteful, organized, comfortable. Hardwood floors, Arts and Crafts furniture, botanical prints on the walls. The living room has floor-to-ceiling bookshelves stuffed with volumes on mythology, archaeology, anthropology.

"It's like her university office," Emma observes, pulling on gloves. "Everything is academic."

We move through the house systematically. The kitchen is clean, minimal. The bedroom is simple—a bed, dresser, more bookshelves. No personal touches. No photos of family or friends. Just books. Hundreds of them.

Garrett is cataloging titles. "Most of these are standard academic texts. Pre-Christian European religion, Celtic and Germanic mythology, archaeological reports. But there's a section here that's different."

He shows us a shelf containing books that look older, more fragile. Some are in languages I don't recognize. German, maybe. Or Old Norse. The bindings are worn, the pages yellowed.

"These are primary sources," Garrett says. "Medieval manuscripts about pagan practices. Some of these are probably quite valuable."

"She's studying original texts," I say. "Going back to the source material."

We continue through the house. A small office off the main hallway is where Eleanor did her work. A desk with a laptop we've already secured. Filing cabinets with meticulously organized papers. More books. Maps on the walls showing various regions of Europe with handwritten annotations.

"Looking for something," Emma says, studying one map. "Archaeological sites, probably. Places where rituals were performed."

An agent calls from the back of the house. "You need to see this."

We follow him to Eleanor's bedroom. At first glance, it

looks normal. But the agent points to the bookshelf against the far wall. "This moves."

He demonstrates, pulling on a specific book spine. The entire bookshelf swings outward on hidden hinges, revealing a small space behind it. A hidden office, maybe six feet by eight feet.

Inside, the walls are covered with maps and photographs and handwritten notes. But these aren't academic materials. This is operational planning.

The largest map dominates the back wall. The Blue Ridge Mountains, topographic detail showing elevation and terrain. And marked on this map, in red ink, are seven locations. Seven X marks spread across hundreds of square miles.

I move closer, my throat tight. One of the locations is circled with additional notes: "First crossing—completed 2/15."

December fifteenth. Four days ago. The day the Caine twins died.

"Jesus," Emma breathes. "Seven locations. Seven planned rituals."

The other six marks have dates beside them. The closest upcoming date is tonight. December nineteenth. Three days before winter solstice.

Garrett photographs everything while I study the map. The locations are remote. Deep in national forest land, accessible only by hiking trails. Places where someone could work undisturbed.

Places where bodies might not be found for days or weeks.

On a small desk in the hidden office, there are

notebooks. I open one carefully. Eleanor's handwriting fills the pages. Not academic notes. Personal journals.

"The first crossing must be twins. Double souls for the initial bridge. The subsequent crossings can be siblings or single children, but they must be prepared properly. The cycle requires seven sacrifices across seven locations to complete the solstice transformation. Each location holds power from previous use. The old gods remember."

I turn pages, my hands steady despite the horror of what I'm reading.

"I've selected the candidates carefully. The Caine twins were perfect—young enough to be pure, old enough to understand their purpose. The Okafor twins will serve as the second bridge. I have three more sets identified. The timing must be precise. Winter solstice is the culmination, but each crossing must happen at specific intervals leading up to it."

Emma reads over my shoulder. "She's planned everything. This isn't reactive. It's systematic."

I flip to another page. This one has a different tone.

"The Shepherd was pleased with my progress when he visited in September. He said my academic preparation has made me uniquely qualified for this work. Unlike his earlier attempts, which relied on intuition and incomplete knowledge, we now have the benefit of rigorous research. I've studied hundreds of primary sources. I know exactly how these rituals were performed. I can replicate them with accuracy our ancestors would recognize."

"The Shepherd visited her," I say. "Three months ago."

"So he's actively involved," Emma replies. "Not just inspiring from a distance. He's checking on her work. Guiding her."

Garrett finds another notebook, this one containing detailed information on individual children. I recognize some names immediately—the Caine twins, the Okafor twins. But there are others. Dozens of profiles on children who attended Greenwood programs over the years. Observations about their personalities, their family situations, their receptiveness to "alternative thinking."

This is documentation of systematic grooming going back years.

"She's been selecting victims since she started the foundation," I tell Emma. "Eight years of identifying candidates."

"But only acting on it now," Emma says. "Why wait?"

I find the answer in another journal entry from last fall:

"The Shepherd says the time is finally right. The planets align correctly this winter solstice for the first time in decades. My research is complete. The locations are identified. The candidates are prepared. And most importantly, the bridge that was never completed can finally be brought home. RC escaped twenty years ago, interrupting a crossing that should have been. Her captors were not fully trained. They didn't understand the complete practice. But I do. And when the seven crossings are complete, when the solstice cycle is fulfilled, RC will return to complete her transformation. She is the keystone. Everything leads to her."

RC. River Collins. Me.

The room tilts slightly. Emma steadies me with a hand on my arm.

"She's been planning to target you all along," Emma says quietly. "The seven crossings aren't the end goal. They're preparation. For you."

I force myself to keep reading. More entries detail Eleanor's belief that my interrupted abduction created a "cosmic debt" that must be repaid. That I'm more valuable now because I've lived with partial transformation for two decades. That my final crossing will be more powerful than all seven of the current victims combined.

"She's insane," I say, though I know that's not quite right. Eleanor isn't delusional. She's utterly rational within her belief system. Every action is calculated. Every step is planned.

She's just operating from a worldview that accepts child sacrifice as spiritual technology.

Garrett has found something else. "Look at this."

It's a calendar. This month—December. The dates of the seven planned crossings are marked. December 15 (completed). December 19 (tonight). December 20. December 21. And then three more on December 22, the winter solstice itself.

"Seven rituals in eight days," Emma calculates. "She's accelerating dramatically at the end."

"Because the solstice is the culmination," I say, still staring at the calendar. "That's when the veil between worlds is thinnest. That's when the transformation is most powerful."

We photograph everything. Document every detail. Secure all evidence.

But as we work, all I can think about is those seven red marks on the map. We found the Caine twins at the first location. The Okafor boys could be at any of the remaining six. Or Eleanor might have already moved them to tonight's location.

We have one address marked for tonight's ritual. Which means we have a chance to stop it before it happens.

But winter solstice is three days away. And Eleanor has planned three more crossings for that day alone.

Seven locations. Seven rituals. Seven crossings.

We've only stopped one.

CHAPTER TWENTY

Eleanor Vance sits across from Emma and me in Interview Room 2, looking remarkably calm for someone facing multiple murder charges. She arrived an hour after the raid on her home, walking into the field office voluntarily with her lawyer at her side. No arrest. No handcuffs. Just a polite phone call from Richard Caldwell of Caldwell and Associates informing us his client wished to cooperate with the investigation. She's dressed professionally in dark slacks and a burgundy sweater, her dark hair pulled back in the same loose bun she wears in her faculty photos. Late forties, minimal makeup, wire-rimmed glasses. She looks exactly like what she is—or was—a university professor turned nonprofit director. Respectable. Educated. Trustworthy.

They've been here for thirty minutes and Eleanor hasn't broken composure once. While her lawyer reviews documents and makes notes on his legal pad, Eleanor sits with her hands folded on the table, patient and serene. Not the posture of someone worried about murder charges. Not the nervous energy of someone caught. She looks like she's attending a faculty meeting where the agenda doesn't particularly interest her but she's too polite to leave.

"My client is cooperating fully," Caldwell says for the third time. "But she maintains her innocence in all charges."

"Dr. Vance," Emma begins, her voice professionally neutral. "We found detailed plans in your home for what you call 'crossings.' Seven rituals planned between December fifteenth and twenty-second. Can you explain what those plans represent?"

Eleanor's expression is serene. "My academic research involves understanding historical practices. I maintain personal notes on sites of archaeological significance. It's part of my ongoing scholarship."

"Scholarship," I repeat. "You wrote about selecting 'candidates.' About preparing them for transformation. You documented specific children who attended your programs."

"I keep observations on the children I work with. It helps me tailor educational programming to their individual needs." Her voice is patient, like she's explaining something simple to someone slow. "Every good educator tracks student progress."

"You documented their 'receptiveness to alternative thinking,'" Emma says. "What does that mean?"

"Some children are more open to non-mainstream ideas. They ask questions about spirituality and nature that go beyond conventional environmental education. I note these traits so I can provide appropriate materials."

Emma slides a photo across the table. The Caine twins, arranged in that clearing. "Titus and Matthew Caine attended your programs. Did you provide them with appropriate materials?"

Eleanor looks at the photo without flinching. "Those poor boys. When I heard about what happened, I was devastated. Their parents trusted me with their education."

"Brenda Caine trusted you," I say. "Did you cultivate that trust specifically so you could access her sons?"

"I cultivate relationships with all the families in my programs. That's good community building."

"Brenda believed her sons were special. That twins carry double souls. Did you teach her that?"

"I discuss traditional beliefs from various cultures. Many indigenous peoples have beautiful philosophies about twins. It's cultural education."

Her lawyer intervenes. "Agent Collins, what exactly are you accusing my client of?"

"Grooming children for ritual sacrifice," Emma says bluntly. "The Caine twins are dead. The Okafor twins are missing. Both sets attended Greenwood programs. Both were identified by your client as having special qualities."

Eleanor's expression doesn't change. "That's absurd. Correlation isn't causation. Many families participate in Greenwood programs. It's tragic that some of those families have experienced loss. But that doesn't make me responsible."

I pull out another document. "You wrote about the Caine twins specifically. 'Perfect for the first crossing.' What did you mean?"

"If you're referring to my personal journals, those are academic explorations. Thought experiments about how ancient peoples might have selected candidates for rituals. I'm a scholar. I think about these questions."

"You think about which children to sacrifice," I say.

"I think about historical practices," Eleanor corrects. "There's a distinction."

Emma shows her the map. The seven locations marked in red. "We found this hidden behind a bookshelf in your home. Why hide it if it's just academic research?"

"I keep my private office private. That's not suspicious. It's personal boundaries."

"The first location is where we found the Caine twins. Explain that coincidence."

"I can't explain tragedies that happened in locations I've identified for historical significance. Many people hike in the Blue Ridge Mountains. It's not unusual for significant events to occur in places with archaeological interest."

She's so calm. So rational. Every answer carefully constructed to maintain plausible deniability. This is someone who has spent years in academia learning how to defend controversial positions.

"A child is in the hospital," I say, changing tactics. "Nine years old. Severe neurological symptoms after attending one of your twilight hike events. What was on that hike?"

"We do plant identification walks. Sometimes we discuss medicinal and toxic plants. It's possible a child touched something inadvisable. These are teaching moments about respecting nature's power."

"You poisoned her."

"I taught her about plants. If she chose to interact with something dangerous despite warnings, that's unfortunate but not criminal." Eleanor's eyes are steady on mine. "Children need to understand that nature isn't always safe. That's a valuable lesson."

Emma leans forward. "Dr. Vance, we have your journals

describing planned rituals. We have the map with seven marked locations. We have documentation showing you identified and groomed specific children. We have your academic papers arguing for the validity of child sacrifice."

"I'm a scholar and educator," Eleanor says. "My research explores controversial historical topics. My foundation provides valuable environmental education. None of that is illegal."

Her lawyer stands. "Unless you're charging my client, we're done here."

"We're building our case," Emma says. "Dr. Vance should remain available for further questioning."

"My client has cooperated extensively. We'll review any formal charges when they're filed." Caldwell gathers his materials.

Eleanor stands, smoothing her dress. She looks at me directly for the first time since entering the room.

"May I say something, Agent Collins? Off the record?"

"Sure," I say with a smile. I know perfectly well that everything in this room is on-record but I keep that to myself.

"I've heard about your career. Your survival of abduction as a child. It's remarkable. You've achieved so much despite that trauma."

"Dr. Vance—" her lawyer begins, but she continues.

"But I wonder if you've ever considered that your captors saw something in you. Something special. That they chose you specifically because you had potential for transformation." She steps closer to the table. "Some debts must be paid in the old ways, Agent Collins. Your captor understood that. That's why you're still here. Not because you escaped. Because you weren't finished."

The room goes silent. Emma stands, moving between Eleanor and me. "That's enough. Agent, would you escort Dr. Vance and her attorney out?"

An agent enters to show them out. But she pauses at the door, turning back to look at me one more time.

Her voice is quiet, almost gentle: "The cycle completes at the solstice. All debts will be balanced. All bridges will be crossed."

Then she's gone, leaving me staring at the empty doorway.

Emma sits back down, watching me carefully. "You okay?"

"She's threatening me. Directly. On record. But with plausible deniability."

"Yes. Which means she's confident that we won't be able to make a case. That whatever she has planned for the solstice will happen regardless of our investigation."

I think about those seven marked locations. About the dates on Eleanor's calendar. About her journal entry saying everything leads to me.

"She thinks she's going to complete my crossing," I say. "That's her endgame. Not just the seven children. Me."

Emma's jaw sets. "Then we make sure that doesn't happen. We find the Okafor boys. We stop tonight's ritual. We prevent every crossing she has planned."

"And The Shepherd?"

"We find him too. Because Eleanor might be the current threat, but he's been orchestrating this for years. We take them both down."

After Eleanor departs with Caldwell—we can't hold her without formal charges being filed—Emma and I return to the conference room where the rest of the team is gathering.

Siwak is at the head of the table. "We have one location marked for tonight's ritual. Same tactics team that handled the Okafor search is ready to deploy. We hit it at dusk, before she can start whatever she has planned."

"What about the other locations?" I ask. "She has three more rituals scheduled for the solstice. We can't just react. We need to be positioned at all of them."

"We'll coordinate with State Police and Park Service. Cover all seven sites simultaneously on the twenty-second. But tonight's our immediate priority."

Garrett pulls up the map location. It's deep in Shenandoah National Park, accessible only by a four-mile hike. Remote. Isolated. Exactly the kind of place Eleanor would choose.

"We go in quiet," Siwak continues. "No lights, no sirens. If she's there, if she has victims, we need to approach without alerting her."

Emma and I will be part of the team. So will Garrett. Aiden will be standing by at the nearest hospital in case we find victims who need immediate medical attention.

As the meeting breaks up, I stay behind, staring at the map with its seven red marks. Eleanor's voice echoes in my mind: *All bridges will be crossed.*

She's so confident. So certain that her plan will work.

Which means she knows something we don't. Has prepared for contingencies we haven't anticipated.

And in three days, on the winter solstice, she intends to complete a crossing that started twenty years ago.

Unless we stop her first.

CHAPTER TWENTY-ONE

The command center is chaos by four PM. Six tactical teams preparing to deploy simultaneously across the Blue Ridge Mountains. Maps spread across tables. Radio checks. Equipment inventories. Weather reports showing heavy snow moving in by nightfall.

Siwak stands at the center coordinating everything. "Team 1 takes the location marked for tonight—here." He taps the map. "Deep in Shenandoah, four miles from the nearest road access. Teams 2 through 6 cover the remaining marked sites. We go in coordinated, we move fast, and we get those boys back."

Emma and I are leading Team 1 with Garrett and four other agents. We've got the location Eleanor plans to use tonight—December nineteenth, one of the dates on her carefully documented calendar.

"What if she's already moved them?" an agent asks.

"Then we find evidence that tells us where," Siwak says. "But according to her journals, she performs rituals at specific times. Tonight is scheduled. She won't deviate from her plan."

I'm not so sure. Eleanor has been methodical for eight years. Building her foundation, recruiting believers, identifying victims. Would she really leave a map showing all her ritual sites where we could find it?

But I keep the doubt to myself. We need to try.

By five PM we're hiking into Shenandoah National Park. The trailhead is remote, accessible only via a forest service road that's barely maintained in winter. Snow is falling steadily now, covering our tracks as we move.

Four miles. In good conditions it would take ninety minutes. In snow, with tactical gear, in failing light—we're looking at two and a half hours minimum.

We hike in silence, conserving energy. The forest is beautiful and hostile. Bare trees reaching toward gray sky. Snow muffling sound. Temperature dropping with the sun.

My radio crackles. Team 2 checking in from their location sixty miles away. "Site located. Clearing with oak trees, fresh carvings on trunks. Evidence of recent activity but no personnel present."

Team 3 reports similar findings twenty minutes later. "Ritual setup complete. Stones arranged, fire pit with warm coals. Recent tire tracks leading away."

Emma and I exchange glances but keep moving. Maybe we're close. Maybe Eleanor just finished her preparations and left. Maybe we'll find something that tells us where she went.

We reach our coordinates at seven-fifteen PM. Full darkness now, only our flashlights cutting through snow and shadows.

The clearing is exactly as Eleanor's map indicated. Oak

trees forming a rough circle. Symbols carved into bark at precise heights. Stones arranged in geometric patterns that match the diagrams in Eleanor's journals.

Fresh carvings. The wood is pale, recently exposed. Someone was here today.

I move to the center of the clearing where a fire pit has been prepared. I crouch, holding my hand near the ashes. Still warm.

"They were here recently," I call to Emma.

Garrett is photographing the carved symbols. "These match the Caine crime scene exactly. Same pattern, same precision."

We fan out, searching the area finding evidence everywhere: footprints in snow, cigarette butts, food wrappers, tire tracks on a service road half a mile away. Signs of multiple people. Signs of preparation and planning.

But no people. No victims.

My radio comes alive. Team 4: "We've got children's items. Blankets, juice boxes, a small shoe. Looks like kids were held here temporarily."

Team 5: "Wooden tokens found near ritual markings. Same design as the one from the Caine scene."

Team 6: "Fresh tracks heading east. We're pursuing."

It's happening at all six sites. Evidence everywhere. Fresh, recent, convincing. But empty. Abandoned just before we arrived.

"This doesn't feel right," I tell Emma quietly.

"What do you mean?"

"We found the map yesterday. Raided Eleanor's house this morning. She's known we were coming for at least twelve hours. Why would she leave all this evidence? Why not clean the sites?"

"Maybe she didn't have time. Maybe we moved faster than she expected."

"Eleanor planned for eight years. Built an entire foundation as cover. Recruited dozens of believers. Systematically groomed children." I gesture at the clearing. "You think someone that careful would leave warm coals and fresh footprints for us to find?"

Emma considers this. "You think she wanted us to find the map."

Before I can answer, Garrett calls out. "Over here. More tracks leading north."

We follow, pushing through snow and undergrowth. Find another campsite, this one with a tarp shelter partially collapsed. More food wrappers. A child's jacket caught on a branch.

My chest tightens. We're so close. They were just here.

Team 6 radios: "Tracks went cold at a creek crossing. Lost the trail."

Team 3: "We found a van hidden under branches. Empty. Running plates now."

We keep searching. Hours blur together. The snow falls heavier. Communication with other teams becomes sporadic as weather degrades radio signals.

At nine PM, while checking yet another abandoned campsite, I hear something.

A child crying.

Emma hears it too. We move toward the sound, weapons drawn, flashlights cutting through darkness. The crying continues—weak, scared, coming from deeper in the woods.

We find another clearing. Smaller than the first. A circle of stones arranged on the ground.

And in the center, a child.

He's lying on his side, barely moving. Dark skin, small frame. Wearing clothes too light for this weather.

I radio immediately. "We've got one of the Okafor boys. Alive. Need medical evac now."

Emma is already beside him, checking vitals. "He's hypothermic. Barely responsive. Pupils fixed and dilated."

The same symptoms. The same poisoning.

The boy's eyes flutter open. He looks at me but doesn't seem to see. His lips move, mumbling something.

I lean closer. "You're safe. We're FBI. We're getting you help."

"They said..." His voice is barely audible. "They said you'd come here..."

"Who said that?"

"They said you'd look in the mountains..." He trails off, his eyes unfocusing.

"Where's your brother?"

"Noah isn't..." He struggles to form words. "Not in the mountains..."

His eyes close. He's unconscious again.

The medevac helicopter can't land in this terrain and weather. We have to carry Liam back to the trailhead. It takes ninety minutes of careful hiking through snow in full darkness.

An ambulance meets us at the access road. I ride with Liam, watching paramedics work. His vital signs are weak but stable. It's likely the same plant-based compounds in his system. The same careful poisoning designed to create compliance without immediate death.

At the hospital, Aiden's team is waiting. They take Liam straight to intensive care. I'm left standing in the hallway, covered in snow, my hands shaking from adrenaline and cold.

Emma arrives twenty minutes later. "Other teams are pulling out. Weather's too dangerous for continued search. We'll resume at first light."

"Did anyone find Noah?"

"No. No sign of him at any of the six locations."

We stand in the quiet hospital corridor. Around us, I hear normal hospital sounds. Beeping monitors. Hushed conversations.

But in my head, I'm replaying Liam's words. *They said you'd come here. They said you'd look in the mountains. Noah isn't in the mountains.*

"It's too easy," I say finally. "Finding the map behind a bookshelf. All the evidence at every site. Liam placed where we'd find him."

"You think it's staged."

"I think Eleanor knew we'd search her house. Knew we'd find the map. Spent months preparing those sites to look exactly right." I turn to Emma. "What if the seven mountain locations are decoys? What if we just deployed every resource we have to chase fake leads?"

"Wait, I think I remember something." Emma pulls out her phone, opening Eleanor's academic papers. She scrolls through one we examined earlier, looking for something.

"Here," she says, showing me a footnote I'd skipped over. "Eleanor wrote: 'While Germanic tribes favored elevated ritual sites in mountain clearings, Celtic traditions emphasized liminal low places—river crossings, valley floors, locations where water meets earth. These were considered the true thin spaces where worlds could intersect.'"

The implication hits me like cold water.

"We've been looking in the mountains," I say quietly. "But Eleanor's research focused on Celtic traditions. She would know—"

"That the real power is in low places." Emma's face is pale. "River, what if all seven marked locations are wrong? What if she prepared them just to distract us?"

My phone buzzes. Unknown number. The same one that sent the message after the Okafor boys were taken.

The mountains are beautiful this time of year. So many agents enjoying the view. Meanwhile, seven crossings proceed as planned. Winter's longest night approaches. - A Friend

I show Emma. She reads it twice, her expression darkening.

"We fell for it," she says. "We deployed six teams to the mountains. Scattered our resources across hundreds of square miles. While Eleanor works somewhere else entirely."

"Somewhere near water. In a valley. A low place." I think about the geography around Charlottesville. Rivers, creeks, valley floors. Hundreds of potential locations. "We have no idea where the real sites are."

"And it's December nineteenth. Three days until winter solstice. According to Eleanor's calendar, she's already behind schedule. She'll be accelerating."

I look through the window into Liam's ICU room. He's surrounded by machines, Aiden and two nurses working over him. He survived. But he was meant to be found. Meant to waste our time while Noah is taken somewhere we're not looking.

"We need to talk to Liam the moment he wakes up," I tell

Emma. "He might know something. Where they were held, what he heard, anything about Noah."

"And we need to rethink everything. Eleanor's research, her academic focus, her belief system. If she's following Celtic tradition, where would she perform these rituals?"

My phone rings. Siwak.

"River, we're pulling all teams back. The mountain sites are a dead end. Everything we found is circumstantial at best. No victims, no Hollow Circle members, no actual evidence of planned rituals tonight."

"Because they were never planning rituals there. It's a diversion."

Silence on the line. Then: "You're sure?"

"Eleanor's entire academic career focused on Celtic practices. These traditions emphasized low places near water for rituals, not mountain clearings. The map we found was meant to be found. She's been planning this misdirection for months."

"Jesus." More silence. "Get back to the field office. Bring everyone. We're starting over."

CHAPTER TWENTY-TWO

Aiden emerges from Liam's room at three AM, exhausted. He's been working for hours. When he sees me still in the waiting area, he sits heavily in the chair beside me.

"He's stable," Aiden says. "We've got him on fluids, warming him gradually, treating the hypothermia. The toxicology is... complicated."

"Same compounds as the Caine twins?"

"Similar. Plant-based alkaloids we're still trying to identify. Whatever it is, it creates a dissociative state without immediately threatening organ function. But combined with exposure and continued dosing, it would eventually be fatal."

"How long until he wakes up?"

"Hard to say. Could be hours. Could be tomorrow." Aiden looks at me carefully. "River, when he does wake up, he's going to be terrified. Disoriented. Whatever he experienced was traumatic."

"I know. But he might be the only person who can tell us where Noah is."

"Then let me be there when you question him. I can help keep him calm, make sure you're not pushing too hard."

It's not standard procedure to have medical staff present during witness interviews. But Liam is nine years old, poisoned, and his twin brother is still missing. Standard procedure can bend.

"Okay," I say. "Thank you."

Aiden squeezes my hand briefly before heading back to check on other patients. I return to my vigil in the uncomfortable waiting room chair.

Emma is at the field office coordinating the new search. Garrett is going through every reference to water and valleys in Eleanor's academic work. Other teams are checking topographic maps for low-lying areas with archaeological significance.

We're racing against a clock we can't see. Eleanor's calendar showed rituals accelerating toward the solstice. If the mountain sites were decoys, what's her real timeline? How many crossings has she already completed while we chased false leads?

My phone buzzes. A text from Leslie: *How's the case? Haven't heard from you in days. We all miss you!*

Guilt washes over me. I've been so consumed with this investigation I've barely thought about Bennett and Ava. About my sister navigating her separation while I chase a killer who recruited her husband to access me.

Case is complicated, I text back. *Will call soon. Love you.*

I wish I could say more because it's not enough. Nothing I can say is enough.

At six AM, a nurse finds me. "Agent Collins? He's waking up."

I follow her to Liam's room. Aiden is already there, adjusting monitors. The boy's eyes are open now, moving around the room with obvious fear.

"Liam," Aiden says gently. "My name is Dr. Watkins. You're in a hospital. You're safe."

Liam's eyes find me. I'm still wearing my FBI jacket, my badge visible. He recoils slightly.

"It's okay," I say, staying near the door. "I'm Agent Collins. We found you in the woods last night. Do you remember?"

He nods slowly. His voice comes out scratchy, damaged from cold. "You were looking for us."

"For you and Noah. Your brother. Can you tell me where Noah is?"

Liam's eyes fill with tears. "They took him away. Said he was special. Said he had to go to the cold place."

I move closer carefully, sitting in a chair where he can see me clearly. "Who took him?"

"The people in robes. The nice lady who taught us about stars."

Eleanor. But I need him to confirm it.

"Liam, I'm going to show you some pictures. Can you tell me if you recognize anyone?"

Aiden gives me a warning look but doesn't intervene. I pull up my phone, display a photo array. Six faces. Eleanor Vance is third.

Liam's finger goes immediately to Eleanor. "That's her. Miss Eleanor. She said we were special. That twins have double souls."

That's the same language Brenda used about her sons.

"Anyone else?" I ask, showing him the next set of photos.

He studies them, his small finger hovering. Then he points to one and starts crying. Not scared crying. Confused, hurt crying.

It's Brenda Caine.

"That's Matthew's mom," Liam says through tears. "Matthew and Titus. They were our friends from the nature program. Their mom was there. In the robes. She was..." He struggles with the concept. "She was happy. She was smiling."

My chest feels tight. "Liam, this is really important. Where did they take Noah?"

"The cold place. They kept saying it. 'The warm one comes first. The cold one comes last.' I was warm. Noah was cold." His tears are falling freely now. "They said Noah was for the cold place. That he'd bridge the water. What does that mean?"

Bridge the water. Rivers and valley floors. Low places where water meets earth.

"You're doing great, Liam. Can you tell me what else you remember? About where you were held?"

His memory is fragmented. Multiple locations. Being moved in vehicles with windows covered. Adults in robes speaking in low voices. Other children—he thinks maybe four or five—but he never saw them clearly.

"There was water," he says. "I could hear it. Not like a river. Bigger. Like..." He searches for words. "Like the ocean but not salty."

A lake. They were held near a lake.

"And rocks. Big rocks standing up. Old rocks. Miss Eleanor said they were from the before-time. From when the old gods lived."

Standing stones. An archaeological site near a lake.

"Stars," Liam continues. His voice is getting weaker. Aiden checks his monitors, concerned. "Every night they made us look at stars. Said we were going to become stars. That our souls would cross over and light the sky."

"What about the sweet drink?" I ask gently. "Do you remember drinking something?"

"Every day. It tasted like honey and flowers. Made everything feel far away. Made me not scared even when I knew I should have been." His eyes meet mine. "I knew it was bad. Knew something was wrong. But I couldn't feel it. Couldn't feel anything."

The plant compounds. Creating compliance. Making children accept their fate.

Aiden steps forward. "River, he needs rest."

"Just one more question." I lean closer to Liam. "Did you hear them say anything about when? About the cold place or when Noah would..."

I can't finish the question.

Liam's eyes are drooping. The effort of talking is exhausting him. "Tonight," he whispers. "I heard them say tonight. Winter's longest night. When the worlds are closest."

Tonight. December nineteenth. Not the solstice. We have even less time than we thought.

"Thank you, Liam. You've been so brave." I stand, giving Aiden space to work.

In the hallway, I call Emma immediately. "We need to find every archaeological site near a lake in Central Virginia. Focus on sites with ancient stone circles or ceremonial structures."

. . .

"On it. How's Liam?"

"He identified Eleanor and Brenda Caine. Says Noah is being held for 'the cold place' near water. Says the crossing is tonight."

"Tonight? But the calendar showed—"

"I know. Either Eleanor changed her timeline or the calendar was part of the misdirection too. Either way, we're out of time."

After hanging up, I stand in the quiet hospital corridor trying to think. Eleanor's fifteen years of research. Her obsession with Celtic traditions. Her carefully documented belief that true liminal spaces exist where water meets earth.

Where in Virginia would she find such a place? Somewhere remote enough for dozens of people to gather without being noticed. Somewhere with archaeological significance. Standing stones. A lake.

My phone buzzes.

Garrett: *Found something. Three archaeological sites in Virginia match the criteria. One is in Albemarle County. Private property. Site of pre-Colonial stone circle discovered in 1970s but never fully excavated. Sits on edge of small lake formed by ancient glacier activity. Checking property records now.*

This is it. This has to be it.

I head for the exit, already texting Emma to coordinate. Behind me, in that hospital room, Liam Okafor is finally safe. But his brother is somewhere dark and cold, drugged into compliance, waiting to be sacrificed by people who believe children are bridges to dead gods.

And we have maybe twelve hours to find him.

CHAPTER TWENTY-THREE

Warren Caine's house looks different in morning light. The manicured lawn is neglected now, snow covering what were probably perfect flower beds. The Christmas wreath is still on the door, and cheerful and grotesque given what happened here.

Emma and I are accompanied by two other agents. We have a warrant for Brenda Caine's arrest. Conspiracy to commit murder. Child endangerment. Kidnapping. The charges will multiply once we can prove her involvement.

Warren answers the door in wrinkled clothes, unshaven. He looks like he's aged ten years in the week since his sons died.

"Agents," he says dully.

"Is your wife here, Mr. Caine?" Emma asks.

"No." He steps aside to let us enter. "Haven't seen her since the funeral. Three days ago."

The house is a mess. Dishes in the sink. Mail piled on the table. The lived-in disorder of someone who's stopped caring about domestic maintenance.

"When did you last speak with her?" I ask.

Warren leads us to the kitchen, moves mail aside to find an envelope. "She left this."

Inside is a handwritten note on floral stationery. Brenda's handwriting, careful and neat:

Warren, I'm going to be with them now. Don't follow. You wouldn't understand. They're not gone. They've crossed over. Transformed. And I will too. By the solstice, we'll all be together in the place beyond. Don't grieve. Celebrate. - B

Emma photographs the note. "Mr. Caine, we need to ask you some questions about your wife's involvement with Greenwood Legacy Foundation and Eleanor Vance."

"I know." He slumps into a chair. "I've been thinking about it constantly. All the signs I missed. All the things she said that I dismissed as New Age nonsense." His voice cracks. "She had something to do with this, didn't she?"

"We believe she was an active participant in their deaths, yes."

Warren puts his head in his hands. For a long moment, he doesn't speak. When he does, his voice is muffled, broken.

"It started about two years ago. She went to some workshop. Meditation and nature connection or something. Came back excited. Said she'd found people who understood her spiritual side. That she'd met this woman, Eleanor, who was so wise about old practices and natural cycles."

"Did Eleanor recruit her specifically?" I ask.

"I don't know. Maybe? Brenda was searching for meaning. She'd left her career when the boys were born, threw herself into being a perfect mother. But I think she felt empty. Like there should be more." Warren looks up, his eyes red. "Eleanor gave her more. Gave her a whole belief system."

Emma takes notes while I listen. This is familiar. The pattern of recruitment. Find vulnerable people searching for purpose. Offer them community and meaning. Slowly introduce more extreme beliefs.

"Tell us about the last few months," Emma prompts.

"She changed. Started talking differently about the boys. Said they were special because they were twins. That twin children have double souls, can walk between worlds, carry gifts others don't have." Warren's hands clench. "At first I thought it was just spiritual talk. Like how some cultures believe twins are lucky or blessed. Harmless."

"When did you start to worry?"

"September maybe. She kept saying the boys had important work to do. That they were being prepared for something special. The way she said it—not like they'd grow up to be doctors or teachers. Something else. Something that made my skin crawl. I asked what she meant. She said I wouldn't understand unless I joined the group."

"Did she try to recruit you?"

"Yes. Wanted me to attend meetings. I went to one. Just once." Warren stands, paces. "It was at someone's house. Maybe fifteen people. They sat in a circle burning sage, talking about pre-Christian practices and cycles of death and renewal. Eleanor was there leading everything. She talked about how modern society fears death but people from back then understood it as transformation."

"What happened at this meeting?"

"They talked about children being pure vessels. About how certain cultures selected young people for ritual purposes. Eleanor kept saying we'd lost touch with necessary sacrifices. That balance requires giving something back to the earth." Warren stops pacing. "I left. Told Brenda I wasn't interested. She said I was close-minded. That I'd never understand the deeper truth."

Emma looks up from her notes. "Did she talk about specific plans? Specific children?"

"Not directly. But she'd say things about our boys. About how honored we should feel that they were chosen. I thought chosen meant for normal success. Good lives. Not..." He can't finish.

"Mr. Caine, this is important," I say gently. "We believe there's a ceremony happening today. Tonight, possibly. Do you know anything about that?"

Warren goes very still. "The solstice."

"What about it?"

"I heard Brenda on the phone weeks ago. Talking to someone about the cycle completing at the solstice. About seven crossings leading up to winter's longest night. I asked her what she meant. Group meditation on significant dates." He looks at us. "It wasn't a metaphor, was it?"

"No," Emma says. "We believe Eleanor and the inner circle are planning ritual sacrifices. Seven children, culminating at the winter solstice."

Warren sinks back into his chair. The weight of understanding crushes him visibly.

"My sons were first," he whispers. "They died first. To start the cycle."

"We believe so, yes."

"And Brenda let it happen. Wanted it to happen. Believed it was an honor." He's crying now, silent tears streaming down his face. "I lived with her for fifteen years.

Had children with her. Thought I knew her. How did I not see?"

"These groups are very good at hiding," Emma says. "They present as normal community organizations."

"There's a boy missing," I say. "Noah Okafor. Nine years old. Twin brother to Liam, who we found last night. We think he's being held for tonight's ceremony. Did Brenda ever mention specific locations? Places where the group met?"

Warren thinks, wiping his eyes. "She talked about sacred sites. Places where ancient peoples performed rituals. She was obsessed with this one place she visited with Eleanor. Said it had standing stones from thousands of years ago. That she felt power there."

"Where was this place?"

"I don't know. Somewhere near water. She mentioned a lake. Said it was on private property but Eleanor had permission from the owner." He struggles to remember. "She took pictures. I saw them once. Old stones arranged in a circle near a lake shore."

"Do you still have access to her phone or computer?"

"Her laptop is upstairs. She took her phone."

Emma and I exchange glances. "Can we see the laptop?"

Warren leads us to their bedroom. It's perfectly neat, undisturbed. Like Brenda just stepped out temporarily. Her closed laptop is on the dresser.

"Do you know the password?" Emma asks.

"Try the boys' names. TitusMatthew, capital T and M, all one word. She used it for everything."

Emma opens the laptop and types. It unlocks.

While she searches files, I look around the room.

Brenda's side of the closet is partially empty. She took clothes with her. Planned to be gone for a while.

On the nightstand are photos. The family at Disney World. The twins' school pictures. A wedding photo of Warren and Brenda, looking young and hopeful.

How does someone go from that to believing their children should be sacrificed to some god?

"Found photo folders," Emma calls. "Hundreds of images from Greenwood events. And here—photos of an archaeological site. Stone circle, lake in background."

She shows me the screen. The images show standing stones arranged in a rough circle, maybe twenty feet in diameter. The stones are weathered, possibly pre-Colonial. Behind them, a small lake reflects sky and trees.

"Can we determine location from these?" I ask.

"No GPS data embedded. But send them to Garrett—he can do image analysis."

Emma forwards the photos while I continue examining the laptop. Five minutes later, her phone rings.

"It's Garrett." She puts him on speaker. "What've you got?"

"Ran the images through topographic analysis software. The treeline patterns and mountain profiles in the background match three possible locations in Central Virginia." We hear typing. "But combining that with the Whitmore donation list and current satellite surveillance... I'm confident it's the Albemarle County property. Rosemary and Daniel Whitmore, 150 acres including a glacial lake."

"How confident?" I ask.

"Ninety percent based on terrain matching. But I just pulled thermal imaging from an NSA satellite pass thirty minutes ago. The Whitmore property currently shows approximately forty heat signatures clustered near the eastern shore of their lake. That's consistent with a large gathering."

Emma and I exchange looks. Forty people. At a private residence. On a winter afternoon.

"Can you see structures?" Emma asks.

"Two large temporary shelters. Canvas or similar material. And what appears to be a fire. Active, based on heat signature."

"They're already there," I say. "Setting up for tonight."

"Sending you the coordinates now," Garrett says. "But River, if there are forty people on site, you're going to need serious tactical support. This isn't a small operation."

After we hang up, Emma pulls up the coordinates on her tablet. The Whitmore property is isolated, accessible only by a private gated road. The stone circle sits half a mile from the main residence, surrounded by forest.

"This is it," I tell Emma. "This is where they'll sacrifice Noah tonight."

Warren appears in the doorway. "There's something else. A calendar. Brenda kept a physical calendar hidden in her drawer. I found it after she left."

He retrieves a small leather-bound planner. Inside, Brenda has marked specific dates over the past year. Notes about "preparation" and "meetings" and "selection process."

And for December nineteenth through twenty-second, she's written detailed entries:

Dec 19: Second crossing. The water's edge. N.O. prepared.

Dec 20: Third crossing. The valley floor.

Dec 21: Fourth and fifth crossings. Simultaneous. The equidistant points.

Dec 22 (Solstice): Sixth and seventh crossings. The completion. All bridges unite. The Shepherd returns.

"N.O.," Emma says. "Noah Okafor. Second crossing is tonight."

"And she knew," Warren says, his voice hollow. "Brenda knew exactly what was planned. These dates. These children. She was part of the planning."

I photograph every page of the calendar. This is evidence. Proof of premeditation, of conspiracy.

"Mr. Caine," I say carefully. "Is there anything else? Anything Brenda said or did that might help us find where this ceremony is happening tonight?"

He thinks, desperate to help. "She talked about water being liminal. That's the word she used. Liminal. Said the ancient Celts understood that places where water meets land are where the veil between worlds is thinnest. That's why they performed rituals at river crossings and lake shores."

"Anything else about this specific site?"

"Just that it was private property. That the owner was sympathetic to the cause." Warren's face crumples. "Whatever she's planning with those people tonight... you have to stop them. You have to make sure no other parents feel what I'm feeling."

"We will," Emma promises.

As we leave, Warren calls after us. "Agent Collins? When you find Brenda... she's not the woman I married. I don't know what she's become. But she's not my wife anymore. She's a monster."

In the car, Emma immediately calls Garrett. "We need property records for every archaeological site with standing stones in Central Virginia. Focus on privately-owned land near lakes. Owners with connections to environmental groups or alternative spirituality."

While she coordinates, I stare at the photos from Brenda's laptop. Those ancient stones. That quiet lake. Somewhere right now, Noah Okafor is being held there, drugged and compliant, waiting for darkness.

My phone buzzes.

Garrett: *Got a hit. Property in Albemarle County. 150 acres, includes glacial lake and confirmed archaeological site with pre-Columbian stone circle. Owned by Rosemary and Daniel Whitmore. Rosemary appears on donor lists for Greenwood Legacy Foundation. Contributed $15,000 last year.*

"That's it," I tell Emma. "That's where they'll be."

Emma is already coordinating with Siwak. Tactical teams. Helicopter support. Medical personnel. We're deploying everything we have.

Because tonight, at the water's edge, Eleanor Vance plans to sacrifice a nine-year-old boy.

And we have maybe eight hours to stop her.

CHAPTER TWENTY-FOUR

The tactical briefing happens at two PM in a rented facility fifteen miles from the target property. Thirty agents crowded into a conference room studying maps and satellite imagery.

Siwak leads the briefing. "The Whitmore property is 150 acres of mostly wooded land. Access is via a single private road, gated. The stone circle sits approximately half a mile from the main residence, on the eastern shore of Whitmore Lake. Satellite imagery shows recent vehicle activity and what appears to be temporary structures—possibly tents or shelters."

He pulls up thermal imaging from a flyover conducted an hour ago. "We count approximately forty heat signatures in the area of the stone circle. That's a lot of people for what's supposed to be private property."

"The Hollow Circle," Emma says. "The whole inner circle gathering for tonight's crossing."

"Do we have confirmation Noah Okafor is on site?" someone asks.

"No visual confirmation. But based on Liam's testimony and Brenda Caine's calendar, this is where he'll be."

I study the map. The stone circle is accessible only by foot from the main road. Heavy forest provides cover but also limits visibility. If Eleanor has lookouts posted, we'll be spotted long before we reach the site.

"Approach strategy," Siwak continues. "Two teams. Team Alpha approaches from the south through forest. Team Bravo takes the eastern shore, using the lake as cover. We time it for dusk—seven PM. Late enough that ceremony preparations should be underway, early enough that we have some visibility."

"What if they start earlier?" I ask. "We have no idea what time the crossing is scheduled."

"Then we move earlier. But Eleanor's journals emphasized astronomical precision. For a winter solstice-related ritual, she'll wait for specific planetary alignments. Probably sunset or just after."

Sunset is at 4:47 PM today. Three hours from now.

"What about the Whitmores?" Emma asks. "The property owners. Are they complicit or just wealthy dupes who let Eleanor use their land?"

"Working theory is complicit," Siwak says. "Fifteen thousand dollar donation, multiple connections to Hollow Circle members. But we'll secure them separately from the main operation."

I'm assigned to Team Alpha with Emma and ten other agents. We'll hike through forest, approaching the stone circle from uphill. If Eleanor has escape routes planned, we'll be positioned to cut them off.

Team Bravo has the more difficult approach, navigating rough terrain along the lake shore. But they'll have better visibility of the stone circle and can move in quickly if needed.

"Rules of engagement," Siwak says, his voice hard. "Children are the priority. We identify victims, we extract them immediately. Eleanor Vance and other Hollow Circle leaders are to be detained if possible, but if they resist, you are authorized to use force. However—" He pauses for emphasis. "—we need Eleanor alive. She's our only link to The Shepherd. We take her in breathing."

After the briefing, teams prepare gear. Body armor. Radios. Medical supplies. It feels like preparing for war, which I suppose it is.

Emma and I do final equipment checks in silence. We've worked together long enough that words aren't always necessary.

"You ready for this?" she asks finally.

"No. But we're doing it anyway."

"River, if Eleanor says anything directly threatening to you—anything about completing your crossing or finishing what was started—you need to maintain professional distance. Don't engage."

"I know."

"I'm serious. She's trying to get in your head. Has been since that first interview. Don't let her."

"I won't."

But we both know that's not entirely true. Eleanor has already gotten in my head. Has been there since I realized my abduction was targeted. Since I understood that The Shepherd has been tracking me for twenty years.

Tonight, at that stone circle, I'll face the woman who believes I'm an unfinished bridge. Who thinks my captivity was preparation for transformation I never completed.

And I have to stay professional. Stay focused. Save Noah Okafor without letting Eleanor's words shake me.

We deploy at three-thirty PM. The drive to the staging area takes forty minutes. By four-fifteen we're hiking through forest toward the Whitmore property.

The woods are beautiful and hostile. Snow covers everything, making travel difficult. Temperature is dropping as the sun lowers. Every branch that cracks under our feet sounds impossibly loud.

We move in careful formation. Ten agents spread across fifty yards of forest. Radio silence except for essential communication.

At four forty-five, we reach the ridge overlooking Whitmore Lake. Below us, the water is dark and still. And on the eastern shore, I can see the stone circle.

Rocks standing in rough formation. Maybe fifteen stones total, varying heights from four to eight feet. They form an uneven ring about twenty feet in diameter. Within that ring, someone has built a fire pit. Flames are already visible as dusk approaches.

And surrounding the stones are people. Dozens of them, dressed in dark robes. They move with purpose, arranging materials, positioning themselves. Preparing.

Through binoculars, I scan faces. Looking for Eleanor. Looking for Noah.

I find Eleanor near the center, directing others. She's wearing a deep green robe, her hair loose. She looks calm. Confident. A professor overseeing a field expedition rather than a ritual murder.

But I don't see Noah. Don't see any children.

"Where are the kids?" Emma whispers beside me.

"Maybe in those structures." I focus on the tents

positioned behind the stone circle. Two large canvas shelters, sides closed. "Being kept separate until the ceremony starts."

My radio crackles softly. Team Bravo reporting their position. They're fifty yards from the stone circle, concealed in brush along the lake shore.

Siwak's voice: "Teams hold position. We move on my signal."

We wait. Watch. The sun drops toward the horizon. The sky turns orange and pink. Beautiful and terrible.

At the stone circle, Eleanor raises her hands. The robed figures fall silent. I can't hear her words from this distance, but I can see her speaking. Teaching. Preparing them.

Then movement from one of the tents. A figure emerges, leading children.

My breath catches.

Four children. Small, drugged, compliant. They walk slowly, helped by adults. I count: three girls and one boy. The boy matches Noah's description.

"We've got visual on potential victims," I radio quietly. "Four children. One matches Noah Okafor."

"Copy," Siwak responds. "Teams prepare to move."

The children are positioned within the stone circle. Each one is placed at a specific point, like compass directions. They don't resist. Don't cry. Just stand where directed, swaying slightly.

Drugged. All of them drugged with Eleanor's plant-based compounds.

Eleanor continues speaking. The robed figures begin chanting something. Low, rhythmic. It drifts across the water and up the hill to our position.

"Now," Siwak commands. "Go go go."

We move down the hillside fast, trying to maintain stealth but prioritizing speed. Team Bravo emerges from the lake shore simultaneously.

Someone in the circle spots us. Shouts a warning. The chanting stops.

Eleanor turns, sees the approaching agents. And smiles.

She was expecting us.

The robed figures don't scatter. They form a protective ring around the children, linking arms. Creating a human barrier.

"FBI! Nobody move!" Team Bravo's leader shouts, weapons drawn.

But the circle doesn't break. They stand firm, chanting louder now. Defiant.

I push through to the front. "Eleanor Vance! Federal agents! Release the children!"

Eleanor stands in the center with the four drugged kids around her. She's so calm. Like this is exactly how she wanted it to unfold.

"Agent Collins," she calls out. "Welcome. We've been waiting for you."

CHAPTER TWENTY-FIVE

"Release the children and no one gets hurt," I saying forcing myself to stay calm. "You're surrounded. There's no way out of this."

"But there is." Eleanor spreads her arms, encompassing the stone circle, the believers, and the darkening sky. "The way has always been here. You just couldn't see it. None of them can." She gestures dismissively at the agents. "But you... you've walked the path before. Felt the pull of transformation. You know what it means to stand between worlds."

She's weaponizing my trauma. Publicly. In front of my entire team.

I keep my voice level. Professional. "These children are drugged. They haven't consented to anything. This is kidnapping and assault. Release them now."

"They're at peace. Willing participants in something greater than themselves." Eleanor takes a step closer to the edge of the human circle. "Just as you would have been if your preparation had been completed twenty years ago."

Behind me, I hear agents shifting uncomfortably. They know about my abduction in general terms. But Eleanor is making it explicit. Making it part of this.

"She was chosen long ago," Eleanor continues, addressing the circle of believers now. Her voice carries across the clearing. "Prepared by those who understood the old ways. But she ran before the transformation could finish. Now she hunts us, driven by the very incompleteness that makes her special."

The believers don't break ranks. Some are crying but their arms stay linked. They're protecting the ceremony with their bodies. Willing to die for this.

Eleanor is stalling. I realize it suddenly. She's keeping us talking, keeping us engaged in dialogue, while time passes. The ceremony has a specific moment—sunset, astronomical alignment, something tied to Eleanor's careful research.

She just needs to keep us here until the right moment arrives.

I glance at the horizon. The sun is nearly touching the mountains. The sun is touching the mountains now, minutes from full sunset

"Where's The Shepherd?" I call out, changing tactics. "He sent you to do this work but he's not here. He's hiding while you take all the risk. While you face the consequences."

Eleanor's expression flickers. First genuine emotion I've seen. "The Shepherd is everywhere. In every tree, every stone, every crossing we complete." Her voice has shifted, become more intense. "You'll understand when you finally accept your purpose."

"My purpose is stopping you."

"Your purpose is completion." Eleanor steps right to the edge of the human barrier now. Close enough that I can see her face clearly in the fading light. "The bridge that was never finished. The crossing interrupted. For twenty years you've been incomplete, Agent Collins. Half-transformed. Walking between what you were supposed to become and what you've forced yourself to be instead."

"I'm exactly what I'm supposed to be. An FBI agent stopping killers."

"You're a woman who escaped transformation and has been running ever since." Eleanor's voice drops, becomes almost gentle. "Don't you feel it? The pull? The knowledge that something was left unfinished? That's why you can't let this go. Why you obsess over these cases. You're trying to save yourself by saving them."

It lands harder than I want to admit, the psychological accuracy of it.

Emma moves up beside me. "Don't engage with her," she murmurs. "She's manipulating you."

"I know."

But Eleanor isn't finished. "Tonight completes the cycle. Seven crossings by winter's longest night. The first has been accomplished. The second—" She glances back at the children behind her. "—happens soon. And the final crossing, the one that matters most, will be you."

"I'm not part of your ritual."

"You've always been part of it. Since you were twelve years old. Since you were chosen and marked and prepared. Your captors failed to complete the work, but the incompleteness remains. It calls to be finished."

Behind me, SWAT is getting into better positions. Emma is coordinating quietly on her radio. But the believers shift too, always keeping the children shielded. This is choreographed. They've practiced for this exact scenario.

"You have thirty seconds to release those children," I say. Final warning. Standard protocol. "After that, we breach."

"You won't breach." Eleanor's confidence is absolute. "You won't risk the children. You won't risk me. You need me alive to find The Shepherd. You need answers I haven't given you. So you'll stand there negotiating while the sun sets and the moment arrives."

She's right. About all of it. We need her alive. We can't risk the children's lives in crossfire. And every second we delay, we get closer to whatever astronomical window she's waiting for.

"Tell me about The Shepherd," I say. Trying to keep her talking, keep her engaged while our teams reposition. "You've spent years preparing for this. Following his guidance. But what does he get from it? What's he building?"

Eleanor's face transforms into joy and reverence. "He's not building anything. He's returning. Coming home from the place beyond. Where he's waited, where he's watched, where all crossings lead."

"He's dead?"

"He's transformed. Crossed over completely. Became what we all aspire to become." She spreads her arms again. "The ultimate bridge. But the veil has been closed too long. Modern society sealed the passages with disbelief. It takes power to tear it open again. Seven sacrifices. Seven bridges. Seven souls to create the pathway home."

"This is insane."

"This is faith." Eleanor's voice hardens. "Something you've never understood. You survived because you wouldn't believe. Wouldn't surrender to what was meant for you. But that stubbornness, that refusal—it's kept you trapped between worlds. Incomplete. Suffering."

Movement behind the human barrier. A figure steps forward, pulling back her hood.

Brenda Caine.

She looks nothing like the last time I saw her—the composed, serene woman at the initial interview. Now her face glows with transcendent certainty. She's not grieving. She's radiant.

And she's holding Noah Okafor's hand.

The boy is barely conscious. His eyes are open but unfocused, his small body swaying. The drug in his system is strong. He doesn't seem to know where he is.

"My sons were the first bridge this season," Brenda says, her voice carrying across the clearing. "Titus and Matthew showed us the way. Their courage, their purity, their double souls opened the path." She squeezes Noah's hand. He doesn't react. "This boy will join them. Will complete the second crossing. Will strengthen the passage."

Warren's desperate voice echoes in my memory: *She's not my wife anymore. She's a monster.*

"Brenda," I call out. "Your sons are dead. Noah doesn't have to die too. You can stop this. You're a mother. You understand—"

"I understand perfectly." Her smile is terrifying. "I understand what you refuse to see. Death isn't an ending. It's a doorway. My sons aren't gone. They've crossed to the place beyond. They wait there with The Shepherd, preparing the way."

"Warren is devastated. Your husband is—"

"Warren is bound by fear. By the limitations modern society places on understanding. He couldn't see what our sons were meant for." She positions Noah in the center of the circle now, between the standing stones. "But I could. I knew from the moment Eleanor told me. Twins have double power. They're perfect bridges."

Eleanor raises her hands. The believers begin chanting —low, rhythmic sounds that aren't quite language. Something older. Something that makes my skin crawl.

The sun touches the mountain peaks. Minutes away from full sunset.

"And when the seventh crossing completes," Brenda continues, her voice rising to match the chant, "when Agent Collins fulfills her destiny, when she finally finishes what was begun twenty years ago—The Shepherd returns. The veil tears completely. He comes home to guide us all."

The chanting grows louder. The believers sway to the rhythm. And the four drugged children in the center of the circle begin to move, responding to the sound despite their altered state.

Emma is beside me, her hand on my arm. "River. We're out of time. We have to breach."

"Children are too close."

"If we don't move now, they die anyway. Poison plus exposure plus whatever Eleanor plans to do—"

"SWAT is ready," someone radios. "Give the order."

I look at the circle. At Eleanor, serene and certain. At Brenda, holding Noah's hand, positioning him in the center of the stones. At the human wall of believers, willing to die protecting this ceremony. At four children who don't understand they're about to be sacrificed.

If we breach, tactical officers will have to go through those believers. Shots will be fired. In the chaos, anything could happen. The children could be hurt, could be killed by panicked believers or by Eleanor in a final act.

But if we wait, if we let this continue, the children die for certain. Eleanor will complete her crossing. Will kill Noah Okafor while we watch.

"Agent Collins," Siwak's voice on the radio. "What's your call?"

Eleanor raises her hands higher. The chanting reaches a crescendo. Brenda is positioning Noah at a specific point in the circle, between two stones. The other three children are being moved into position by robed figures.

The sun is half-hidden behind the mountains now. The light is failing fast.

"Agent Collins," Siwak repeats. "Give the order or stand down. Right now."

I look at Eleanor one more time. She's looking back at me, her expression is knowing. She thinks she's won. Thinks I can't give the order to breach because I won't risk the children. That my own trauma, my need to save them, will paralyze me.

She's betting on my incompleteness and on the wounded twelve-year-old girl still inside me.

But she's wrong about what that girl became.

"Breach," I say into the radio. "All teams go. Get those children out."

CHAPTER TWENTY-SIX

The word leaves my mouth and everything explodes into motion.

"Breach! All teams go!"

SWAT rushes the stone circle from multiple angles. The believers' linked arms break under the assault. Some scatter immediately, running into the darkening woods. Others try to hold their ground, forming tighter circles around the children, but tactical officers push through with overwhelming force.

I run toward the center where Eleanor stands. Emma is beside me, weapon drawn. Around us the clearing erupts into chaos—shouts, commands, the sounds of people being tackled and restrained.

Eleanor doesn't move at first. She stands in the middle of those weathered stones watching the collapse of her ceremony with an expression I can't read. Not panic. Something else that makes my skin crawl.

Two SWAT officers reach the children first. Noah Okafor is barely conscious, his legs giving out as an agent scoops him up. The other three children are similarly limp, drugged into compliance. Officers carry them away from the stones, away from the believers, toward the waiting medical team.

Brenda Caine lunges after Noah, screaming. "No! You don't understand! He needs to—"

An agent tackles her to the ground. She keeps screaming, words about bridges and her sons and transformation that dissolve into incoherent sobbing.

I push through the crowd toward Eleanor. She's still standing in the exact center of the circle, her green robe billowing in the winter wind. Our eyes meet across the chaos.

She smiles.

Then she bolts.

Not toward the woods where everyone else is headed. She runs toward the lake shore where the tree line is thicker and the terrain more difficult. For someone in a robe she moves fast, her feet finding sure purchase on the snowy ground like she's practiced this route.

"Eleanor! Stop!" I chase after her, dimly aware of Emma shouting something behind me.

Eleanor reaches the trees and disappears into shadow. I follow without thinking, without waiting for backup, without considering that this might be exactly what she wants me to do.

The forest swallows me immediately. The canopy blocks what little light remains from the setting sun. I can hear Eleanor ahead, branches cracking under her feet, but I can barely see her.

My flashlight cuts through the darkness in a narrow beam. I sweep it back and forth, catching glimpses of movement. A flash of green fabric. A shape darting between trees.

"Eleanor! There's nowhere to go! The entire area is surrounded!"

No response except the sound of her running, and somehow that makes it worse. She should be panicking, should be making noise, but she's moving with purpose through terrain she clearly knows.

I follow, my breath coming hard in the cold air. The ground is uneven, roots and rocks hidden under snow. I stumble once but catch myself against a tree trunk, bark rough under my palm.

Eleanor knows this forest. That becomes obvious from how confidently she navigates through it even in darkness. She's scouted these woods, planned routes, and prepared for a possibility that is just dawning on me.

The trees thin slightly and I catch up enough to see her more clearly. She's maybe fifty feet ahead, moving along what might be a deer trail. Her robe is hiked up to her knees now.

"Stop running! You can't escape this!"

She glances back but doesn't slow down. I can see glimpses of her face with my flashlight. She's eerily calm as if all of this is going according to a plan.

We run for what feels like forever but is probably only a few minutes. My radio crackles with confused chatter from the command post. Emma calling my name. Siwak demanding to know my position. I should respond but I can't spare the breath and I don't want to lose sight of Eleanor.

She takes a sharp turn off the trail, pushing through under growth. I follow, branches scraping my face and jacket. The terrain slopes upward and my legs burn with the effort. Snow is deeper here, untouched by foot traffic, and it slows us both down.

Then suddenly she stops.

We've reached a clearing. Small, maybe thirty feet across. The ground is relatively flat, covered in undisturbed snow that looks gray in my flashlight beam. Around the edges stand more stones—not arranged in a circle like the ones by the lake, but scattered in a pattern that seems random.

Eleanor stands in the center with her back to me, breathing hard but not as hard as she should be after that run.

"Turn around slowly," I say, drawing my weapon and training it on her back. "Hands where I can see them."

She complies, turning to face me. Her hands rise to shoulder height, empty and open. Her green robe is torn from branches, her hair has come loose, but her expression is still composed. Still certain of something.

"You followed me," she says. "Just as I knew you would."

"On the ground. Now."

"Take a moment, River. Look around. Really look." Eleanor's voice is gentle, almost kind. "Don't you recognize this place?"

I keep my weapon trained on her, but something in her tone makes my skin prickle. I risk a quick glance around the clearing without taking my eyes off.

The scattered stones. The way the trees form a rough circle around the flat ground. The slope of the hill behind us. Something about the shape of this space tugs at memory I've spent years trying to bury.

"Get on the ground, Eleanor."

"There was a structure here once. Small. Temporary. Long gone now, of course. But the stones remain. The trees remember." She takes a step closer and I tense. "This is where it happened, River. Where you were brought twenty years ago. Where you were held. Where you were supposed to transform."

My heart stutters. No. She's lying, trying to manipulate me, trying to—

But I *do* recognize it. Not consciously, not in a way I can articulate, but my body knows this place. The exact angle of the slope. The way sound carries in this particular clearing. The smell of the earth and old snow and pine.

This is where I was held captive when I was twelve years old.

"You're lying."

"Am I?" Eleanor tilts her head, studying my face like I'm a particularly interesting specimen. "Your captors chose this location carefully. It had been used for generations before them. The Shepherd taught them its significance. This is where bridges are built, River. Where the boundaries between what is and what could be become thin enough to cross."

My hands are shaking. I tighten my grip on the weapon, trying to steady myself. "Shut up."

"I brought you back here deliberately. You needed to remember. To understand what you were meant for." Eleanor's voice drops lower, more intimate. "This is where your transformation began. Where it should have been completed. The fact that you escaped doesn't change what was started here. The mark remains. The incompleteness remains."

"I said shut up!"

I hear movement at the edge of the clearing. My peripheral vision catches it and I start to turn, but Eleanor is speaking again and I can't afford to look away from her.

"You're not alone, River. Others believe as I do. Others understand what The Shepherd has been teaching all these years."

They emerge from the trees. Three figures, two men and one woman, all wearing dark clothing and carrying weapons. Handguns, pointed at me. They move with purpose, spreading out to surround the clearing.

I'm trapped. My weapon is still trained on Eleanor but now I have threats from three other directions.

"Drop the gun, Agent Collins," one of the men says. He's older, maybe sixty, with gray hair and steady hands. His weapon doesn't waver. "We don't want to hurt you. We want to help you finish what was started."

"FBI!" I shout, though I have no idea if anyone can hear me this deep in the woods. "Drop your weapons now!"

They don't drop them. They close in, maintaining distance but tightening the circle. I'm calculating angles, trying to figure out if I can get to cover, knowing that three against one in an open clearing means I'm probably going to die here.

Eleanor is still standing in the center, watching with that same serene expression. "The Shepherd sent them years ago. They've been waiting. Watching you build your career, following your cases, preparing for the moment when you'd return to this place. Tonight was always meant to end here, River. Not at the stone circle. Here. Where it began."

"This is over," I say, trying to keep my voice steady. "You're all under arrest. Backup is thirty seconds behind me. You can't—"

"We're willing to cross," the woman says quietly. She's younger, maybe forty, with dark hair and eyes that shine with absolute conviction. "All of us have accepted what comes next. We're bridges too. If we have to become that tonight to help you finish your transformation, we're ready."

They're not bluffing. I can see it in their faces. These are people who genuinely believe that killing me or dying themselves serves some greater purpose.

"The solstice is tomorrow," Eleanor continues, like she's discussing academic theory instead of murder. "But this moment works too. This location holds enough power. If they help you cross here, where your journey began, it completes the cycle beautifully. The Shepherd will be pleased."

My radio crackles. Emma's voice, distant and distorted: "...River... position... responding..."

They hear it too. The older man's finger moves to his trigger.

"She's not alone," he says to Eleanor. "We need to move now."

"No," Eleanor says firmly. "We wait. We do this properly. River needs to understand what's being offered before—"

The woman's gun shifts slightly, pointing more directly at my chest. "She'll never understand. She's refused for twenty years. We should finish this."

Everything happens in the space between heartbeats.

The woman's finger tightens on the trigger. I see the minute shift of her hand, the way her breath catches, the certainty in her eyes that she's about to do something holy.

I drop and roll left, squeezing off two shots as I move.

The first shot goes wide. The second catches her in the

shoulder and she spins, her weapon firing into the trees as she falls.

The two men are firing now. I hear the shots, feel one round tear through my jacket sleeve without hitting flesh, another kick up snow near my head. I'm scrambling for cover behind one of the stones, firing back, trying to hit something in the chaos.

More shots. One of the men goes down, but I didn't fire that shot. Emma's voice shouting commands. Flashlights cutting through the darkness from multiple directions. The cavalry has arrived.

The older man drops his weapon and raises his hands. The other one is on the ground, clutching his leg where a bullet caught him.

The woman I shot is still down. Not moving.

I push myself up, my ears ringing from the gunfire. Emma is beside me suddenly, her hand on my shoulder, asking if I'm hit. I shake my head, unable to find words.

Agents flood the clearing. Someone is cuffing the two men. Someone else is checking the woman, calling for medical, their voice urgent and then less urgent. The tone that means it's too late.

I killed her.

I shot her and she's dead.

Eleanor is on her knees in the snow now, hands behind her head, an agent holding her at gunpoint. But she's looking at me, and that serene expression hasn't changed. If anything, she looks satisfied.

"You see?" she says, her voice carrying across the clearing even through the chaos. "This place transforms everyone who comes here. You were meant to return. Meant to shed blood on this ground. The cycle continues, River."

Emma is pulling me away, but I can't stop looking at the woman on the ground. Her eyes are still open, staring at nothing. She died believing she was doing so for some purpose.

And I killed her at the exact spot where they brought me yeas ago.

Eleanor is right about one thing. This place changes everyone who comes here.

I just don't know what it's changed me into.

CHAPTER TWENTY-SEVEN

The command post is chaos. Forty-two people arrested. Four drugged children being treated by medical teams. Evidence bags are everywhere—ceremonial objects, notebooks, phones with incriminating messages. We've disrupted the largest ritual sacrifice attempt in Virginia history.

I gave my statement about the shooting two hours ago. Justified use of force, they said. Three armed suspects, I was outnumbered, she fired first. Clean shoot. I'm cleared to continue working.

Emma tried to get me to take the night off. Said I should process what happened before jumping back into interviews. But sitting alone with my thoughts means seeing that woman's face. Means remembering Eleanor's satisfied expression. Means standing in that clearing knowing I shed blood on the same ground where I was held captive twenty years ago.

So I work instead.

But all I can think about is what Eleanor said. *The Shepherd chose your captors.*

Emma and I sit in a makeshift interview room—actually a van that's been repurposed with recording equipment. We're processing Hollow Circle members one at a time, taking statements, building cases.

Most of them are cooperative now that the ceremony has been stopped. The outer circle members are horrified to learn children were meant to die.

"I thought we were just learning about ancient practices," a woman in her fifties tells us, crying. "Eleanor talked about connecting with pre-Christian traditions. About understanding cycles of death and renewal. It was academic. Historical. I never thought..." She can't finish.

The inner circle members are different. True believers. They speak about transformation and bridges and the necessity of sacrifice with utter conviction. Brenda Caine is among them, still insisting her sons died with honor.

But none of them will talk about The Shepherd. When we mention him, they go silent. Some smile knowingly. Others look frightened. But nobody gives us information.

"He's protected by layers of secrecy," Garrett says during a break between interviews. "Classic cult leadership. The inner circle knows he exists but most of them have never met him. They receive instructions through Eleanor and other intermediaries."

"Someone must have met him," I insist. "Eleanor said he visited her three months ago. That's recent contact."

"We're working on it. Going through phone records, emails, Eleanor's calendar. If there was a meeting, we'll find evidence."

At midnight, we interview a man in his thirties who's

been asking for a lawyer but also hinting he has information to trade. His name is Corey Thomas and he's been with the Hollow Circle for two years.

"I want immunity," he says before we even sit down. "Full immunity for anything I tell you."

Emma and I exchange glances. "That depends on what you've done. And what you tell us."

His lawyer, a public defender who looks exhausted, intervenes. "My client is willing to provide information about the organization's leadership structure in exchange for consideration on charges. He's never harmed anyone directly. Never touched a child. His participation was limited to attending meetings and ceremonies."

After twenty minutes of negotiation and consultation with the prosecutor's office, we reach a preliminary agreement. Corey will provide full cooperation. In exchange, the most serious charges will be dropped pending verification of his information. It's contingent on everything he tells us being truthful and useful.

Only then does Corey start talking.

"I met him. The Shepherd. Three times."

My pulse quickens. "When?"

"Once last year. Once in the summer. And again in October." Corey looks between us. "He's a real person."

"Describe him," Emma says, already pulling up a laptop to take notes.

"Older. Maybe seventy, seventy-five. Tall. Thin. White hair but he still moves like he's younger. Sharp eyes. Very intelligent. When he talks, everyone listens." Corey pauses. "He's been doing this longer than any of us have been alive. That's what Eleanor said. That he started the Hollow Circle in the 1970s. That everything we practice came from him."

"Where did these meetings happen?"

"Different places. Last October it was at Eleanor's property. He came at night. Maybe ten of us were there. He talked about the winter solstice. About how this year was special. That the planets aligned correctly for the first time in decades. That we had to prepare for seven crossings."

Emma types rapidly. "Did he give specific instructions?"

"He told Eleanor which children to select. Said twins were essential for the first crossing. That it set the tone for everything that followed." Corey wipes his forehead. "He talked about bridges. About how certain souls are naturally suited for transformation. About how the work we were doing would tear the veil and let him return."

"Return from where?" I ask.

Corey looks uncomfortable. "That's the part that always confused me. He talked like he was already gone. Already crossed over. Like his physical body was just a vessel he was using temporarily. He said when the seventh crossing is completed, when the bridges were all in place, he'd return to his full power."

Emma and I share a look. This is starting to sound less like criminal conspiracy and more like genuine delusion.

"Did he mention Agent Collins specifically?" I ask, trying to keep my voice neutral.

Corey nods. "In October. He talked about someone specific. An FBI agent. Said she was the key to everything. The bridge that was never completed." He pauses, choosing his words carefully. "He said this agent had been taken twenty years ago by his followers. That they'd been preparing her for transformation but she escaped before it finished."

My chest goes tight. Twenty years ago. An escaped victim who became an FBI agent.

He's talking about me.

"He said she'd find her way back eventually," Corey continues, not seeming to notice my reaction. "That the incompleteness would drive her to hunt people like us. That when she finally understood what she was meant to become, she'd complete the crossing willingly." He leans forward. "He's obsessed with her. Has been following her career for years. Every case she solves, every child she saves—he sees it as evidence that she's special. That she was correctly identified all those years ago."

Emma's hand finds my arm under the table. A silent question: Are you okay?

I'm not okay. But I need to hear the rest.

"Did he say where he is now?" I ask, keeping my voice steady. "Where we can find him?"

"No. He shows up, gives instructions, then disappears. Eleanor said he moves between places. That he's been preparing for decades. Building strength in the place beyond." Corey shakes his head. "I know how that sounds. Like religious nonsense. But when he talks about it, you believe him. He's that convincing."

We interview Corey for another hour, extracting every detail he can remember. Physical description, speech patterns, specific things The Shepherd said. It's more information than we've had before, but it's still not enough to identify him.

After Corey is processed, Emma and I stand in the cold outside the command van. The scene is winding down now. Arrestees transported to holding. Evidence tagged and secured. The stone circle empty except for forensic techs documenting everything.

"He's been tracking you since your escape," Emma says quietly. "Everything Eleanor said, everything this Corey guy confirmed—your abduction wasn't random. You were specifically targeted. Chosen."

"I know."

"River, that means for twenty years you've been on his radar. While you were building your career, working cases, living your life—he was watching. Waiting."

"I know."

"That doesn't terrify you?"

I look at her. "Of course it terrifies me. But what am I supposed to do? Live in fear? Change careers? Pretend I don't know?" I shake my head. "The Shepherd wants me to believe I'm incomplete. That I need transformation to be whole. But I'm already whole, Emma. I survived. I built a life. I help people. That's completion."

"Eleanor didn't think so."

"Eleanor is wrong." But my voice lacks conviction. Because some part of me, some wounded twelve-year-old part, wonders if they're right. If something was left unfinished. If the nightmares and hypervigilance and inability to trust are evidence of incompleteness.

My phone rings. Siwak.

"We've got something," he says without preamble. "Forensic analysis of Eleanor's laptop found deleted emails. Messages to someone with an encrypted address. Discussing plans, timelines, your background. The encryption is sophisticated but our tech team is working on breaking it."

"How long?"

"Could be hours. Could be days. But River, the content we can see? This person has detailed information about your abduction. Things that were never made public. Things only your captors would know."

My hands go cold. "Send me what you have."

After hanging up, I tell Emma. She looks as disturbed as I feel.

"If he knows details from your abduction, if he was in contact with your captors—" She doesn't finish the thought.

"Then he's been part of my life since I was twelve." I stare at the dark forest surrounding us. "He's been there all along. Watching. Waiting for me to find my way back."

"EVERY HIGH-PROFILE CASE," Emma says quietly. "Every time your name made the news. He was watching. Following your career. Waiting for the right moment."

The thought makes my skin crawl. Not that he controlled my path, but that he's been a silent observer all these years. Watching me build a life while planning to destroy it.

"We need to find him," I say. "Not just to close this case. To end this. Whatever connection he thinks exists between us, whatever transformation he believes I need—it ends when we arrest him."

"Agreed. But River, if he's been planning this for decades, if he's as intelligent and patient as everyone says—he's not going to be easy to find."

Garrett approaches with a tablet. "We've compiled everything we have on The Shepherd. Witness descriptions from the 1994 case. Corey's statement tonight. References in Eleanor's research. It's not much, but it's a start."

I take the tablet, scrolling through information. The composite sketch from various descriptions shows an older man with sharp features and intelligent eyes. Could be anyone. Could be anywhere.

But buried in Eleanor's notes is something that catches my attention. A reference to "the original crossing site" and coordinates that don't match any of the seven locations we found.

"What's this?" I show Garrett.

He pulls up a map. "Those coordinates are in western Virginia. Middle of nowhere. There's nothing there according to satellite imaging. Just forest."

"Eleanor mentioned this place was where The Shepherd performed crossings before she was born. Before anyone alive now was born." I zoom in on the location. "What if this is where it started? His first rituals. The place he considers most sacred."

"You think he'd go back there?" Emma asks.

"If tomorrow is the winter solstice, if that's when he believes the veil is thinnest—yeah. I think he'd want to be at his most powerful location." I look at Siwak, who's joined our group. "We need to check this site. Tomorrow. Before the solstice."

"That's a five-hour drive, and the last hour is mountain roads. We'd need to leave before dawn to get there by noon."

Siwak considers this. "River, we've already stopped Eleanor's planned crossings. The children are safe. We have forty-two arrests. The case is solid. We don't need to chase a maybe lead across the state."

"But The Shepherd is still out there. Still obsessed with completing my crossing." I meet his eyes. "This doesn't end until he's arrested. You know that."

Siwak is quiet for a long moment. Then he nods. "Take a small team. Emma, Garrett, two support agents. Coordinate with local law enforcement when you get there. But River—if this turns into another standoff, if there's any danger—you call for backup immediately. No running off alone. Understood?"

"Understood."

We prepare to leave within the hour. While others pack gear and coordinate logistics, I stand at the edge of the stone circle one last time. The rocks cast long shadows in the portable lights.

Eleanor wanted to add four more deaths to their history. We stopped her. But The Shepherd remains. And tomorrow, at the place where it all started, I might finally understand what they see in me. What they believe I was meant to become.

And maybe, finally, I can prove them wrong.

CHAPTER TWENTY-EIGHT

The hospital wing devoted to the four children looks like a fortress. FBI agents stationed outside. Medical staff cleared and vetted. Parents allowed in only after thorough security checks. We're not taking chances after everything that happened.

I stand outside Noah Okafor's room watching through the window. He's awake now, sitting up in bed with his parents on either side of him. His mother holds his hand like she'll never let go. His father keeps touching Noah's face, his hair, his shoulder. He's in need of constant reassurance that his son is real and alive.

Liam is in the next room. The brothers will be reunited later today once the doctors are satisfied both boys are stable enough for the emotional intensity of seeing each other.

Dr. Aiden Watkins finds me in the hallway and gives me a kiss. He looks exhausted but relieved. "All four children are responding well to treatment. We've flushed most of the compound from their systems. They're dehydrated and malnourished, but those issues are manageable."

"What about long-term effects?"

"Too early to say definitively. But based on what we're seeing, I'm cautiously optimistic. The dissociative symptoms are fading. They're becoming more aware of their surroundings, more responsive." He pulls up a tablet, shows me charts I don't fully understand. "The compound they were given is sophisticated. Botanical in origin, derived from plants we're still working to identify. It creates a dissociative state, suppresses normal fear responses, makes subjects highly suggestible."

"So they weren't scared because they couldn't be scared."

"Exactly. Combined with ritualistic language and environmental manipulation, the children basically experienced reality through a filter. Everything felt distant, dreamlike. They were compliant because their normal self-preservation instincts were chemically disabled."

I think about Liam saying he knew something was wrong but couldn't feel it. About Noah being led to that stone circle without protest. They were robbed of their ability to fight back.

"Is it permanently damaging?" I ask.

"We don't think so. But they'll need extensive therapy. What they experienced will have psychological impact even if the physical effects are temporary." Aiden hesitates. "River, there's something else. Dr. Hayes in toxicology asked to speak with you. She found something unusual in the compound analysis."

Dr. Elizabeth Hayes, the medical examiner, is waiting in her lab when I arrive. She's the same ME who performed the Caine twins' autopsy, and now she's analyzing the toxicology results from the surviving children

"Agent Collins, thank you for coming." She gestures to a chair. "The hospital sent me blood samples from all four children for forensic analysis. I've been examining the botanical compound in their systems."

"Can you identify the plants?"

"Some of them. Datura stramonium—jimsonweed. Atropa belladonna—deadly nightshade. Mandragora officinarum—mandrake. All highly toxic plants with documented historical use in shamanic practices and witchcraft trials." She pulls up molecular structures. "But the combination is unique. Whoever formulated this understood actual pharmacology. They knew exactly which compounds to extract and in what ratios."

"Eleanor Vance could have researched this."

"Possibly. But here's what concerns me." Dr. Hayes pulls up a different file. "This compound has a very specific chemical signature. A particular ratio of alkaloids that creates a unique metabolic fingerprint. When I ran it through our database looking for similar cases, I got a hit."

She shows me the screen. A case file from 2003. My case file. From when I was rescued.

"Your toxicology report from twenty years ago shows trace amounts of a compound with the exact same signature. The concentration pattern is unusual—much lower than we'd expect given the length of your captivity."

The lab feels suddenly too cold. "You're saying my captors used the same drug."

"I'm saying whoever formulated this compound twenty years ago and whoever formulated it today either learned from the same source or are the same person." Dr. Hayes meets my eyes. "This isn't something you find in a textbook, Agent Collins. This is specialized knowledge passed directly from teacher to student."

"But why would the concentrations be lower if I was held for two years?"

"That's what's interesting. Based on the metabolites in your system, they were dosing you intermittently, not continuously. Probably because you were there so long—they didn't need you constantly sedated. They could control you through fear and isolation. The current victims were dosed heavily and continuously because they only had them for days or weeks. Different strategies for different timeframes, but the same fundamental formula."

"Because The Shepherd taught both groups."

"That would be my hypothesis, yes." She hesitates. "Agent Collins, based on the trace amounts in your system and the timeline of your captivity, they'd only just started dosing you when you escaped. A few more days and you would have been as compliant as these children. Unable to fight back. Unable to refuse whatever they intended."

I force myself to breathe normally. "Thank you for telling me."

"I thought you should know. For the investigation, obviously. But also..." She trails off, then continues more gently. "You survived because you acted before they could take away your ability to act. That's significant."

After leaving the lab, I sit in my car in the hospital parking lot for a long time. The same drug. The same formulation.

The Shepherd didn't just know about my abduction. He orchestrated it. Trained my captors in the specific methodology. Taught them which plants to use and how to prepare them. Gave them the tools to transform me into someone compliant and suggestible.

But they didn't have enough time. I escaped while I could still think clearly, while I still had the will to fight. If I'd been drugged longer, I would have become like those four children.

My phone rings. It's Emma.

"River, we've got members starting to break. One of the inner circle wants to deal. Says he has information about The Shepherd's visit to Eleanor. Can you get back to the field office?"

"On my way."

I start the car, forcing myself to focus on the work ahead. There will be time later to process what Dr. Hayes told me. Time to confront the reality that I came much closer to losing myself than I'd realized.

CHAPTER TWENTY-NINE

The interrogation room is standard FBI. It's windowless, there are cameras in two of the corners, and a table bolted to the floor. The man sitting across from Emma and me is named Roger Whitfield, age forty-seven, one of Eleanor's inner circle members. He's been in custody for thirty-six hours and his lawyer has spent that time negotiating a deal.

"My client is prepared to provide information about the organization's leadership," the lawyer says. "In exchange for reduced charges and consideration for a minimum security placement."

"That depends on the quality of information," Emma replies. "Start talking and we'll see what it's worth."

Roger looks uncomfortable but determined. He's forty-seven with sandy brown hair going gray at the temples, wearing wire-rimmed glasses that keep slipping down his nose. Everything about him seems ordinary—soft-spoken, unremarkable, the kind of person who blends into a crowd.

If I passed him on the street, I'd think accountant or middle manager. Not someone involved in ritual child sacrifice.

"I joined the group four years ago. My wife had died, I was looking for meaning, someone invited me to a nature workshop. It seemed harmless at first. Meditation, environmental education, traditional stories about the seasons. Eleanor was charismatic. Intelligent. She made you feel like you were part of something important."

"When did you realize it was more than environmental education?" I ask.

"Gradually. There were different levels of involvement. Outer circle members just attended workshops and hikes. But if Eleanor thought you were serious, truly committed, she'd invite you to private meetings. Smaller groups. That's where the real teachings happened."

"What teachings?"

Roger shifts in his seat. "She talked about how modern society has severed humanity from natural rhythms. How we've forgotten that death and life are linked. How certain practices once considered sacred are now dismissed as primitive." He pauses. "She taught us that transformation requires sacrifice. That some souls are meant to facilitate passage between what is and what could be."

"Did she specify what kind of sacrifice?" Emma asks.

"Not at first. She used metaphors and talked about letting go of attachments and surrendering the ego. It wasn't until much later that I understood she meant literal death."

"When did you understand that?"

"Maybe a year ago. There was a ceremony. Eleanor talked about children being uniquely suited for this work because they're not corrupted by modern thinking yet. She said twins especially carried power because they're naturally dual—two souls, one unit. That's when I started to realize what she was planning."

Emma leans forward. "And you stayed involved anyway."

"I know how that sounds. But by then I believed. She was so certain, so articulate about the logic behind it. And I'd already committed so much—left my job, sold my house, devoted my life to the group. Walking away would have meant admitting I'd been wrong about everything."

"You chose your ego over children's lives," I say flatly.

Roger flinches but doesn't argue. "Yes. That's exactly what I did."

His lawyer intervenes. "My client acknowledges his guilt and poor judgment. He's prepared to provide testimony about others who were more directly involved in the planning and execution."

"Tell us about The Shepherd," Emma says.

Roger's expression changes. He becomes both fearful and reverent. "He's the source of everything. All of Eleanor's knowledge, all the practices she taught us, came from him. She talked about him constantly. Said he'd been teaching the true way for longer than any of us had been alive."

"Did you ever meet him?"

"Once. Three months ago, he came to evaluate Eleanor's progress. She was nervous that day, wanted everything perfect. Maybe ten of us were invited to be present."

"Describe him," I say, pulling out a notepad.

"Older, maybe mid-seventies. Tall, thin, white hair. But he moved like someone much younger. Very alert. Sharp eyes that seemed to look right through you." Roger pauses, remembering. "When he spoke, everyone listened. His voice had this quality—calm but absolutely authoritative. He talked about the winter solstice being significant this year.

About how the timing was finally right after years of preparation."

"Right for what?"

"For tearing open the veil. That's how he described it. Said Eleanor's work setting up seven locations was excellent. That she'd identified the correct candidates. He specifically praised her selection of the Caine twins for the first ceremony."

Emma and I exchange glances. "He was directly involved in planning specific murders."

"He didn't use those words. He talked about 'facilitation' and 'transformation.' But yes, he approved which children Eleanor had selected. Told her the sequence in which they should be... processed."

"Did he mention Agent Collins?" I ask, keeping my voice steady.

Roger looks at me directly for the first time. "Yes. He was obsessed with you. Called you the incomplete work. Said you'd been chosen correctly twenty years ago but the execution was flawed. That your survival created an imbalance that needed correcting. He told Eleanor that once the seven were complete, you would return to finish what was started."

"How did he know I'd get involved in the investigation?"

"He said you always come for the children. That it's your nature now because of what happened to you. That you'd be drawn back to this work inevitably." Roger hesitates. "He said he'd been following your career for years. Knew which cases you worked, which successes you achieved. Said everything you'd become was evidence that you were correctly identified as special."

My hands clench under the table. Emma continues the questioning.

"Where is he now? Where can we find him?"

"I don't know. He came for that one meeting and then disappeared. Eleanor had a way to contact him—some kind of secure email—but I never saw the details."

"Did he use any other names? Any identifying information?"

Roger shakes his head. "Just The Shepherd. Eleanor said he's used different names in different places over the decades. That he moves between communities, building networks, teaching selected individuals. The 1994 case you're investigating. Eleanor mentioned that as one of his earlier attempts. Said he'd learned from mistakes made then and refined his approach."

We question Roger for another hour, extracting every detail he remembers. Physical descriptions, specific phrases The Shepherd used, his mannerisms and speech patterns. It's more than we had before but still not enough to identify him definitively.

After Roger is processed and returned to holding, Emma and I brief Siwak on what we learned.

"So The Shepherd is real, active, and has been orchestrating ritualistic murders for at least thirty years," Siwak summarizes grimly. "And he's specifically fixated on Agent Collins as an unfinished project."

"That's what the evidence suggests, yes," Emma says.

"We need to identify him. I'm authorizing full resources—work with Behavioral Analysis, get a detailed profile. Go through the 1994 case files again with this new information. Find connections between Eleanor Vance and the suspects from that case."

Agent Mercer, who's been consulting on the investigation, speaks up. "I've been reviewing my notes from 1994. The Hartley children—Jennifer and Michael—were killed using methods nearly identical to what we've seen with the Caine twins. Symbols carved in trees, ceremonial positioning of bodies, evidence of plant-based compounds in their systems. We investigated dozens of suspects but never made arrests. The case went cold."

"Do you have photos from the crime scene?" I ask.

"In my files. I'll pull everything."

AN HOUR LATER, we're gathered around a conference table covered with materials from the Hartley case. Crime scene photos, witness statements, evidence logs. Mercer has organized everything chronologically.

"This photo was taken at a community meeting we held trying to find leads," Mercer says, showing us an image of maybe fifty people gathered in what looks like a church basement. "We were asking if anyone had seen suspicious activity in the area where the children were found."

I study the faces in the crowd. Most are blurry, background figures. But near the edge of the frame, partially visible, there's a woman. Dark hair, sharp features, looking directly at the camera.

"Can we enhance this?" I ask.

Garrett takes the photo and uploads it to image enhancement software. The technology now is vastly superior to what existed in 1994. He processes the image, increasing resolution, sharpening details.

The woman becomes clearer. And my breath catches.

"That's her," I say quietly. "The woman who took me. I'm certain."

Emma leans closer. "You're sure?"

"I've seen her face in nightmares for twenty years. That's her."

Garrett continues processing. There's someone standing slightly behind the woman, mostly obscured by her and other people. A tall figure. Male. Older. He's turned partially away from the camera but his profile is visible.

"Enhance that section," Mercer says, his voice tight.

Garrett isolates the figure and processes it. The image sharpens. We can see white hair, a lean build, sharp features. The man is watching the meeting with an expression of calm interest. He's not obviously hiding but he's positioned himself to be less visible.

"That could be The Shepherd," Emma says. "Based on Roger's description. The age, height, build all match."

"He was there," Mercer breathes. "Thirty years ago, he was at our community meeting. Probably watching the investigation. Seeing how close we were to identifying him."

I stare at the image. This is the man who trained my kidnappers. Who's been tracking me for two decades. Who orchestrated Eleanor's entire plan. He's right there in a photo from 1994, watching investigators scramble to solve murders he committed.

"Can we run facial recognition?" Siwak asks.

"Already on it," Garrett says, uploading the enhanced image to databases. "This will take time. The angle isn't ideal and he's partially obscured. But if he's in any system—driver's license, passport, criminal records—we might get a match."

We wait. The software runs through millions of faces.

Minutes stretch into an hour. Garrett watches the screen, periodically adjusting parameters.

"Anything?" Emma asks.

"Multiple possible matches, but nothing definitive. The partial profile makes it difficult." Garrett pulls up the top ten matches. "These men all have similar facial structures and would have been the right age in 1994. But without a full face or better angle, I can't narrow it further."

I study the possible matches. Any of them could be The Shepherd. Or none of them. The face that's haunted the periphery of my life for twenty years, and we still can't identify him with certainty.

"Keep running it," Siwak orders. "Try different databases. And get that image to Agent Mercer's old contacts in West Virginia. See if anyone recognizes him."

As the meeting breaks up, I stay at the table staring at that enhanced photo. The woman who took me and the man who trained her, standing together thirty years ago. They were already doing this work back then. They were already selecting children and already performing their rituals.

And somewhere out there, he's still at it.

Still waiting for me to find my way back to him.

CHAPTER THIRTY

Dr. Patricia Reeves's office is decorated with the kind of deliberate calm that's supposed to make trauma processing feel safe. It has soft lighting, comfortable chairs, and a white noise machine in the corner masking sound from the hallway. I've been coming here twice a month for five years. Today is an emergency session.

"You killed someone four days ago," Dr. Reeves says, not as a question but as an opening. "At a location that turned out to be where you were held captive twenty years ago. And you discovered your abduction was specifically orchestrated by a man who's been tracking you ever since. That's a lot to process."

"I'm managing."

She gives me the look that means she's not accepting that answer. "River, you shot someone. That woman died. Regardless of the justification—and I understand you were defending yourself—taking a life has psychological impact. You can't just grit your teeth through that."

"I know." I look at my hands. They're steady now but they

shook for hours after the shooting. "She was going to kill me. She believed murdering me would be holy. Would help me transform. She died thinking she was doing me a favor."

"How does that make you feel?"

"Angry. Confused. Sad." I pause. "Guilty that I don't feel worse. She's dead and part of me just feels relief that it was her instead of me."

"That's normal. Survival instinct doesn't disappear just because the threat does." Dr. Reeves makes a note. "Tell me about returning to that clearing. About recognizing it."

This is harder. I've spent twenty years trying not to think about that place. "I didn't recognize it consciously at first. But my body knew. The way sound carries in that space. The angle of the ground. Even the smell." I close my eyes, can see it perfectly. "Eleanor brought me there deliberately. She wanted me to understand that the place still exists. That what happened there matters."

"Does it still matter?"

"Of course it does. I was held prisoner there. Drugged. Prepared for something I still don't fully understand." I open my eyes. "And now I know it wasn't random. The Shepherd chose my kidnappers and told them what drugs to use on me."

"How does knowing that change things for you?"

"It means I've been connected to this network my entire life. They have been watching me, waiting for me to grow up and become whatever they think I'm supposed to be." My voice is rising and I force myself to breathe. "It means I've never been free. Not really. Because he's been there the whole time. Following my career. Watching me save other children while planning to reclaim me."

Dr. Reeves is quiet for a moment. When she speaks, her

voice is gentle but firm. "Let me ask you something. What does it mean to you if your survival wasn't luck? If it was resistance?"

I don't understand the question. "What do you mean?"

"You escaped before they could fully implement their plan. Before the drugs took complete effect. Before you lost your ability to fight back." She leans forward slightly. "Eleanor told you that you're incomplete because you escaped. But what if that framing is wrong? What if you're not incomplete—you're unbroken?"

The words hit differently than I expect. "I don't follow."

"They tried to transform you into something compliant and suggestible. Into someone who would accept death as transcendence. But you refused. You fought back. You escaped. That's not incompleteness, River. That's resistance. You broke their pattern by refusing to be what they wanted you to become."

I sit with that for a moment. All this time I've been thinking about what was left unfinished in that room. What mark or change or transformation they intended that didn't happen. But Dr. Reeves' perspective changes something.

"You're saying I won."

"I'm saying you survived on your terms, not theirs. And everything you've built since—your career, your life, your ability to help other children—that's evidence that their plan failed completely. You didn't become what they wanted. You became what you chose." She pauses. "The Shepherd can claim you're still connected to his work. But the truth is, you've been free this whole time. And he's been trying to reclaim something he never actually had."

The relief that floods through me is unexpected and overwhelming. I've spent two decades feeling like I'm living with something unfinished. Something incomplete. But Dr. Reeves is right. I'm not incomplete. I'm whole in a way they never intended me to be.

"They're trying to reclaim me," I say slowly, working through the realization. "But I was never theirs to begin with."

"Exactly."

We sit with that for a while. Outside Dr. Reeves's window, Charlottesville goes about its normal business. There are people out there who don't know about ritual sacrifice networks or men who've been orchestrating murders for decades. There are people living ordinary lives untouched by this darkness.

But I'm not separate from them. I'm one of them, living my own ordinary life between cases. Going to dinner with Aiden. Playing with my niece and nephew. Building something normal despite everything I've seen.

That's what The Shepherd can't accept. That I escaped his design and built my own life anyway.

"There's something else I need to process," I say. "My brother-in-law was recruited to the network specifically to provide access to me. He took my nephew and niece to Eleanor's programs. Put them in proximity to someone grooming children for murder."

"How does that make you feel about Chris?"

"Furious. Betrayed. He was family and he exposed my sister's children to danger because he was looking for meaning." I shake my head. "But he's also a victim in his own way. Eleanor manipulated him. Targeted him because of me."

"Have you spoken with your sister about this?"

"Not really. Not beyond the basics of the investigation. She's filing for divorce. I don't know what to say to her."

"Maybe start with listening," Dr. Reeves suggests. "This affected her differently than it affected you. Her marriage, her trust in her own judgment, her sense of safety for her children. She needs support, not solutions."

AFTER MY SESSION ENDS, I drive to Leslie's house. It's midafternoon, the kids are at school. When Leslie opens the door, she looks exhausted. Older somehow than the last time I saw her.

"River. Come in."

The house is neat but impersonal. Chris's things are gone. The family photos that used to crowd the mantle have been taken down. The space looks less like a home and more like a temporary dwelling. A place Leslie is living in while she figures out what comes next.

"How are you holding up?" I ask.

Leslie laughs without humor. "I don't know. I'm angry constantly. At Chris for being so stupid. At myself for not seeing it. At you sometimes, which isn't fair, but I can't help it."

"You're angry at me?"

"Because if you weren't FBI, if you hadn't survived your abduction, Chris would never have been recruited. Eleanor would never have targeted our family. My boys would never have been exposed to—" She stops, breathing hard. "I know that's not logical. I know it's not your fault. But when I look at my children and think about what could have happened, I need someone to blame."

I sit with that. Don't defend myself or explain. Just let her be angry.

"Chris keeps calling," Leslie continues. "Leaving messages about how sorry he is. How he didn't know. How he was manipulated. And maybe that's all true, but it doesn't change what he did. Doesn't change that he had an affair with someone from that group. That he took our children to Eleanor's programs while he was sleeping with Amanda. That he chose his spiritual crisis and his mistress over our family's safety."

"Are you going through with the divorce?"

"Yes. Even if he didn't know about the murders, even if he was manipulated—he still cheated on me. He still exposed our children to danger. He still ignored every red flag because he was so desperate for meaning and validation from people who turned out to be part of a death cult." Her voice breaks slightly. "I don't know how to trust him again. Every workshop he attended, every 'business meeting,' he might have been with Amanda or at one of Eleanor's ceremonies. Our entire marriage was already falling apart and I didn't even know it."

Leslie looks at me, really looks at me for the first time since I arrived. "How do you do it? Trust people after everything you've been through?"

The question catches me off guard. "I don't know that I do. Not completely."

"But you're with Aiden. You work with Emma and your team. You function in the world."

"I test people," I say slowly, working through it as I speak. "I give them small pieces of trust and see what they do with it. And I accept that some people will fail—Chris failed spectacularly. But others won't. Emma has proven herself hundreds of times. Aiden shows up consistently. My therapist maintains boundaries and helps me process without judgment." I pause. "You start small. You test. You give people chances to prove themselves. And you accept that rebuilding trust is slow work."

"How do I trust my own judgment again? I chose Chris. Built a life with him. Had children with him. And I was completely wrong about who he was."

"You weren't wrong about who he *was*. You were wrong about who he *became*. People change. Sometimes they change in ways we can't predict or control." I lean forward. "Chris made his choices. You didn't make them for him. You're not responsible for his decisions."

Leslie is crying now, quiet tears streaming down her face. "I'm so angry, River. And so scared. Scared that Eleanor or someone else from that network will come after my children. I'm terrified that I won't see the danger until it's too late and that I'll never feel safe again."

I move to sit beside her on the couch. Put my arm around her shoulders. We sit like that for a long time, my sister crying against my shoulder while I hold her the way she held me when we were kids and I had nightmares.

"We'll get through this," I tell her. "You and the kids. It won't be fast and it won't be easy. But you'll get through it."

"How can you be sure?"

"Because I did. And because I'll be here to help."

When I leave an hour later, Leslie seems slightly steadier. Not healed, not close to okay, but slightly more grounded. She walks me to the door and hugs me tightly.

"Thank you for coming. For listening."

"Always."

I drive back to my apartment as the sun sets. The case is

winding down. Arrests are being processed, evidence is being catalogued, and interrogations are continuing. If all goes well with the trial, Eleanor Vance will spend the rest of her life in prison. Brenda Caine and the other inner circle members will face decades of incarceration. The Hollow Circle network is dismantled.

But The Shepherd remains out there. Somewhere.

The difference now is that I understand what Dr. Reeves helped me see. I'm not incomplete. I'm whole. I built a life they never intended me to have. And every day I continue living on my own terms is another day their plan fails.

They can track me all they want. They can believe I'm destined for their transformation. But I've already chosen who I'm going to be.

And it's nothing they intended.

CHAPTER THIRTY-ONE

The courtroom is packed for Eleanor Vance's preliminary hearing. Media fills the back rows, sketch artists capture every detail, and family members scatter throughout the gallery. Security is heavy. There are federal marshals at every door as well as metal detectors and thorough bag searches. Everyone's nervous about people trying to disrupt the proceedings.

Eleanor sits at the defense table in civilian clothes—gray slacks, white blouse, her hair pulled back neatly. She looks like a professor attending a faculty meeting, not someone facing multiple felony charges. Her lawyer, Richard Caldwell, sits beside her reviewing documents.

I'm in the gallery with Emma and Siwak. We'll testify today as the prosecution presents evidence to establish probable cause for trial. This is where the government has to prove they have enough evidence to proceed with criminal charges.

The judge enters and everyone stands. Judge Margaret Videen is known for running an efficient courtroom. No nonsense, no theatrics, just careful attention to evidence and law.

"Be seated," Judge Videen says once she's settled. "We're here for the preliminary hearing in United States v. Vance et al. This hearing will determine whether there is probable cause to believe the defendants committed the crimes charged and whether this case should proceed to trial. Mr. Ross, you may begin."

The prosecutor, Assistant U.S. Attorney Michael Ross, stands. He's mid-forties, experienced with complex conspiracy cases and known for being methodical and thorough.

"Thank you, Your Honor. The government will present evidence that the defendants engaged in a systematic conspiracy to kidnap and endanger children under the guise of operating an educational foundation. The charges include conspiracy to commit kidnapping, kidnapping of minors, child endangerment resulting in death, administering controlled substances to minors, and conspiracy to commit murder."

Caldwell rises immediately. "Your Honor, the defense maintains that our clients were engaged in protected religious expression and educational activities. We'll demonstrate that any harm that occurred was unintended and resulted from tragic accidents, not criminal intent."

Judge Videen nods. "Noted for the record. Mr. Ross, present your evidence."

Ross proceeds methodically. He introduces documents showing the Greenwood Legacy Foundation's eight-year operation. Eleanor Vance's academic credentials and her extensive research into ritual practices. Financial records showing systematic recruitment efforts. Testimony from outer circle members who believed they were participating in environmental education, unaware of the inner circle's true intentions.

"The Caine twins, Titus and Matthew, were found deceased on December fifteenth," Ross continues, displaying crime scene photos on the courtroom monitors. "Medical examination revealed they'd been administered plant-based alkaloids and left in subfreezing temperatures until they died of exposure. The Okafor twins, Liam and Noah, were abducted on December seventeenth. Four additional children were rescued on December nineteenth during an operation where law enforcement prevented the defendants from continuing their pattern of planned killings."

He presents more evidence over the next hour. The map found in Eleanor's hidden office with seven marked locations. Brenda Caine's calendar documenting specific dates and identifying children by initials. Witness testimony from Hollow Circle members about meetings with someone called The Shepherd who provided instructions. The botanical compound analysis showing identical formulations to substances used in a 1994 cold case and in the 2003 abduction of an FBI agent.

Then it's my turn to testify. I'm sworn in and take the witness stand. Eleanor watches me with that same serene expression she's maintained throughout the proceedings.

Ross begins his questioning. "Agent Collins, please state your role in this investigation."

"I'm the lead investigator for the FBI's Crimes Against Children unit. I was assigned to investigate the deaths of Titus and Matthew Caine."

"Can you walk the court through what your investigation revealed?"

I describe the timeline in detail. Finding the twins' bodies in that clearing with symbols carved into surrounding trees. The connection to a 1994 cold case with identical methodology. The discovery that both sets of victims had attended programs run by Eleanor Vance's Greenwood Legacy Foundation. The abduction of the Okafor twins. The tactical operation at the stone circle where we rescued four children and arrested seventeen individuals.

"Agent Collins, did you identify a pattern of behavior by the defendants?"

"Yes. The defendants operated a sophisticated multi-layered organization. Most participants believed they were involved in legitimate environmental education. But Eleanor Vance maintained a smaller inner circle that was gradually indoctrinated into extreme beliefs about transformation through death. The structure ensured most members didn't realize the true purpose until they were deeply committed to the group."

"In your professional opinion as a federal agent with extensive experience in crimes against children, was this operation systematic and intentional?"

"Absolutely. Eleanor Vance spent eight years building this organization. She identified specific children based on criteria she'd developed. She groomed their families through seemingly benign educational programs. She prepared multiple ceremonial locations in advance. She orchestrated a sequence of planned murders timed to coincide with the winter solstice. This was methodical, premeditated, and executed with extensive planning."

Ross introduces more evidence through my testimony. Eleanor's journals describing the selection process. The hand-drawn organizational chart found in her office showing connections between members. The emails discussing preparations and progress reports.

"Agent Collins, the defense has suggested this was religious expression protected by the First Amendment. Do you agree?"

"No. Religious freedom doesn't protect child endangerment or murder. The defendants weren't practicing their faith in ways that affected only themselves. They were selecting, drugging, and killing children. That's criminal activity regardless of the spiritual beliefs underlying it."

Caldwell's cross-examination focuses on my personal connection to the case. He stands, approaching the witness stand with careful precision.

"Agent Collins, you were abducted as a child, weren't you?"

"Yes, when I was twelve years old."

"And your kidnappers used similar methods to those alleged in this case?"

"Based on toxicology analysis comparing my case file from 2003 to the current victims, yes, the same botanical compound was used."

"Isn't it possible that your personal trauma affected your objectivity in this investigation? That you saw connections that might not exist because you were looking for them?"

"No. The connections are documented through physical evidence. The chemical analysis proves the compounds are identical. Eleanor Vance's own writings reference The Shepherd as her mentor. The same individual appears in photographs from the 1994 case. This isn't about my perception—it's about documented evidence."

"But you pursued Eleanor Vance alone into the woods after the tactical breach, against standard protocol. Wasn't that driven by personal feelings rather than professional judgment?"

"I pursued a fleeing suspect who was attempting to escape custody. That's my job."

"A fleeing suspect who deliberately brought you to the location where you were held captive twenty years ago. That must have compromised your professional judgment."

"I wasn't aware of the location's significance until after I'd secured the suspect. My actions were appropriate given the circumstances and were later reviewed and approved by my superiors."

Caldwell continues pressing on the personal angle but I hold steady. Everything I did was documented, witnessed by other agents, and found to be within policy. My history doesn't negate the physical evidence or the systematic nature of the crimes.

After I'm excused, other witnesses testify. Dr. Elizabeth Hayes, the medical examiner, explains the botanical compounds and their effects. Aiden takes the stand next, and I watch him shift into his professional demeanor—the calm, authoritative physician who treated the rescued children. He describes their medical condition upon arrival at the hospital, the treatment protocol required to counteract the drugs, and his prognosis for their recovery. When Caldwell tries to suggest the children weren't in real danger, Aiden's response is measured but firm: without immediate intervention, all four children would have died within hours. As he steps down, his eyes find mine for just a moment—a brief connection before he returns to the gallery. Emma details the evidence seized from Eleanor's home and the surveillance operation that led to the final confrontation. Garrett presents the financial records showing Eleanor's donor cultivation and the paper trail connecting her to The Shepherd.

Ross rests his case after three hours of testimony. "Your Honor, the government has established probable cause that the defendants engaged in a criminal conspiracy resulting in the deaths of two children and the endangerment of at least six others. We ask that this case proceed to trial."

Caldwell begins his response. "Your Honor, the defense maintains—"

Eleanor stands abruptly. Her chair scrapes against the floor, the sound cutting through the courtroom.

"Your Honor, I need to speak." Her voice is calm but carries throughout the room.

Judge Videen's expression hardens. "Dr. Vance, you are not recognized. Please sit down."

"This court doesn't understand what's at stake." Eleanor ignores her lawyer's hand tugging at her sleeve. She turns to face me directly. "Agent Collins knows. She's always known, even when she pretends otherwise."

"Bailiff—" Judge Videen begins.

But Eleanor speaks faster, her words rushing out before she can be stopped. "I'm accused of harming children, but what I offered was transformation. Freedom from the limitations modern society places on existence. Those children felt peaceful. They transitioned without fear or pain. That's more than most people experience in death."

Caldwell is on his feet. "Your Honor, my client is clearly—"

Then Eleanor turns to me.

"The Shepherd will come for you, Agent Collins," she says, her eyes staring into mine with absolute certainty. "He always completes what he begins. You're the unfinished bridge. And bridges are meant to be crossed."

"Remove the defendant!" Judge Videen's gavel comes down hard.

Marshals move forward but Eleanor doesn't resist. She sits calmly, her message delivered, still looking at me with that serene satisfaction.

The courtroom erupts. Caldwell is objecting to his own client's outburst. Ross is standing, likely preparing to use Eleanor's statement against her. Media members scribble notes frantically. Judge Videen gavels repeatedly for order.

Emma's hand finds my arm from where she sits in the gallery. I can feel her silent question: Are you okay?

I nod slightly, but I'm not okay. Eleanor just threatened me in open court, on the record, with absolute confidence that The Shepherd will finish what was started twenty years ago.

Judge Videen restores order after several minutes. "Dr. Vance, you are held in contempt of court. That outburst was inappropriate and will be noted in the record." She turns to address the room. "I've heard sufficient evidence today. The government has established probable cause to believe the defendants committed the crimes charged. This case will proceed to trial. The defendants will remain in custody pending trial proceedings. We're adjourned."

Her gavel comes down with finality.

As the marshals lead Eleanor out, she glances back at me one more time. Not threatening now. Almost pleased, like everything is proceeding according to plan.

Outside the courthouse, reporters shout questions. Did Eleanor threaten you? Are you concerned for your safety? What did she mean about The Shepherd?

Siwak handles them with practiced efficiency. "The FBI takes all threats seriously. Agent Collins's safety is a priority. The defendants will be held accountable for their crimes. That's all I can say at this time."

In the car afterward, Emma drives while I process what happened. The preliminary hearing was supposed to be routine—establishing probable cause, moving the case toward trial. Instead, Eleanor used it as a platform to deliver her message.

"That was calculated," Emma says, breaking the silence. "She knew what she was doing. Making that statement on the record, ensuring it would be reported. She wants everyone to know you're still a target."

"She wants me scared."

"Are you?"

I think about Eleanor's absolute certainty. About The Shepherd orchestrating operations from wherever he is. About being marked as unfinished business since I was twelve years old.

"Yes," I admit. "I'm scared. But I'm also done running from it."

Eleanor's words echo in my head: *Bridges are meant to be crossed.*

Not if I have anything to say about it.

CHAPTER THIRTY-TWO

The press conference happens three days later at FBI headquarters in Washington D.C. Siwak stands at the podium with the SAC from Behavioral Analysis and representatives from the U.S. Attorney's office. I'm seated behind them with Emma and Garrett, visible but not speaking.

The room is full of reporters. National media has picked up the story—ritual sacrifice conspiracy, children drugged and left to die, FBI agent with personal connection to the case. It has everything the news cycle loves.

Siwak begins with a prepared statement. "On December nineteenth, the FBI concluded a major operation dismantling a criminal network operating under the guise of the Greenwood Legacy Foundation. Seventeen individuals have been arrested and charged with conspiracy to commit kidnapping, child endangerment, and related federal crimes. Four children were rescued and are receiving ongoing medical care. Two children tragically died before we could intervene."

He continues with statistics. Eight years of operation. Hundreds of families exposed to Greenwood programs. Twenty-three children across five states who went missing in proximity to Greenwood activities—cases now being reopened and investigated for potential connections.

"The organization's leader, Dr. Eleanor Vance, operated a sophisticated recruitment system. Most participants believed they were involved in environmental education and alternative spirituality. A smaller inner circle was gradually radicalized into beliefs about ritual sacrifice and transformation through death."

A reporter raises her hand. "Is it true Dr. Vance threatened Agent Collins in court?"

Siwak's expression doesn't change. "Dr. Vance made inappropriate comments during her arraignment. The court found her in contempt of court. We take all threats against federal agents seriously and have implemented appropriate security measures."

"Can you comment on The Shepherd? Reports say he's been orchestrating these activities for decades."

"The investigation has identified an individual using that moniker who appears to have been training and directing various groups over a thirty-year period. We're actively working to identify and locate this person. Anyone with information should contact the FBI tip line."

More questions. About the botanical compounds. About other potential victims. About whether this network extends beyond Virginia. Siwak and the SAC handle each one professionally, revealing enough to satisfy public interest while protecting investigative details.

After forty minutes, the conference ends. We're escorted

out through a back entrance to avoid additional media attention.

In the car back to Charlottesville, I stare out the window watching the landscape pass. Winter has settled in fully now. Bare trees, gray sky, the kind of cold that makes everything feel brittle.

Emma breaks the silence. "You did good up there. Staying visible without having to answer questions directly."

"I hate press conferences."

"Everyone hates press conferences. But they're necessary. Public needs to know we're handling this."

My phone buzzes. A text from Leslie: *Saw you on the news. You okay?*

I reply: *Fine. Talk later.*

Another text, this one from Aiden: *Proud of you. Dinner tonight?*

Yes. My place at 7.

Emma glances over. "How's your sister holding up?"

"As well as can be expected. Divorce paperwork is filed. She's getting therapy for herself and the kids. Bennett had nightmares for a few days after learning that the nice lady from nature camp was arrested, but he's resilient."

"And Ava?"

"Too young to fully understand. Leslie's keeping it vague —just saying that some activities got canceled and they're trying different programs now."

We drive in silence for a while. Then Emma says casually, "Found something interesting in Eleanor's personal effects."

I turn to look at her. "What kind of something?"

"Letters. Dozens of them. All addressed to an inmate in the federal system." Emma keeps her eyes on the road.

"Eleanor was receiving instructions. Guidance on recruitment strategies, which children to target, timing for the winter solstice operations. Whoever she was writing to has extensive knowledge and decades of patience."

My chest tightens. "The Shepherd."

"Eleanor referenced him by that name in several letters. Asked for his approval, reported on her progress." Emma pauses. "River, if he's been in federal prison this entire time, that changes everything. He's contained, not wandering free. But it also means he's been orchestrating murders from inside."

"Have you identified him?"

"Siwak won't release the name yet—not even to the investigative team. He's restricting access until we finish building the full case. Could be days, could be weeks while we go through years of correspondence and cross-reference with known crimes."

"He's been part of my life since I was twelve. I deserve to know his name."

"Siwak knows. But he's worried about the personal connection compromising the case. Legal advised him to compartmentalize the information until they're ready to move." Emma's voice softens. "It's not about trust. It's about making sure nothing can be challenged in court later."

I look away, frustrated.

Emma's hands tighten on the steering wheel. "River, you'll probably need to recuse yourself from that part of the investigation. Your personal connection could compromise prosecution."

"I know. But I still need to be there when you interview him. Even if it's just observing through the glass."

"We'll make that happen," Emma promises.

We reach Charlottesville as the sun sets. Emma drops me at Aiden's apartment. I climb the stairs feeling the weight of the past few weeks settling into my bones. The investigation is officially closed. The press conference is done. The arrests are complete.

But The Shepherd remains. Somewhere in the federal prison system, an older man with white hair and sharp eyes is reading about Eleanor's arrest. About the failed winter solstice operations. About me testifying in court.

And he's planning what comes next.

Because that's what The Shepherd does. He plans. He waits. He builds networks of believers who will act on his instructions even when he can't act directly.

Eleanor said he always completes what he begins.

I intend to make sure that particular pattern finally breaks.

CHAPTER THIRTY-THREE

Aiden's apartment smells like garlic and rosemary when I arrive. He's at the stove stirring something that looks like risotto, still in scrubs from an earlier shift. When he sees me, his expression softens.

"Long day?"

"You could say that." I shed my jacket and badge, leave my service weapon in the lockbox I keep in his closet. "What are you making?"

"Mushroom risotto. Thought you could use comfort food." He continues stirring, the motion meditative. "I saw the press conference. You looked composed."

"I felt like I was drowning."

"But you didn't show it. That's what matters in those situations." He adds more stock to the pot. "How are you really doing?"

The question catches me off guard. Most people ask how I'm doing as a pleasantry. Aiden asks because he actually wants to know.

I sit at his small kitchen table. "Exhausted. Relieved the case is closed. Scared that The Shepherd is still out there. Angry that Eleanor threatened me in open court. Processing the fact that I killed someone." I pause. "Mostly I'm just tired, Aiden. Tired of looking over my shoulder. Tired of being the unfinished business in someone else's plan."

He plates the risotto and brings it to the table, sits across from me. For a few minutes we eat in silence. The food is excellent, rich and creamy with perfectly cooked mushrooms.

"I need to say something," Aiden begins, setting down his fork. "And I need you to really hear it."

My stomach tightens. "Okay."

"I've been patient through this case. Understood when you couldn't answer calls or had to cancel plans or disappeared for days at a time. That's part of being with someone in your line of work—I accept that." He meets my eyes. "But River, you shut me out completely. For two weeks, I barely heard from you except for brief texts. When you did see me, you were somewhere else mentally. I know the case was intense, but I felt like I was watching you disappear."

"I was working—"

"I know. But there's working and there's using work to avoid processing trauma. You do this every time things get dark. You throw yourself into cases and shut out everything else."

"That's not fair. This wasn't just another case. My abduction was connected. My brother-in-law was recruited to provide access to me. I had to kill someone at the site where I was held captive. This was personal in ways most cases aren't."

"Which is exactly why you needed support. Instead, you isolated." Aiden's voice is gentle but firm. "You texted me facts. Updates on the investigation. But you never told me how you were feeling. Never let me help carry any of it."

I want to argue but he's right. I know he's right. This is the pattern Dr. Reeves has been trying to help me break for years. When things get overwhelming, I retreat. Convince myself that processing alone is safer than being vulnerable with people who might leave.

"I'm afraid," I admit quietly. "Afraid that if I let you see how damaged I am, you'll realize you made a mistake. That I'm too much work. Too much trauma. Too much everything."

"River, I've known about your trauma since our second date. You told me you were abducted and held captive for two years. You've had nightmares at my place. I've seen you check locks three times before bed. I know exactly who you are, including the damaged parts." He reaches across the table, takes my hand. "What I don't know is if you'll ever let me really be there for you. If you'll ever trust me enough to share the hard things instead of carrying everything alone."

"I don't know how to do that."

"Then learn. We learn together." He squeezes my hand. "But I need to know you're willing to try. Because I love you, River. I love you enough to be patient through the hard times. But I can't love someone who won't let me in at all."

The words hang in the air between us. He loves me. He just said he loves me. In the two years we've been together, neither of us has said it out loud. We've danced around it, implied it, shown it through actions. But he just put it into words.

"I love you too," I say, the words feeling strange and terrifying and true. "That's why I shut you out. Because if something happened to you because of me, because The Shepherd decided to hurt me by hurting people I care about, I couldn't live with that."

"So your solution is to push me away preemptively? To make sure I'm never close enough to be hurt?"

"When you say it like that, it sounds dysfunctional."

"Because it is dysfunctional." Aiden's smile is sad. "River, I'm an ER doc. I see the worst of what humans do to each other every day. I understand danger and risk and the fact that life doesn't come with guarantees. But I'd rather risk being hurt while being close to you than be safe because you've pushed me away."

I think about Dr. Reeves asking how I trust people. About telling Leslie you start small, you test, you give people chances to prove themselves. Aiden has proven himself hundreds of times. Shown up consistently. Respected my boundaries while gently pushing back when I retreat too far.

He's earned trust. But I have to choose to give it.

"I'll work on it," I tell him. "On letting you in instead of shutting you out. It won't be perfect. I'll probably still retreat sometimes. But I'll try."

"That's all I'm asking."

We finish eating. I help him clean up the kitchen, the rhythm of washing and drying dishes strangely grounding. Normal domestic activity after weeks of intense investigation work.

As I'm putting away the last plate, something shifts in me. A realization that's been building for months. Maybe years.

"Move in with me," I say before I can talk myself out of it.

Aiden turns from the stove where he's wiping down surfaces. "What?"

"Move in with me. To my apartment. Or we find a new place together. I don't care which." The words are tumbling out now, pushed by adrenaline and terror and the strange courage that comes from being exhausted enough to stop overthinking. "You're right that I shut people out. That I isolate. But maybe that's partly because I keep everyone at arm's length physically too. If we lived together, I couldn't retreat as easily. I'd have to practice being present. Being vulnerable."

"River—"

"I know it's fast. I know I just spent two weeks barely talking to you and now I'm asking you to share my space permanently. I know it doesn't make logical sense." I force myself to meet his eyes. "But I don't want to keep doing this. Keep pretending I'm fine alone. Keep telling myself that distance equals safety. It doesn't. It just equals loneliness."

Aiden sets down the dish towel and crosses to where I'm standing. He takes both my hands, his touch warm and steady.

"Are you sure? Because this is a big step. There's no taking it back once we do this."

"Well, one of us could then move out if it doesn't work out," I say with a coy smile. He tilts his head, slightly annoyed.

"I'm kidding," I admit "And yes, I'm sure."

He kisses me, soft and sweet and full of promise. When he pulls back, he's smiling. "Then yes. Let's do it. Your place or new place?"

"New place. Somewhere neither of us has old habits. Fresh start."

"Fresh start," he agrees. "We'll start looking this weekend."

The relief that floods through me is unexpected. I just committed to something that should scare me more than it does. Cohabitation means less control, less privacy, less ability to retreat when things get hard. But it also means partnership. Support. Someone to come home to who knows exactly who I am and chooses to stay anyway.

We move to the couch and he pulls me against his side. I let myself relax into his warmth, his steady presence. Let myself be held instead of always holding myself together.

"This doesn't mean I'm suddenly going to be good at this," I warn him. "At sharing space and being vulnerable and not retreating when things get hard."

"I know. But you'll be trying. That's what matters."

We stay like that for a long time, watching the snow fall outside his window. The case is closed but not finished— The Shepherd remains out there, Eleanor's threats still echo in my head, the investigation continues in different forms.

But right now, in this moment, I'm not alone. I'm choosing connection over isolation. Choosing to let someone see me completely and trusting they won't leave.

It's the scariest thing I've done in years.

It's also the most hopeful.

Tomorrow we'll start looking at apartments. Tomorrow I'll get back to work and face whatever comes next. Tomorrow I'll continue processing everything that happened and learning to carry it without letting it crush me.

But tonight, I'm exactly where I need to be. With

someone who knows the worst of me and stays anyway. Someone who's willing to build a life with me despite all my sharp edges and broken pieces.

Someone who calls it love instead of damage.

And maybe, eventually, I'll learn to see it that way too.

CHAPTER THIRTY-FOUR

Two weeks after the preliminary hearing, life starts finding a new rhythm. I'm at the field office finishing paperwork on the Hollow Circle case—witness statements, evidence logs, the endless documentation that comes after arrests. Emma sits across from me organizing files for the prosecution team, her desk covered with color-coded folders.

"Coffee?" she asks, standing and stretching.

"Please."

She returns a few minutes later with two cups from the break room. We drink in comfortable silence, the kind that comes from working together through hell and coming out the other side.

"I need to tell you something," Emma says finally, setting down her cup. "I got offered a promotion."

I look up from my paperwork. "That's great. What kind of promotion?"

"Supervisory Special Agent. Crimes Against Children unit. It would mean staying in Charlottesville, better pay, more responsibility. I'd be coordinating investigations across multiple teams, mentoring junior agents." She pauses. "Siwak recommended me after how I handled the Hollow Circle case."

"You should take it."

"I'm not sure I want it." Emma stares at her coffee. "The emotional toll of these cases. It's getting harder. Every missing child, every abuse case, every investigation like this one where we don't get there in time. I don't know if I want to carry that responsibility for multiple teams."

"You already carry it. You're one of the best investigators I know. Those kids need someone who actually cares about getting it right, someone who won't take shortcuts or give up when things get complicated. Someone like you."

Emma looks at me directly. "You really think I should do it?"

"I think you'd be excellent at it. And I think you'd regret passing it up because you were afraid of the hard parts." I lean back in my chair. "The cases are going to be difficult whether you're a line agent or a supervisor. At least as a supervisor, you can make sure investigations are handled properly. You can protect victims by ensuring the team does thorough work."

"That's a good point."

"Plus, I could use someone in management who actually understands what field work requires. Someone who won't make unreasonable demands because they've forgotten what it's like to be on the ground."

Emma smiles slightly. "So this is self-serving advice."

"Partially. But mostly I just think you'd be good at it."

She's quiet for a moment, considering. Then she nods.

"Okay. I'll accept it. Starting next month after this case goes to trial."

"Congratulations, Supervisory Special Agent Bertanelli."

"It's weird. A year ago I was hiding what happened with Daniel, convinced my career was over. Now I'm getting promoted." Emma's expression shifts to something more serious. "That's because of you, you know. You believed me when it mattered. Helped me through the worst of it. I wouldn't be here without that."

"You would have gotten here on your own. You're strong and competent and good at your job. I just helped speed up the process."

"Still. Thank you."

WE RETURN TO OUR PAPERWORK. An hour passes in comfortable silence. I'm finishing up the last witness statement when my phone buzzes. A text from Aiden: *Finished my shift. Still good for tonight? Moving truck is reserved.*

I reply: *Yes. See you at 6.*

Tonight Aiden is moving his things into our new apartment—the bigger place we found last week, a two-bedroom with actual closet space and a kitchen that fits more than one person. Fresh start like we discussed. We're both moving in this weekend.

The thought still makes me nervous. Sharing space, sharing life, being vulnerable in ways I've avoided for years. But Dr. Reeves says growth happens outside comfort zones. And Aiden has proven himself patient and steady and willing to work through my complicated history.

My phone rings. Siwak.

"Collins, can you come to my office? We need to talk."

Something in his tone makes my stomach tighten. "On my way."

Emma looks up as I stand. "Everything okay?"

"Don't know yet. Siwak wants to see me."

I walk to Siwak's office with a growing sense of unease. When I enter, he's standing by the window rather than sitting at his desk. Never a good sign.

"Close the door," he says.

I do. "What's going on?"

"We need to talk about your abduction case. The prison letters Eleanor was writing—we finally got clearance to move forward." He turns to face me. "My team has been building the case for two weeks. Going through years of correspondence, cross-referencing dates with known crimes, preparing for interview strategy. Legal has been advising on prosecution angles."

"And?"

"The recipient is an inmate at FCI Lewisburg in Pennsylvania. He's been there for fifteen years, serving a life sentence for kidnapping and murder. Multiple victims across several states in the 1990s." Siwak picks up a file from his desk. "River, we think we've found The Shepherd."

The room feels suddenly too small. "Who is he?"

Siwak opens the file. Inside is a surveillance photo taken from prison security cameras. It shows Eleanor Vance sitting across from someone in an institutional visiting room. The image is dated three months ago—November, right before her winter solstice operation began.

The man she's visiting is older, maybe mid-seventies, with white hair and lean features. Even in the grainy surveillance photo, his eyes are sharp and intelligent.

I've never seen him before. But somehow I feel like I have. Like his face has been haunting the periphery of my life for twenty years.

"His name is William Strickland," Siwak continues. "Arrested in 2009 for a series of kidnappings and murders across Virginia, West Virginia, and Pennsylvania between 1994 and 2008. He was connected to at least eight deaths, all involving ritualistic elements. Sentenced to life without parole."

William Strickland. The Shepherd. The man who's been directing operations from inside prison for fifteen years.

"He trained my kidnappers," I say quietly.

"We believe so. The botanical compounds match. The methodology matches. And we found references in Eleanor's letters to 'the incomplete work from 2003' that needed to be finished. She was asking him for guidance on how to 'complete the bridge.'" Siwak's expression is grim. "River, he's been tracking you since your escape. Using contacts on the outside to monitor your career."

My hands are shaking. I sit down in the chair across from Siwak's desk. "How long has Eleanor been visiting him?"

"Prison records show she started visiting three years ago. Initially as part of academic research—she told the prison she was studying incarcerated individuals with alternative spiritual beliefs. But the visits became more frequent. By last year, she was going monthly."

"And the prison didn't flag this?"

"She had legitimate academic credentials. Her research was approved through proper channels. Nothing about her visits seemed suspicious until we connected her to the Hollow Circle crimes." Siwak sits down. "But here's what concerns us most. Strickland's visitor logs show dozens of people over the past fifteen years. Many using different names but similar patterns of visits. We think he's been recruiting and training followers from inside, just like he did with Eleanor."

"How many?"

"We're still tracking them down. But based on visitor patterns and mail records, potentially twenty to thirty individuals who had sustained contact with him. Some might be peripheral—curious academics or spiritual seekers. But others..." Siwak trails off.

"Others are true believers who've been receiving instructions."

"Yes."

I stare at the surveillance photo. William Strickland. The Shepherd. The man responsible for two decades of my nightmares. Not some shadowy figure moving between communities. An inmate in federal prison, contained but still dangerous. Still orchestrating murders through devoted followers willing to act on his instructions.

"We're coordinating with Bureau of Prisons to interview him," Siwak continues. "But it needs to be handled carefully. He's been in the system long enough to know how to protect himself legally. He'll lawyer up the second we approach him about anything beyond his original conviction."

"I want to be there."

"River—"

"I know I can't conduct the interview. I know my personal connection creates problems. But I need to be there. Need to see him, hear his voice, understand what he believes and why he's fixated on me." My voice is steady despite the fear coursing through me. "I've earned that right."

Siwak considers this for a long moment. "You can observe. Through the glass, not in the room. And only if the interviewing agents agree."

"Who's doing the interview?"

"Haven't decided yet. Probably someone from Behavioral Analysis with experience in cult cases. Maybe Agent Mercer since he's been tracking this network since 1994." Siwak closes the file. "River, this is a major development. If Strickland has been directing operations from inside, he's more dangerous than we thought. He's patient, intelligent, and has a network of followers we haven't fully mapped yet."

"When does the interview happen?"

"Could be as early as next week. Legal wants to finish reviewing all the correspondence first. We get one shot at this—if he invokes his rights and refuses to talk, we might never get answers about the full scope of his network."

I stand, legs steadier than I expected. "Keep me updated. Every development, every discovery. I need to know."

"You will be." Siwak stands as well. "And River? I know this is personal. But you've handled this case professionally despite that. Don't lose that now. We're close to understanding the full picture. Don't let your need for answers compromise the investigation."

"I won't."

I leave his office and walk back to my desk on autopilot. Emma looks up as I approach.

"What happened? You look like you've seen a ghost."

"They found him. The Shepherd. He's been in federal prison for fifteen years." I sink into my chair. "His name is William Strickland. Eleanor was visiting him, receiving instructions. He's been orchestrating everything from inside."

Emma's expression shifts through shock and realization. "Jesus. That means—"

"He's been tracking me since my escape. Using followers on the outside to monitor my career. Directing Eleanor specifically to involve me." I pull up my computer, searching the FBI database for William Strickland. His mugshot from 2009 appears—the same face from the surveillance photo, just fifteen years younger.

Sharp eyes. Lean features. The face of someone absolutely certain of his beliefs.

"What happens now?" Emma asks.

"They interview him. Try to get information about the full network. Map his followers and prevent future operations." I stare at the photo. "And I watch from behind glass while someone else asks the questions I've been wanting to ask for twenty years."

"River—"

"I know. It's the right call. I'm too close, too compromised. My testimony would be torn apart in court if I conducted the interview." I close the database. "But knowing that doesn't make it easier."

My phone buzzes. Another text from Aiden: *Everything okay? You usually respond faster.*

I reply: *Long day. Tell you tonight.*

Tonight. Moving in together. Starting a new chapter while the old one finally reveals its darkest secrets. William Strickland has been the invisible architect of my trauma for two decades. And now I finally have a name, a face, a location.

He's in FCI Lewisburg in Pennsylvania. Locked up,

contained, supposedly unable to hurt anyone. But he's been hurting people from inside for fifteen years.

And he's been waiting for me. I'm the incomplete bridge. His unfinished work. The girl who escaped.

Emma's voice breaks through my thoughts. "You're not alone in this. Whatever happens with Strickland, whatever we discover about his network, you have people backing you up."

"I know."

"Do you? Because you have a tendency to internalize everything. To carry it all yourself." Emma leans forward. "Strickland is locked up. Eleanor is locked up. The Hollow Circle is dismantled. You won. You survived. And now we're going to make sure he never hurts anyone else."

I want to believe that. Want to trust that prison walls and legal proceedings and FBI resources can protect me from someone who's spent twenty years planning my death.

But William Strickland has proven himself patient and adaptable. He's waited decades for the right opportunities. He's built networks that operate independently of his physical presence. He's created believers so devoted they'll die rather than betray his teachings.

Eleanor's words from the courtroom echo in my head: *The Shepherd will come for you. He always completes what he begins.*

If she knew that he was in prison, what did she mean exactly? Does he have plan that he's set in motion that we haven't discovered yet?

The question isn't whether William Strickland will try to finish what he started.

The question is *when*. And *whether* I'll see it coming in time to stop it.

THANK you for reading River's Hollow. I hope you enjoyed the book. Can't wait to find out what happens to River next? **Get River's Reckoning Now!**

The man who's haunted her for twenty years finally has a name.

Getting answers means looking evil in the eye.

FBI Agent River Collins just closed the biggest case of her career—a cult that murdered children in ritualistic ceremonies. But the investigation revealed something far worse.

The mastermind has been in federal prison for fifteen years.

And he's been orchestrating everything from inside.

The Shepherd. The man who trained River's childhood

captors. Who's been tracking her FBI career through a network of devoted followers.

He believes River is the unfinished work that must be completed.

Now prison records reveal dozens of visitors. Years of correspondence. Instructions for operations River hasn't discovered yet.

And when people close to River start disappearing, she realizes that the Shepherd's endgame is already in motion.

River Collins survived once by running.

This time, she's done running.

This time, she's going to end it.

Perfect for fans of Mary Stone, Elle Gray, and dark psychological thrillers with complex female protagonists.

The explosive conclusion to The Shepherd arc.

Get River's Reckoning Now!

IF YOU ENJOYED THIS BOOK, please don't forget to leave a review on Amazon and Goodreads! Reviews help me find new readers.

If you have any issues with anything in the book or find any typos or mistakes, please email me at Kate@kategable.com. Thank you so much for reading!

INTERESTED IN READING a new standalone psychological thriller? Check out my new book, **The Neighborhood Watch!**

Everyone has secrets. Some neighborhoods collect them.

When Brooke Sullivan and her family move into the upscale community of Desert Oaks, the gates, the sunshine, and the smiles feel like a dream come true. The HOA president drops off a welcome basket. The "Neighborhood Watch" offers a home-insurance discount and a safety app that connects every Ring camera on the block. All Brooke has to do is turn on Sharing.

Then a break-in rattles the street, and Brooke's doorbell clip "solves" the crime. She is invited behind the curtain, where she glimpses The Vault—a private archive of neighbors' videos, fines, and quiet little files. What looks like community is something else entirely. Surveillance. Leverage. Control.

When Brooke tries to walk away, the Watch reminds her who she used to be. The sealed court record. The new name. The people she has been hiding from. If she talks, they expose her past. If she stays silent, she becomes complicit.

To save her family, Brooke will have to turn the cameras back on the people who installed them. But in Desert Oaks, the lights never go out. And the Watch is always watching.

Perfect for fans of Freida McFadden and Lisa Jewell, The Neighborhood Watch is a razor-sharp suburban thriller about belonging, power, and the price of safety.

1-click The Neighborhood Watch Now!

ALSO BY KATE GABLE

Standalone Psychological Thrillers
The Other Mother
The Neighborhood Watch

FBI Agent River Collins Mystery Thriller
River's Edge (Book 1)
River's Shadow (Book 2)
River's Hollow (Book 3)
River's Reckoning (Book 4)

Detective Kaitlyn Carr Psychological Mystery series
Girl Missing (Book 1)
Girl Lost (Book 2)
Girl Found (Book 3)
Girl Taken (Book 4)
Girl Forgotten (Book 5)
Gone Too Soon (Book 6)
Gone Forever (Book 7)
Whispers in the Sand (Book 8)

Girl Hidden (FREE Novella)

FBI Agent Alexis Forest Mystery Thriller
Forest of Silence
Forest of Shadows
Forest of Secrets
Forest of Lies
Forest of Obsession
Forest of Regrets
Forest of Deception

Detective Charlotte Pierce Psychological Mystery series
Last Breath
Nameless Girl
Missing Lives
Girl in the Lake

ABOUT KATE GABLE

Kate Gable loves a good mystery that is full of suspense. She grew up devouring psychological thrillers and crime novels as well as movies, tv shows and true crime.

Her favorite stories are the ones that are centered on families with lots of secrets and lies as well as many twists and turns. Her novels have elements of psychological suspense, thriller, mystery and romance.

Kate Gable lives near Palm Springs, CA with her husband, son, a dog and a cat. She has spent more than twenty years in Southern California and finds inspiration from its cities, canyons, deserts, and small mountain towns.

She graduated from University of Southern California with a Bachelor's degree in Mathematics. After pursuing graduate studies in mathematics, she switched gears and got her MA in Creative Writing and English from Western New Mexico University and her PhD in Education from Old Dominion University.

Writing has always been her passion and obsession. Kate is also a USA Today Bestselling author of romantic suspense under another pen name.

Write her here:
Kate@kategable.com
Check out her books here:
www.kategable.com

Sign up for my newsletter:
https://www.subscribepage.com/kategableviplist

Join my Facebook Group:
https://www.facebook.com/groups/833851020557518

Bonus Points: Follow me on BookBub and Goodreads!

https://www.bookbub.com/authors/kate-gable

https://www.goodreads.com/author/show/21534224.Kate_Gable

- amazon.com/Kate-Gable/e/B095XFCLL7
- facebook.com/KateGableAuthor
- bookbub.com/authors/kate-gable
- instagram.com/kategablebooks
- tiktok.com/@kategablebooks

Printed in Dunstable, United Kingdom